BY THE BOOK

A.J. MCCARTHY

Black Rose Writing | Texas

First printing

This is a work of fiction. Names, characters, businesses, places, events, and incidents are either the products of the author's imagination or used in a fictitious manner. Any resemblance to actual persons, living or dead, or actual events is purely coincidental.

ISBN: 978-1-68433-587-9
PUBLISHED BY BLACK ROSE WRITING
www.blackrosewriting.com

Printed in the United States of America
Suggested Retail Price (SRP) $19.95

By the Book is printed in Calluna

*As a planet-friendly publisher, Black Rose Writing does its best to eliminate unnecessary waste to reduce paper usage and energy costs, while never compromising the reading experience. As a result, the final word count vs. page count may not meet common expectations.

This novel is dedicated to my dear friend, Thelma. I've never known anyone with a more caring and beautiful soul. Love you forever.

Other Titles by A.J. McCarthy

Sins of the Fathers
Cold Betrayal
Legacy of Fear

BY THE BOOK

BY THE BOOK

CHAPTER 1

The figure glided to the bed on soft-soled feet. The face of the intended victim was at ease, lashes dark against her pale cheeks. The curve of her lips suggested a pleasant dream. Jennifer Danvers slept the sleep of the dead, the intruder thought. The pun provoked a smile; a hand stifled a chuckle.

Jennifer's face was familiar, chosen with great care, and it inspired a sense of excitement; the adventure had begun at last. It had taken months of planning and hour upon hour of research. A few hiccups were expected along the way, but the killer didn't question the likelihood of reaching the goal.

Despite a sense of elation, the hands were steady as the person leaned over the bed and wrapped latex-covered fingers around Jennifer's throat. Her lovely blue eyes opened, startled, and her hands grabbed her assailant's wrists as she struggled to free herself, to no avail. Training and preparation were on the killer's side.

"You should be honored." The words were spoken with a smile, even as the fingers increased their pressure, and terror-filled eyes pleaded for mercy. "You're perfect. The most perfect I've found. We'll go down together in history."

It was over within minutes, too quick for the killer's satisfaction, and the young woman's body slumped, lifeless, on the bed. The act completed, the murderer took a few moments to relish the sight of her: the slack mouth, the bulbous eyes staring back, as if in wonder. Exhilaration flowed through the killer's veins. *So powerful, so clever, so much in control.* A laugh escaped, a brief staccato burst.

"No one will ever suspect me. They never do. I'm invisible." The words were addressed to the body on the bed, as if expecting a response. "I may not come across as being special, but I can do whatever I want to, and I'll prove it. You've been an enormous help. Thank you."

The corpse received a bright grin as a reward.

"Oh, I can't forget. I have a few things to take care of, haven't I?"

From a pocket, a pair of tweezers were removed. Unzipping a bag pinned to the front of the person's white coveralls, a small, red plastic heart was extracted. Jennifer's mouth was opened, and the heart was lodged against her tonsils. Thin lips curved into a smile of admiration before closing the victim's mouth and blocking the heart from view. Next, the tweezers were used to pull a crisp piece of paper from the bag. The killer squatted, placed it beneath the bed, and pushed it under as far as possible, taking care not to bend or tear it.

"There. Once upon a time."

CHAPTER 2

Detective Josh Riddell stood in the bedroom's doorway as his partner, Clint Weller, looked over his shoulder. Josh clenched his fists on lean hips, his tall frame alert and tense. Clint, of a similar height and build, his hands thrust into the front pockets of his jeans, was no less disturbed by the scene. The men studied the space before venturing farther into the room. The two patrol cops who had secured the scene were in the living room, trying to calm the victim's friend.

The detectives, from the homicide division of the Ottawa Police Service, were among the first to arrive at the scene. The call had come in at 10:05 on Saturday morning, when Jennifer Danvers' co-worker and close friend, Susan Watson, had dropped by the house.

Josh glanced at his partner, noting his uncombed light brown hair, the wrinkled shirt, and the jeans with a small rip in the knee. He caught a whiff of women's perfume. Knowing Clint, he had spent the night with someone new and had dressed in haste when he received the call. Josh, on the other hand, had been awake for hours, taken his morning run, had his breakfast, and was ready for the day in navy chinos and a freshly washed cotton shirt.

The detectives, pulling on blue latex gloves, approached the bed, and gazed at the body. The memory of another corpse, also a young woman in the prime of her life, struck Josh. He looked toward the curtained window and inhaled a deep breath.

"You okay?"

"Yeah, I'm good." Josh swung his gaze back to his partner and gave him a small nod before returning his attention to the body on the bed.

The girl was in her late twenties, with blond hair, and what might have been a pretty face. Now, it could only be described as grotesque, with bulging eyes, blue lips, and a neck ringed with bruises. Experience told Josh the cause of death was strangulation, but the coroner had to make the last call.

Blankets covered her legs. One bare foot peeked out from underneath. Bright blue pajamas, somewhat rumpled, concealed her upper body. Josh's gaze swept the room. Apart from the bed and a small night table, a six-drawer dresser in a matching dark mahogany was the only other piece of furniture.

The top of the dresser held a small assortment of items: a hairbrush, a tube of lipstick, and an open jewelry box. Josh took a step closer. The victim didn't have a lot of jewelry, but much of it resembled gold. The stones could have been diamonds or Zircon. His knowledge didn't extend that far. Either way, it hadn't interested the killer.

He crossed back to the bed and glanced at the nightstand. A lamp, an alarm clock, and a bodice-ripping romance novel were the items adorning it. He bent to study the row of books on the lower shelf. Romance was definitely her genre of choice.

The closet door, ajar, caught Josh's attention. He eased it open with his elbow and learned the victim was tidy and didn't go for clutter. Neatly arranged clothing and footwear were displayed before him.

Nothing seemed disturbed.

"Looks like she was sleeping when she was attacked." Clint's thoughts mirrored Josh's. "No sign of her being dragged around."

"Didn't put up much of a fight. Either she was asleep, or she was familiar with the killer. She could have argued with her boyfriend."

"One hell of an argument. When that happens, I go wash the car to get out of the line of fire. I don't strangle her."

Josh didn't offer a response and guessed Clint didn't expect one. He circled around the bed and used his cell phone to move the curtain aside a few inches.

"No sign of damage here." He turned and observed Clint stepping into the bathroom across the hallway. A moment later, his partner emerged, met Josh's gaze, and shook his head.

The two men didn't touch the body or any object in the room, avoiding contamination of the crime scene. They made their way to the hallway where Josh took a mental inventory of his emotions. He reminded himself he needed to be at his best at a time such as this.

"You okay?" Clint said.

"Just fine. Thanks for asking. But don't ask again." Josh softened the blow of his words with a pat on his friend's shoulder. "Why don't you interview the woman who found her? I'll take the uniform."

With a nod, Clint moved to the living room and spoke to the patrol cop who stood at attention in the middle of the room. A look of relief spread across the police officer's face. He glanced at the woman who sat on the couch, sobbing into her hands, before leaving her in Clint's care and making his way over to Josh.

"Fill me in," Josh said after introducing himself.

Officer Travers went through the specifics of the initial call and their arrival on the scene. The door had been locked, the victim was dead, and had been for a while, according to the young cop.

"You check outside?" Josh jerked his head toward the door.

"Yeah, Jim and I did the rounds. Saw nothing out of place. No evidence of forced entry at any of the doors or windows. It's as if the killer walked in, did the job, and walked back out."

Josh grimaced. It would not be the first time someone known by the victim entered a dwelling and committed a crime. They needed to explore that angle, but the crime scene team had yet to arrive, and he knew they might find evidence to support another theory.

Clint came up behind him, holding a notebook with his distinctive scrawl covering the exposed page.

"What do you have?" Josh turned to face his partner.

"Jennifer Danvers, twenty-eight years old. An accountant employed by a small firm. Worked with the woman over there. They were good friends."

Their gazes turned toward the puffy-faced woman who sat with her shoulders curled inward, a tissue clasped in her fist.

"They've been friends three years," he continued. "No boyfriend at this time, and any previous boyfriends don't raise suspicions, at least not in Ms. Watson's mind. No known enemies, no recent incidents. She was well-liked, worked hard, minded her own business. Worked late last night. It's a busy time of year, and they expected her at the office for a while this morning. Never showed up. Ms. Watson phoned a few times, didn't get an answer, came to investigate. Rang the doorbell several times, no response. Peeked in the bedroom window, saw a woman on the bed, called 9-1-1." He snapped the notebook shut and shoved it into his shirt pocket.

Josh's attention was drawn to the front door as a group of people entered, all of them dressed in white Tyvek coveralls, and each carrying bags or cases in various shapes and sizes. These contained the tools of the trade of a forensic team, ranging from cameras to swabs to specially designed lighting equipment. Clint stepped forward to lead a group to the bedroom, while others fanned throughout the other rooms, moving into their roles without instruction.

On their heels, another visitor arrived; a tall, trim man in his early forties, with an aura of professionalism. He wore a navy-blue suit and a crisp white shirt, a tag dangling from his breast pocket, looking as if he was ready to attend a business meeting on a Monday morning, not a murder scene before noon on a Saturday. Josh didn't need to check his ID. He was well acquainted with the coroner.

Dr. Chris Abbott paused for a moment on the threshold and gazed around the room until he spotted Josh. He moved into the house, and Josh stepped forward to shorten the distance between them. They shook hands but didn't exchange pleasantries other than a nod.

"What do we have?" The doctor's gaze explored his surroundings, searching for details to make his job easier.

"A young woman, Jennifer Danvers, age twenty-eight. No sign of either forced entry or struggle. Her friend called it in around ten this morning. The body's in the bedroom." Josh gestured toward the hallway.

There was no need for further explanation. Josh didn't do the medical examiner's job for him by offering unsolicited theories of how the victim had died. In turn, Dr. Abbott didn't tell Josh how to handle his investigation. The doctor mumbled about getting there before the body was disturbed and hurried toward the bedroom.

Josh turned to Clint.

"They don't need us here. We'll go canvas the neighbors. With any luck, someone saw something last night."

They got as far as the second house when Josh's cell phone vibrated in his pocket.

"Detective Riddell? This is Eddie DeLorme, CSI. You should come back to the scene. We've found something unusual."

CHAPTER 3

Josh stood beside Jennifer's round kitchen table. A grim-faced Clint stood on the opposite side. Two plastic evidence bags lay on the surface between them. A technician had labeled and registered both bags in the log. The first contained a small, red plastic heart, half of an inch in width. Josh lifted the bag by the corner between his thumb and forefinger and dangled it between them.

"Interesting. Not unusual. How many times have we seen a killer leave behind a souvenir?" Josh's gaze narrowed on the contents.

"They often leave one or take one with them," Clint said.

Josh grunted. "Yeah, it adds something to the case, but it's this that intrigues me." He set down the bag and picked up the other one. "I've never seen anything like it. It's either going to make our job easier or much more complicated."

Inside the bag was a single piece of paper, a page from a paperback novel.

"Listen to this. 'Jennifer's lifeless body lay in the center of the bed. Around her throat was a necklace of bruises, and her eyes were glassy, staring vacantly at the ceiling.' Do you believe this?" Josh's eyes widened.

"You think it's fake?" Clint said. "Somebody set it up to look like a page out of a book, to throw us off? A computer-generated thing?"

"I don't know. It looks legit, as if it's been pulled out of a novel." Josh pointed out the slight raggedness on one side of the paper.

"Still might have been set up somehow."

"You're right," Josh said. "It's possible. We'll check it out. We have to go to HQ and move on this."

"I'll call Jenkins and Newbury. Get them to canvas."

"I'll tell the doc we're taking off." Josh headed toward the bedroom.

• • •

They drove the fifteen minutes to the station in silence. Josh knew Clint, like him, ran over the details of the murder in his mind, and they would compare their mental notes when the time came.

The headquarters of the Ottawa Police Service was located downtown on the corner of Elgin and Catherine Street, just off the Queensway, the major highway that cuts through Ottawa. It was quiet compared to the usual craziness of a weekday, but the ringing of telephones welcomed the two detectives, along with the voices of some of their coworkers shouting across the room.

Josh headed straight to his desk. His colleagues considered him one of the lucky ones with a window location, even though his view was nothing more than the rush of traffic on the busy highway.

"I'm going to..." Josh stopped and glanced over his shoulder, thinking his partner followed a few steps behind him. Instead, Clint leaned against a filing cabinet, smiling and chatting with a rookie detective, Linda Benson, an attractive, blond woman who had joined the homicide department a few weeks ago.

Josh's boss had made noises about having her assigned to their team. They wanted her to learn the ropes from experienced detectives. Josh had mixed feelings for the idea. She appeared to be competent, but he worried she might be a distraction for his partner, a worry that was apparently justified.

"Clint? May I interrupt you for a few minutes?"

The other man glanced his way, flashed another smile at the female cop, and sauntered over to Josh's desk. "It's important to make the recruits feel welcome, don't you think?"

Without making a comment, Josh settled in front of his computer as Clint perched on the low cabinet behind Josh's shoulder, giving him an unobstructed view of the screen.

Within moments, a website appeared before Josh, and he typed in 'T.L. McGinnis', the name printed on top of the page found under the victim's bed. His quest earned him two results. The author had two published novels, *Murder by the Dozen* and *Stalked*. The former held their interest, since it was the title displayed on the opposite side of the page.

A few clicks later, Josh found a tiny amount of biographical information on the writer. T.L. McGinnis lived in the small, nearby town of Navan and was working on a third novel.

After a quick reference to another website, Josh had the directions to find him. One last search was needed to see if the name appeared in their database as having any prior arrests or convictions. None appeared. Josh stood and glanced at Clint. Without a word, they headed to the car.

Their first stop was at a local bookstore.

"Yes, I have a copy of that book, but only one," the shopkeeper told them, leading them through the store. He was a tall man in his early forties, pudgy, dressed in beige; pants, shirt, and sneakers. "Actually, you're lucky I have it. It wasn't a national bestseller, but it had decent sales. And, since the author is a nearby resident, I have copies on hand to encourage local talent. I like to do that, you know. I'm not one of those big bookstore chains. I can't afford to carry more than a few selections on the shelves, but if there's any particular book someone wants, I'll order it and have it in the store within a few days, a week tops."

Josh exchanged a glance with Clint.

"Do you have any information about the author?" Josh's tone was hesitant, afraid to send the bookstore owner into another long rant.

"No, I don't. Although, I'm a big fan of the genre. I love to solve the mystery before I get to the end, don't you? What's your interest in this book? I must say, you've got me intrigued." The man's smile exposed yellowed teeth.

They came to a stop in front of a display of fiction novels, and the man removed a paperback from the shelf. He clutched it to his chest, holding it hostage.

"Someone recommended it to me, that's all." Josh itched to grab the book from the man's hands and make his escape.

"Oh? Just this one?"

"Yes. Can I buy it, please?"

The man handed him the paperback, his expression curious, and the three of them returned to the cash register. Josh paid for the book and thanked him, sensing the man's gaze on his back as they left the store.

Clint took over the wheel, while Josh settled into the passenger seat.

"A little creepy, wasn't he?" Clint checked his side mirror before pulling out into traffic.

"That's one word for him. I could find a few others. Remember to jot down his name. Let's get a move on. We've wasted too much time."

Josh turned his attention to the novel. What he read made him grunt and shake his head.

"What's it say? Anything interesting?" Clint shot him a worried glance.

"Keep driving. I want to read this."

"Josh…"

"I'll tell you in a minute."

"I'm a patient man, but please tell me what's in the book."

They had almost reached their destination. Josh ignored Clint's threatening tone, closed the novel, and turned toward his partner.

"It's unbelievable." His voice was just above a whisper. "It's like a premonition or, I hate to say it, but a set of instructions."

"What are you talking about?"

"Everything is the same. The name, the occupation, the MO, everything."

"Do we need backup?" Clint frowned. He slowed the car and pulled to the side of the road.

Josh stared through the front windshield, not noticing the new spring foliage on the trees, or the tidy, older homes on each side of the car. Like Clint, he wondered if the author of the book was the killer. Only an idiot or a masochist would leave such an obvious clue. There had to be another connection.

"No, we'll check it out first. But we'll be careful."

The countryside evolved into a rural area, dotted with farms, both new and old. There were mature trees lining the road, their branches almost touching overhead. Navan was a quaint, quiet suburb, a half hour drive from downtown Ottawa. It wasn't considered a hotbed of criminal activity or a hideaway for murderers, Josh thought.

Clint drove at a snail's pace as they peered at the numbers on the mailboxes. The one they searched for stood out from the others and brought a trace of a smile to Josh's face. Shaped to resemble a large golden retriever, the mailman would have to flip up the dog's nose to insert the mail, while its left ear took the place of the traditional flag. The number 157 was emblazoned on the hound's flanks, 'McGinnis' imprinted on his collar.

Clint pulled the car into the driveway. Behind the leafy branches of two immense trees, a two-story farmhouse was hidden. The property seemed to have been renovated by someone with more concern for aesthetics than farming. The exterior of the residence had white wood siding with a dark-green wraparound veranda. Cheery flower boxes graced the lower-level windows and immaculately maintained grounds surrounded the home. The lush grass and flower gardens promised to be abundant once the season was in full bloom.

Josh noted the absence of farm animals and the presence of two other buildings; a barn and perhaps a storage shed. There wasn't any activity near either of them.

"Delightful place," Clint said. "Not somewhere you'd find a cold-blooded killer."

"You can find killers, cold-blooded and otherwise, almost anywhere," Josh drawled.

"Right. But I have a hard time believing this guy could've done it. He'd have to be crazy to leave a clue like that."

Josh noticed Clint looking at the small silver-gray Toyota parked in the driveway. His partner pulled the pad from his pocket and noted the license plate number.

"Okay, let's get it over with." Josh shoved open the car door. "See what T.L. is like."

As he approached the door, Josh was on his guard. Clint would also be aware of the danger and of the weapons tucked into their shoulder holsters. They flanked the doorway as Josh pressed his finger to the doorbell. An answering bark sounded from inside the house. It was only one bark, followed by silence.

The detectives exchanged looks, and Josh's hand closed around his weapon, knowing he was ready to react in a split second, if necessary. A few moments later, the lock clicked, and the door opened wide enough for the occupant to see who was on the veranda.

"Yes? May I help you?"

Josh's shoulders relaxed somewhat. The voice belonged to a delicate-looking woman with light brown hair pulled back into a high ponytail. She had wary, green-gray eyes and rimless glasses perched on top of her head. Her complexion was clear, unhampered by makeup. An oversized t-shirt and lightweight sweatpants covered her slight frame. Josh pegged her at around thirty years old, judging by the maturity in her eyes and voice. Otherwise, she could pass for someone much younger.

The dog, an old golden retriever, which explained the mailbox and the lack of furious barking, lumbered over to the door and tried to nudge his overweight frame into the small space.

"Sit, Cooper."

The dog complied and settled at her feet, but his tail wagged as if he looked forward to making the acquaintance of the newcomers. Josh smiled at both the animal and its owner before getting to the business at hand.

"We'd like to speak with Mr. McGinnis, please."

The wariness in her eyes sharpened. "Mr. McGinnis isn't here. Can I ask why you're looking for him?"

Josh ignored her question. "When do you expect him back?"

The woman countered with more questions. "Who are you? Why do you want to see him?"

Josh glanced at Clint before reaching into his jacket pocket and removing his identification. He opened the case and presented it to her.

"My name's Josh Riddell. This is my partner, Clint Weller." He nodded in Clint's direction.

Josh noticed the change wash over the woman as she looked at his badge and ID card. The blood drained from her face, and her eyes widened in alarm. It was a reaction that was not unfamiliar to him.

"We should come inside, Miss. Let's sit down, and we'll tell you why we're here." Clint's tone was warm and reassuring.

She shifted her panic-stricken gaze from one man to the other. "Is it my parents? Has something happened to them? Please tell me they're all right."

Before Josh responded, she flung the door open and wrapped her hand around his forearm, squeezing with a surprising strength.

"Is it Monty? It's Monty, isn't it? I should have known."

Josh saw she was headed for a full-blown panic attack, and he wanted to head it off at the pass. He gently removed her hand and placed his own on her upper arms. He bent until his eyes were level with hers.

"Miss, listen to me. As far as I know, your parents and Monty are safe. All we want to do is talk to Mr. McGinnis. You don't have to worry."

Josh didn't know if what he said was true. Her parents might have driven their car off a bridge, or Monty may have suffered an aneurism, but his words had the desired effect and that was the most he hoped to achieve. The woman relaxed to a certain degree, and her eyes focused on his. She stiffened her arms and gave them a shrug, just enough to give him the message to remove his hands. He complied without hesitation.

"I told you Mr. McGinnis isn't here. What do you want with him?"

Despite her brave show, there remained a tinge of apprehension in her voice. From Josh's experience, having two homicide detectives at your door, making enquiries, made people apprehensive.

"Are you his wife?" Josh glanced at her left hand to find it bare. "Or his sister? Daughter?"

"It depends on which Mr. McGinnis you're looking for."

"Mr. T.L. McGinnis."

Her reaction surprised Josh. Her eyes widened once again, her shoulders straightened, and her head snapped back as if he had tried to slap her. She seemed at a loss for words.

"So, which is he, your husband, boyfriend, father, or brother?" Josh persisted. Her evasiveness intrigued him.

"I'm afraid the answer is none of the above." She paused, and Josh saw a mixture of fear and curiosity in the woman's eyes. "I'm T.L. McGinnis."

CHAPTER 4

The scene was surreal. They were in a room that had been all but abandoned in the recent past, having fallen victim to her mother's decorating tastes many years ago with no sign of rescue. Now, apart from herself, two strange men occupied it, looking uncomfortable with their tall frames folded into the overstuffed floral-patterned armchairs. The detectives' serious faces blended in with the paisley wallpaper and the abundance of framed pictures and posters that surrounded them.

She should have kept them in the kitchen, Tierney thought, her befuddled brain straying from the unknown crisis at hand.

She probed her mind for an explanation for two police officers showing up unannounced at her door. *If her parents and Monty were safe, whatever they had to say didn't affect her, did it? But homicide detectives? Could something have happened to one of her neighbors? If that was the case, this visit was routine, a duty performed in the pursuit of suspects.* A shudder ran through her at the thought of a homicide so close to her home.

"Ms. McGinnis?"

Tierney flinched and forced herself to focus her attention on the detective who had spoken. *Josh Riddell, was it?* She figured he was the lead detective, or at least the one who asked the most questions. The other one appeared to follow his lead.

She didn't know if it was a good thing. *Of which one should she be more nervous? Why should she be nervous of either of them? She had done nothing wrong. But they were so serious, and she had a terrible sensation about this visit.* Tierney placed her hand on her stomach and felt it churn under her palm.

Cooper was his usual relaxed self. As the men sat, the dog ambled over to the blond-haired man, Mr. Weller, and gave him a cursory sniff. Next, he crossed to visit the dark-haired detective and, deciding he would do, lowered himself onto the man's shoes, laid his head on his paws, and fell asleep.

"Cooper! Don't do that." Tierney stood, prepared to launch herself at the animal.

The man held up his hand and gave a deep-throated chuckle.

"It's okay. I don't mind."

She returned to her seat, aware that the only way to remove Cooper from the man's feet would be to drag him away. Since he was a large dog, the maneuver could be awkward and embarrassing. Tierney glanced at the detective. He was tall and broad-shouldered, his hair trimmed short, his eyes a warm brown, a sharp contrast to his disheveled partner.

Detective Weller removed a notebook and pen from his pocket. "Miss, what's your full name, please?"

"It's Tierney. Tierney McGinnis."

"That's an unusual name." Weller spoke in a conversational tone.

"My parents are fans of the silver screen. They named me after Gene Tierney, a big star in the 1940s." She recited this by rote, a standard answer to an often-asked question.

"And the L?" Weller asked.

"Laura."

"Another movie star?"

The question came from Detective Riddell, and Tierney thought she detected a trace of amusement in his voice, although his expression remained benign. She incessantly explained to people the origin of her name and the obsession her parents had with the stars of the 1940s. It tended to make her defensive.

"No, it was the name of one of Gene Tierney's most famous movies."

"Ah, I see," Josh said, as if this made perfect sense.

The other detective scribbled more notes. Tierney didn't understand the relevance of these questions or of her answers, and her nerves buzzed throughout her body. "I'm sorry if I sound impatient, but may I ask what this is regarding?"

"You can, and we're getting to that, Ms. McGinnis. I just have one other question for you," Riddell said.

"Go ahead."

"Are you the author of the book, *Murder by the Dozen*?"

The question sent Tierney's stomach into a tailspin. *What was going on?* "Yes, I am."

"You wrote that book?"

Tierney blinked at Detective Weller in surprise. "I did. Why? What of it?" Her voice rose in alarm. She hadn't expected such a reaction to her response and didn't grasp how to interpret it.

Detective Riddell spoke after casting a dark look at his partner. "We just needed to establish that you're the author."

A heat rose from the base of Tierney's spine, working its way up her body. The detectives seemed shocked and almost disgusted by her statement. She didn't comprehend what interest they had in her book, and her thoughts tripped over themselves trying to find a reason. As she watched, Josh's features regained their blandness, and her stomach took up its dance again.

A few moments passed, and the uncomfortable silence made her impatient with the cloak and dagger act. Tierney stood, hoping to gain the advantage by forcing them to look up at her. "Now, gentlemen, unless you're willing to tell me the reason for your presence here, it's time for you to leave my home."

The eyes of the blond-haired detective narrowed, and she saw a glint within them she hoped wasn't amusement. If he laughed, she might lose it.

"Miss McGinnis, please sit, and I promise we'll explain," Detective Riddell said. "We understand your concern and we'll get to the point of our visit."

Tierney had difficulty interpreting the glance that passed between the men. She dug her fingers into the arms of the chair as she lowered herself into it.

"We're investigating a homicide that took place during the night," Josh said. "We found..."

"A homicide? Who? Someone I know? What does it have to do with me?"

Her mind raced, not able to connect the dots between herself, her book, and a recent homicide.

"Please, let me finish," Josh said. "I'm getting there. At the scene of the crime, we found a page from your book, *Murder by the Dozen.*"

"Okay. So? It sold well." Her gaze bounced from one cop to the other, her expression puzzled. "There are copies in plenty of houses. Will you question all the authors of all the books on people's bookshelves?"

"There are aspects of the case that are very particular," Weller said.

"I don't understand." And she didn't. *Why had his tone changed? Was it sympathy in his voice?*

Detective Riddell leaned forward in his chair, resting his elbows on his knees. The movement made the dog open his eyes and lift his head, but seeing it was business as usual, he lowered it back onto Josh's feet. The detective didn't seem to notice. His attention focused on Tierney, as hers did on him.

"We didn't find it on a bookshelf. We found only one page and no trace of the rest of the novel. I'm afraid someone left it there as a clue."

"A clue? What kind of clue? What are you saying?"

"The victim's name was Jennifer, a twenty-eight-year-old accountant. Someone strangled her to death in her sleep."

For the second time that day, Tierney experienced the sensation of blood draining from her face. She didn't speak as Josh finished his explanation.

"The page we found was an excerpt from chapter one of *Murder by the Dozen.*"

CHAPTER 5

"You must have made a mistake. It had to be a random page found in the room."

Tierney's voice was thin and unsteady, her frame stiff with shock. Her hands gripped the arms of the chair as if she was on a roller coaster ride.

"That's what I'd like to think, but there are too many things that match up. The name of the victim, her age, her profession, even her coloring. Jennifer Danvers was a blonde with blue eyes. And she died by strangulation, as did the victim in the book." Josh paused for a moment. "We found something else interesting. There was an object in the victim's throat."

Tierney's fingers fluttered across pale lips, her words a mere breath. "A plastic heart?"

"Yes." Josh observed a parade of emotions cross Tierney's face: doubt, fear, confusion. He could see she hunted for a credible explanation, something to make it go away.

When she spoke, it was in a low voice pulsing with disbelief. "It must be a coincidence. It has to be. How could someone plan something like this? I don't understand."

"Yes, it may be, and we may have considered that possibility if we hadn't found only one page under the bed. Why just one? Why not the entire book? It seems the killer tried to leave us a message. I'm sorry. It's obvious this is upsetting for you, but we need all the information we can get if we want to catch the perpetrator."

"I don't know what I can tell you. I have no idea who bought the book. There's no way I can trace it." Tierney wrung her hands, knotting and unknotting her fingers.

"We're aware of that, but you can help in other ways, just by answering our questions. Could you do that?" Josh was careful to keep his voice soft and conciliatory.

"Of course."

"Good." From the corner of Josh's eye, he noticed Clint's pen poised over his notepad. "First, were you acquainted with the victim, Jennifer Danvers?"

"No. No, I've never met her."

"You didn't base her on anyone in real life?"

"Yes...no...I mean she's fictional."

"And you've never heard of Jennifer Danvers?"

"Never."

"Has anyone discussed the character from your book with you?"

"No. Not that I remember." She ran her hands over her head, dislodging strands of hair from her ponytail.

"Has anyone approached you in the recent past with questions about the book? Did you receive any mail? Phone calls?"

"I get letters from readers, but I can't put my finger on one that seemed unusual."

"Do you keep copies of the letters?" A spark of hope shot through Josh. A traceable letter would be a godsend.

"Yes. I erase nothing. I'll find them for you." She moved to rise from the couch only to settle back down with Josh's next words.

"We'd appreciate that, but you can do it in a few minutes. First, we need you to concentrate. Is there anyone you're aware of who might resent you or wish you harm?"

"You think someone is doing this to get back at me?" Tierney's gaze widened.

"We have to explore all the possibilities," Josh said. "Can you think of anyone?"

"No. I'm not aware of any enemies." Her gaze flicked from one detective to the other.

"Keep it in mind, and if you think of anyone, you can let us know."

"I understand. I will." Tierney's hands resumed their wringing.

"I'd appreciate seeing those letters now," Clint said.

"Sure, no problem." Rising, Tierney swayed on her feet and clutched the back of the chair to steady herself. Josh was quick to react, grabbing her by the elbow, rousing Cooper from his comfortable nap and sending him grumbling over to his doggie cushion.

"Thank you. I'm all right," Tierney mumbled, pulling her arm from his grip before heading along a short hallway off the living room.

Josh glanced at Clint with raised eyebrows before taking a moment to scrutinize the room. An inordinate number of knickknacks crowded various shelves and cabinets; many of them tacky souvenirs found in shops on Hollywood Boulevard. Vintage framed movie posters decorated the walls. They could be classics and worth a few bucks. It seemed Tierney McGinnis was also a fan of the silver screen, Josh reflected.

"What's your take on it?" Clint interrupted his partner's browsing.

"I think she got a hell of a scare."

"Too far-fetched to consider she's the killer, isn't it?"

"Yeah, but I'm not willing to write off the fact she's connected somehow."

"Right." Clint said. "But do you think..."

Josh caught a movement out of the corner of his eye and turned to see Tierney coming back to the living room carrying a laptop computer. The woman seemed more composed as she sat and opened the device under the watchful eyes of the two detectives.

"Are you referring to e-mail letters?" Josh said.

"Yes, the only mail I receive from readers is through my website."

"You have a website?" Josh didn't see the need to tell her they had already checked out her site.

"Most authors do, although mine may be different." Tierney's eyes focused on the screen as she logged into her computer.

"How is it different?" Clint said.

"I don't have any pictures of myself on the site. Nor do I give out any information to show whether I'm a man or a woman. I just refer to the books, give a synopsis, accept e-mail correspondence, that sort of thing."

"Why don't you give out personal information?" Clint said.

"I'm a private person. I'm not looking for fame or notoriety. It also makes me seem a little mysterious. I see it in the letters I get. It intrigues people. It helps to keep away the crazies out there."

Tierney's expression froze, and Josh realized the irony of what she had said struck her. If what he and Clint suspected was true, there was someone out there who was crazy enough to re-enact a murder scene from a novel.

"This is horrible. I might be responsible for this poor girl's death."

Tierney dropped her head into her shaking hands, knocking the computer off her lap. Clint snatched the laptop before it landed on the floor as Josh stood and took a step closer to her.

"Miss McGinnis..." He stopped, not sure what to say.

Josh glared at Clint, hoping to get an offer of help. Josh was out of luck. His partner stood to the side, holding the computer, and indicating with his head that he should step up to the task. Josh shot him an exasperated glance before he settled on the sofa next to the distraught woman and laid his hand gently on her shoulder.

"Miss McGinnis, I understand you're upset, but, if you want to help, you need to stay calm."

"But it's as if the killer followed my instructions." She lifted her stricken face to stare at him, her hands clenched into fists.

"We don't know that for sure. It's possible it was a coincidence." Josh didn't think he sounded convincing. It was difficult, when you knew, deep down, your words were empty platitudes. "Besides, they weren't instructions. It's a novel. It's fiction. It isn't supposed to be copied. Unfortunately, there are sick people who get their kicks in strange ways."

"This is horrible," Tierney said, her voice muffled by her hands once again.

With a low grumble, Cooper, the faithful pet, decided it was his duty to offer his mistress the support she needed. When his wet nose nudged her hands, Tierney wrapped her arms around his neck and clung to his fur. Josh removed his hand from her shoulder as the dog looked up at him with a doleful you-owe-me-one expression.

Josh allowed her a few moments before he redirected her thoughts to the matter at hand. "Let's get to the e-mails."

Tierney drew herself up and looked around for her computer, not seeming to comprehend how it had vanished. She gave Clint a small, watery smile when he placed it back on her lap. Her fingers fumbled for the glasses on top of her head. She slid them into place and got on task.

"Yes, here they are. You can scroll through them, but I'd be surprised if you find something useful in there." Her voice trembled.

"Would it be okay if you forwarded them to my office, and we went through them on our own?"

Tierney nodded. "I don't see why not. There's nothing personal in there."

The keys clicked as her fingers flew across them. She asked the detective for his e-mail address and sent the messages. Meanwhile, Josh used the time to study Tierney and consider his next move.

He couldn't help feeling sorry for her. He wasn't heartless, often sympathizing with witnesses, in particular if they were distressed. As was the case today, he had to fight to suppress his sympathy, needing to maintain his role as a cop. Ms. McGinnis was a witness and potential suspect in a homicide case and had to be treated as such.

Josh didn't have to dig too deep to analyze his emotions and recognize from where they came. This case had stirred memories from the moment he had laid eyes on Jennifer Danvers' body. And, because of that, he didn't relish the thought of upsetting Tierney any further. His gaze met Clint's, and he realized his partner planned to take the task off his shoulders.

"We bought a copy of your book before coming here," Clint said. "We haven't had time to read it yet. Would I be right in guessing there are twelve murders that occur in the novel?"

"Yes. That's why it called *Murder by*...oh my God, you don't think...do you?" She splayed her hands over her chest, and her horror-filled gaze fixed on them. Josh and Clint held their poker faces in place.

"It's too early for us to think anything. It was a simple question." Josh saw his words did little to calm her nerves. She understood why Clint had asked, and her mind had leaped to the right conclusion. The shell-shocked expression returned to her face, and he suffered a stab of guilt for having helped put it there.

"What about the heart? What's the significance?" Clint said, intervening.

Tierney straightened and stared over his shoulder at a poster featuring Lauren Bacall and Humphrey Bogart in *The Big Sleep*, but her gaze turned inward. "It was the killer's calling card. His wife had passed away while on the waiting list for a heart transplant. He worked as an intern in a hospital, and he used his connections to gain access to medical records. He targeted people who might have been donors, based on their blood type."

Josh and Clint exchanged a glance.

"Do you think it's the same?" she said. "Someone's preying on people for the same reason?" Her voice rose in volume as she spoke, worry creasing her forehead.

"We know nothing yet," Josh told her. "These are questions we have to ask, and they may lead us somewhere, or they may not. Whatever you can tell us might be helpful."

"Ms. McGinnis," Clint drew her gaze back to him. "I wondered how the killer got into the victim's home. I mean the fictional killer in your book."

"He broke a basement window in the back of the house earlier in the day, before she returned from work, and hid inside until she came home and went to sleep." Tierney looked up at the two men. "He enjoyed that, the anticipation, the waiting, and the buildup, until he performed the final act." Shock and disbelief laced her voice. "How did the murder happen this time? How did the person get in? Was it a basement window?"

"We don't have that information yet," Josh said. "The team is still checking it out."

Josh was vague in his answers. He still hadn't learned where Tierney McGinnis fit into the picture, and he didn't intend to show her his cards just yet.

"Do you live here alone?" Josh asked.

"It's my parent's home, but they're never here. When they retired, they bought an RV so they could spend their time traveling. I gave up my full-time job as a teacher last year to devote myself to writing and moved here to make ends meet."

"You're not married?" Josh said.

"No."

"A significant other?"

"No."

Clint's head was bent over his notepad, and his indecipherable script covered the page.

"What about this Monty person you mentioned? Who is he?" Josh continued.

"He's my brother." Shock had voided Tierney's voice of emotion.

"Ex-boyfriends?"

"There's one I was seeing until a few months ago, but I assure you he's not a killer."

"We need his name, just to eliminate him from the suspect list. We also have to know where you were last night."

As Josh expected, the question stunned her.

"You believe I killed that girl?" Her hand lay across her throat.

"It's routine, Ms. McGinnis," Clint said. "We have to question everyone who's involved in the investigation. As a crime writer, you should be able to appreciate that."

"I never expected anyone to ask me that question."

"Can you tell us where you were?" Josh asked, since Clint had smoothed the way for him.

"I was with friends, Faye and Jim, most of the evening. I got back here around ten thirty."

"We'll need your friends' contact information."

Clint jotted the details in his notebook, and Josh decided they had enough answers for now. Tierney was still in shock, and there was no need to push her any further today. They had work to do on other fronts. He looked at Clint and nodded. The men stood in unison, and Tierney followed suit.

Clint handed her two business cards. "If you remember something, no matter how small, that might connect someone to this case, please call us."

"I have to caution you, it's very important you don't discuss the case with anyone," Josh added.

The woman stared at the cards in her hand as if she wanted to memorize them, but Josh realized her mind was elsewhere, and the impact of the murder would linger for hours, if not days.

"Is there someone you'd like us to call?" he said. "A friend? Your parents? You shouldn't be alone."

"No. I'll be all right." Her words didn't match her tone of voice.

"What about your brother?"

"He's away on a business trip. Don't worry. I'll be fine," she persisted, her voice gaining strength.

"Okay." Josh spoke with reluctance. He glanced at Clint, and they headed to the door, but Josh pulled up short when a small hand was laid on his arm. He turned to face Tierney.

"Will you let me know what happens? If you're able to catch this person, I mean."

Josh smiled. "Yeah, sure. No problem. You'll be hearing from us again."

It was only after the door closed behind them that Josh understood Tierney could have taken his last statement as either a promise or a threat.

CHAPTER 6

Alone, Tierney sank into the depths of the armchair Josh Riddell had occupied. The warmth from his body surrounded her, but it did nothing to ease the chill inside her soul. She had never imagined anything as horrible as being told someone had used her book as a road map to murder. The only thing worse would be if it happened again. She understood the same thoughts ran through the detectives' minds. *How could this be happening?*

Tierney had taken up writing out of pure pleasure. She was an avid reader, her favorite novels being of the crime and mystery genres. This second career, along with her passion for gardening, had filled her off-work hours.

Her first book, *Stalked*, had taken a while to come to fruition. The fact she was a first-time author didn't help. After many years of sending out numerous submissions, Tierney found an agent willing to take a chance on her. Several months later, she had a publishing contract signed, sealed, and delivered. She considered herself lucky. Many debut authors were not so fortunate.

Stalked didn't become the bestseller Tierney had dreamed of, but it sold relatively well, and, once she lowered her expectations, its modest success satisfied her. She followed it with *Murder by the Dozen*, which was more successful, allowing her to change her career plans.

Tierney scanned the room, with its tacky souvenirs and too-busy wallpaper, and felt the need for her family, or anyone willing to provide a shoulder on which to cry. She realized she had made a fool of herself in front of the police detectives, but she hadn't been able to help it, with her emotions running rampant. She sensed she had made them uncomfortable, in particular Detective Riddell.

Tierney thought of Faye, her closest friend, and considered contacting her, but she couldn't bring herself to make the call. She sat and stared at the wall, trying to absorb the fact that, because of her, or because of something she had written, a young woman was dead.

If her book had not caused the murder, might it have been another? Was the mind behind the killing already warped beyond redemption, or had her novel pushed it over the edge? What was it that drove people to take another life? She couldn't imagine hurting another living being. Yes, she wrote novels relating to crime and murder, but they were a product of her imagination.

At a time such as this, Tierney wished her imagination had led her down a different path.

CHAPTER 7

Josh drove while his partner sat in the passenger seat, his brow creased. The tension was palpable, each wrapped in their own thoughts. Clint broke the silence.

"You okay?"

Josh glanced at him. "Yeah, I'm fine."

"You sure?"

"I'm sure. Let it go." Josh did not tamp down the frustration in his tone.

"What do you think?" Clint twisted in his seat to face his partner.

"Of her?"

"Yeah, of her. Who else?"

Josh pinched his bottom lip. "I don't know. I don't think she's the doer, that's for sure, but there's got to be a connection. And I don't mean the fact the murder was a carbon copy of the first chapter in her book. There's a closer connection. We just have to find it."

"You think she's working with the killer? Coaching him or something? Why leave the page under the bed? It's a link to her."

"No. It's not the impression I got. I don't believe she's involved with the murder, not directly. But I figure the person chose her book for a reason. I think the killer knows her, or knows of her, and used her book to make the link to her."

"Why?"

"I can't say, not yet. It's just a perception. I mean, how many crime writers are there? Thousands? Tens of thousands? But she lives within a half hour of the crime. What are the chances?"

Silence fell in the car until Clint spoke. "She's kind of cute, isn't she?"

Josh rolled his eyes. "We're in the middle of an investigation. Can't you keep your mind off women for a while?"

"What? I just said she's cute. There's nothing wrong with that. Don't tell me you didn't notice."

Josh sighed. He knew Clint well enough to realize that if he didn't make a comment, his partner would not leave him alone. "All right. She's cute. Okay? But she's not my type, and at a time like this, she shouldn't be yours either."

"I wasn't thinking of making a move. I just wanted your opinion." Clint gazed out the window at the scenery that changed from rural to urban. "Besides, it's time you changed your type."

"You can't change your type. Your type is your type." Josh rubbed the back of his neck. His partner picked the worst times to discuss something unrelated to the case. When he spoke again, Clint's voice was serious.

"You think there'll be more?"

Josh's hands tightened on the steering wheel. "Yeah. That's an awful feeling I have. I'm afraid there'll be more. We have to figure out when, who, and how."

"Should be easy," Clint said.

Josh caught his partner's sarcasm. "It won't be, and the worst part is, we may not have much time."

"If you're right that this is not a one-time deal, and if you're right that the killer knows Ms. McGinnis, she may be in danger."

"That's another thing bothering me. We have to make headway. You go through the e-mails. I'll get someone to canvas the bookstores."

"You think someone will remember selling the book?"

"It's not likely, but we have to do it. We also have to contact the hospitals to see if anyone has died while waiting for a heart transplant in the last six months or a year."

"Then what?" Clint said.

"I'll catch up on my reading."

• • •

Josh didn't spend a lot of time reading fiction. Police reports and the sports page were more his style, but Tierney McGinnis' tale of a serial killer intrigued him. He had expected a TV-style cops and robbers story with stereotypical personalities. Instead, unique characters peppered the story, and the plot was well-timed. The action was intense, and although there were violent scenes, they were not gratuitous.

A pad and pen rested at Josh's elbow, and he took basic, point-form notes as he read. He planned to list the names, sex, age, coloring, and profession of each of the victims in the book along with the manner of death. Because of the reason behind it, he didn't enjoy the exercise, but he hoped his worst fears would not be realized. In fact, Josh hoped what he was doing was an enormous waste of time and the most he got out of it was a chance to read an enjoyable book.

After a few hours and three murders, Josh set the book aside, stretched long and hard, and made his way to the kitchen. It was not a lengthy journey. His apartment was small, but the right size for a single man who didn't spend much time there.

It was mid-evening, and Josh had forgotten to eat dinner. Despite the common beliefs regarding bachelors, Josh cooked on a regular basis, avoiding fast-food as much as possible.

He put together a dinner of lamb chops, a baked potato, and steamed asparagus, while his thoughts were in Tierney McGinnis' farmhouse. He sat in her living room, watching her absorb the shock of the news they had delivered, knowing she harbored the same fears as he did.

As he shook seasonings onto his chops, he wondered if she had bothered to prepare herself a meal tonight or had thoughts of the murder wilted her appetite. Josh hated to drop such a bombshell on her, but he told himself there was no choice. Their job was to solve a murder, and Tierney was a key element in the crime.

He pulled the potato from the oven and dropped it on the counter before running his singed fingers under icy tap water. Josh believed his professionalism had faltered a little that afternoon. Ms. McGinnis may not have noticed, but Clint had. He would also have understood the cause, but they had been friends and partners for several years. Clint had his back.

Josh stared at his meal; his appetite vanished. His thoughts had turned to another woman, one that didn't resemble Tierney but who had also needed his help, and he could not give it to her. Not in time.

CHAPTER 8

Clint had also taken his work home with him, but the setting was different. His apartment was more spacious than Josh's, and there had been more time spent on decorating. Not his own time, but that of the *femme du jour*.

He found women had a strange desire to put their own stamp on what they thought of as their nest. If they suspected another bird had arranged the twigs in a certain way, it compelled them to rearrange them and add a few extra twigs of their own. As a result, Clint's apartment was an eclectic mix of many personalities. He liked to describe his style as avant-garde garage-sale.

Clint's approach to cooking also differed from Josh's. The useless-in-the-kitchen method worked for him. His girlfriend of the moment would shake her head in frustration, but the maternal instinct would shoot through her veins, she would take him under her shapely wing and save him from the horrors to which his previous girlfriends had subjected him. This technique served him well, and he rarely had to eat takeout or fast food either.

Josh told him he was a feminist's nightmare, and someday he would get his comeuppance. Clint shrugged off his friend's comments. If it worked, why change it?

However, this evening, Clint set aside his personal time and devoted an hour to poring over the e-mails sent to Tierney McGinnis' website. He searched for hidden clues or allusions but saw nothing to raise his suspicions. Someone intent on murder did not advertise the fact, but for the life of him, Clint didn't see any comments that even hinted at evil. The letters were your basic fan mail. Tierney's books seemed to be well received, and most of the correspondence was impersonal.

One letter, however, was from a woman who expressed a desire to meet the author and strike up a relationship of a romantic nature. She said she loved men who had both a violent streak and a vivid imagination. She left her name and phone number and was even kind enough to send Tierney a photograph that Clint suspected was digitally enhanced.

He chuckled when he imagined the reaction of the woman if she met the real T.L.. It led him to wonder if the killer also considered T.L. McGinnis a man and what bearing it could have on the case.

The ringing of his cell phone shook Clint from his thoughts. The display told him it was Josh, and he didn't bother with the formality of saying hello. "Yeah, I just finished going through them."

"How did it go?" his partner said.

"There was nothing special, except a lady that wants to get it on with Mr. McGinnis."

"With Tierney's father?"

"No, with her. She thinks she's a man, like we did."

"Yeah, right. I get it," Josh said.

"Did you read the book?"

"Not yet. Not the entire thing, but I've gotten through three murders so far."

"And?"

There was a moment of silence before Josh spoke, his tone sober.

"I hope the killer got bored after the first chapter and stopped reading."

CHAPTER 9

The Chateau Lafayette Tavern, better known as The Laff, had resided in the heart of downtown in the Byward Market since 1849, making it even older than the City of Ottawa. Clint had been a regular visitor since he was old enough to go to bars. The exterior of the establishment may not have attracted a lot of attention, but its reputation for excellent food, wonderful music, and a great atmosphere drew people to the inside.

It was Friday night, and they had granted him downtime from work. Deciding to spend it here had been a simple decision. He needed something to distract him from the investigation, at least for a few hours.

On occasion, he convinced Josh to join him and his friends for a beer, but prying his partner away from a case wasn't easy, and tonight had been no different. Unlike Clint, who needed an outlet to take his mind off the strain of his job, Josh dug his claws in deeper. The most he did to relax was to catch a sports game on TV or go fishing.

Clint saw two of his buddies, Chad and Barry, lounging at a table, a half-full pitcher of beer between them. A four-piece band played 80s rock on the opposite side of the room, but the sound filled every corner. People shouted over the music; a few danced where they stood, and the staff worked their way through the crowd, holding pitchers of golden liquid or platters of food high in the air.

The two women walked into the bar an hour later. It was a chance moment when Clint looked in their direction and spotted them. They were both average height, one blonde and one brunette. The blonde's curves and full, blood-red lips drew the attention of more than a few men in the immediate vicinity, and she knew it. Her smile radiated confidence.

The brunette was slim, her clothing understated. Her makeup was either nonexistent or as unobtrusive as her jeans and sweater. And her expression as her gaze swept over the inhabitants of the bar made it obvious she wished she was anywhere else but there. When the blonde grabbed the other woman's elbow and steered her on a different course, Clint leaped from his stool and pushed his way over to them.

"Hello, ladies." He directed his attention to the curvy blonde. He didn't miss the step back the other woman took as he leaned closer to them. "We have two seats at our table, if you'd like to join us."

The blonde's gaze swept over him and drifted to the table he had pointed out with a sweep of his arm. If her smile was any sign, she approved of the company. Before her friend had a chance to express an opinion, she grabbed her hand and tugged the brunette along behind her as Clint led them through the crowd.

His friends made room for the two women, found stools to accommodate them, and acquired filled glasses to quench their thirst. Clint found himself in the envious position of being seated between the two of them, but he figured he had earned it. If he hadn't stepped forward, they'd be at someone else's table.

The blond, Karen Berg, held an animated conversation with the male occupants of the table, uncovering names, occupations, and marital status in record time. She'd make an excellent interrogator, Clint thought.

Her friend, who he discovered went by the name Lydia Sandford, remained silent while Karen entertained the troops. Her quietness didn't discourage Clint.

"So, either you've been here before, and you hate it, or you've never been, and you hate it."

Lydia turned her dark brown eyes toward him, his frankness startling her. "I don't hate it. I just don't..." She shrugged her shoulders and diverted her gaze.

"You just don't what?" Clint hoped to put her at ease with his winning smile. Although, he wouldn't place any bets on how winning it might be tonight.

"I'm not a bar person. I'm more of a homebody, I guess." She focused her attention on the glass of beer in front of her.

"Nothing wrong with that. That's usually where I am, when I'm not working, that is." Her uneasy gaze, once again, shifted to another area of the bar, anywhere else but at him. "Ah," he said. "You don't like cops." It wasn't a question.

"That's not true. I have nothing against them," Lydia blurted.

Clint smiled and nodded, but he doubted she spoke the truth, for whatever reason that might be. He was not deterred. He set his sights on the prize and pulled out and dusted off his considerable charm.

Clint joined in the conversation with the others and told a few entertaining stories, giving it his all. Lydia eventually rewarded him with the sound of her laughter and a smile that reached her eyes.

The evening ended with an unmistakable softening-up of the woman's attitude toward Clint, and he hoped it had less to do with consuming alcohol and more to do with a genuine attraction she had for him. He knew his fascination with her wasn't a result of the beer.

"I hoped we could get together some night for dinner. I'd like to get to know you better. What do you say?" Clint walked beside Lydia through the parking lot.

Karen and Chad were several steps ahead of them, the blond with her hand tucked in the crook of Chad's arm, her body pressed closed to his. She flicked a knowing glance over her shoulder at her friend, but her chatter continued non-stop.

He returned his gaze to Lydia in time to see her slight frown. "No pressure," he said. "Two new friends going out to dinner."

When she turned to stare at him, he blasted her with a killer smile, full of innocence.

"All right. Just two new friends," she said.

●　●　●

Clint rolled out of bed, after having spent ten minutes waking up and deciding what to do with his Saturday. It was supposed to be a day off, but he needed to check in with the team to see if they had any news. His specific interest was the investigation into the bookstores and hospitals.

Without a doubt, Josh would call him to discuss the case. That thought drove him from his bed and into the shower. As he took his first fortifying sip of coffee, his phone chirped.

"Hey," Clint said.

"You're sounding chipper this morning. You said you were going to The Laff last night."

"I did." He pinned the phone between his ear and his shoulder as he dropped bread into the toaster.

"I assumed you'd still be in bed at this hour."

"You hoped to wake me up? Sorry to disappoint."

"It must have been a slow night."

"Not at all. It was great."

A moment of silence hung in the air. "My powers of detection tell me you met someone. You have company this morning?"

Clint chuckled. "Your powers of detection are particularly sharp, but I'm alone. Hopefully, that'll change soon."

"Oh."

"What do you mean by that?"

"Nothing. All I said was 'oh'."

"Yeah, but the way you said it makes it sound as if I told you I have lice."

"Well, come on, Clint, figure it out. You meet these women in bars. They're desperate women looking for a poor schmuck they can sink their fake fingernails into. They're hoping it's dark enough and you're drunk enough you won't notice they've been around the block a few times."

"Josh, that has to be the most sanctimonious, sexist twaddle I've ever heard. You haven't even met this girl, and you already imagine the worst. For once, you might reserve judgment, at least until you've laid eyes on her."

"You're right, Clint. I'm sorry. I shouldn't have spoken in such a manner. You're a grown man and should be able to make an intelligent and well-thought-out decision on your romantic affiliations with no interference from me. I apologize if I upset you."

After a moment of silence, laughter erupted between them.

"No, I was wrong before," Clint said. "As far as sanctimonious twaddle goes, that was the best."

CHAPTER 10

During the week that followed Jennifer Danvers' murder, Tierney's emotions swayed from guilt to despair to resignation and back again. She tried to concentrate on her writing but found the little she wrote didn't work for her. She started over countless times but came back to where she had left off the previous week. Her life went from bad to worse when she received a call from her agent, Ron Wallace.

"Hey, I'm so glad to find you at home. Working on your manuscript, I hope?"

Tierney held back a groan. She had expected Ron to get in touch with her. Under normal circumstances, she screened the calls, but her distraction made her forget to check the display.

"Hi, Ron. Yes, by coincidence, that's what I'm doing."

"Great. I'm getting calls from the publisher, and they're getting antsy, wondering if you'll make the deadline."

Tierney picked up the question in his voice, and she pictured him leaning back in his chair, his thin legs resting on his desk, his eyes narrowed behind thick glasses, and his sparse hair ruffled.

"I'm doing my best." She was unable to give him more without lying outright.

"Is everything okay? Are you having problems on another front?"

"Everything's fine." She grimaced. That was an unmitigated lie.

"You want me to help you? Write it for you? I know a lot about crime," he said.

Tierney had trouble describing his laugh. It was somewhere between disturbing and eerie. Ron was a good agent and businessman, but his bedside manner left much to be desired. She finished the conversation and disconnected with a new resolve to be more diligent screening her calls.

Tierney read every news story she could find, poring over the articles that followed the murder. She cried as she read Jennifer Danvers' obituary and imagined the faces of the family members listed there. She watched the television news reports. They made no mention of Tierney's book, or, for that matter, any book connected with the crime.

She assumed the police had decided not to reveal too many details to the press. Tierney understood why. Releasing information such as the plastic heart or the novel muddled the investigation with crank calls and exposed their hand to the killer. She realized the media received only the basics from the authorities, and that was fine with her. The fewer people aware of her connection to the murder, the better.

Within days, the articles became shorter and harder to find, until they dropped off altogether. If the police didn't come up with fresh information, they would use the front pages for more newsworthy stories.

A few days after the killing, she received an impromptu visit from Faye. It was not unusual for her friend to pop in unannounced, and Tierney was always happy to see her. They had been acquainted for several years, ever since the woman had moved to the neighborhood with her husband.

She was a sharp contrast to Tierney, with short, dark curls and a tall, stocky build. Her character was also far from that of the quiet introvert. Faye worked as a negotiator for a trade union, and she could be as tough as nails. Yet, the woman had a heart of gold and would move heaven and earth for someone she considered a friend.

"What's up? You look as if you haven't slept in days." Faye didn't mince her words, as usual.

Tierney ran her hand through her hair and straightened her t-shirt.

"I've been working hard on my manuscript," she lied. "Ron's been putting pressure on me."

"I didn't think your deadline was that close."

"They moved it up on me. I'm working day and night to get through it." Tierney worried how she would extract herself from her tangled web of lies. She made a mental note to put on a little makeup so unexpected visitors wouldn't notice the circles under her eyes. Under normal circumstances, she discussed everything with Faye, and she didn't blame her friend for being suspicious.

"Does this have anything to do with that visit we had from the police?" Faye crossed her arms over her chest and narrowed her eyes.

"No, not at all. I already explained that to you." Tierney had needed to deflect her friend's questions after the police had checked her alibi. Her cover story was that Jennifer was her accountant, and the authorities had to investigate everyone who had been in recent contact with the victim.

"Anyway, enough about me. How are things with Jim and the kids?" Tierney forced a smile. Faye's husband was a lawyer, and they had two young children, a boy and a girl. Tierney often called on Jim for advice on legal scenes in her books, and he helped her by looking over her contracts.

Tierney listened with half an ear as Faye regaled her with stories of her preschool children. She wished she could contribute more to the conversation, but the murder lurked in the back of her mind.

"So, Jessica jumped on the back of the winged elephant, and they flew off into the sunset."

"Good. That must've been fun," Tierney said.

"What did I just say?" Faye's expression turned fierce.

"Um...the kids...the kids were at the park?" She winced, suspecting Faye had caught her in a lie.

"I've never seen you like this before. This had better be about the book, because if there's something bigger going on, I'll be very, very upset with you for not telling me."

Tierney smiled and hoped Faye never learned the truth. She had seen her friend upset in the past, and it was not pleasant.

CHAPTER 11

It took a full week to release Jennifer's body to the family, and they scheduled the funeral for the following Tuesday, ten days after her death. Tierney realized it would be difficult to attend the ceremony, but she also understood it was something she couldn't avoid. In her view, she owed it to this stranger.

Still, as she climbed the steps into the church, she had a horrible foreboding that everyone would turn and point an accusing finger at her.

With lowered eyes, Tierney slipped into a back pew seconds before six solemn men, dressed in black, shuffled past with the casket. Most of them were young, possibly friends or coworkers. One of them was over fifty, maybe an uncle or a friend of the family. It was obvious their sadness ran deep, as expected when someone they knew and loved had been murdered.

The group continued up the center aisle of the large, gilded Catholic church. It burst at the seams with people. She wondered how many of them knew the family, and how many were there for the same reason as her. Not because they were acquainted with the victim, but because they felt sorrow for the circumstances under which she had died and sympathy for a family with much brighter dreams for their daughter or sister or cousin.

An elderly priest who had a special connection to the family performed the service. He had baptized Jennifer in this place of worship. Here, she had taken her first communion and celebrated her confirmation. There was a eulogy from her brother, who spoke stoically but with a tremor in his voice, which drew audible sniffles throughout the church. Another eulogy followed, this time from her friend, Susan Watson, the woman who had found the body. People openly sobbed. Tierney was no exception.

As she fumbled in her bag to grab a tissue, Tierney glanced over her shoulder and encountered the grim gaze of Detective Josh Riddell. Her initial reaction was surprise at seeing him until she realized he had an excellent reason to be present. He was the investigating detective. He had every right to come to the funeral, and, by the expression in his eyes, Josh considered her out of place in the church. Tierney turned forward, feeling like a schoolgirl caught playing hooky.

As the procession left the church, Tierney had the misfortune to end up next to the cop as they joined the crowd for the brief walk to the cemetery, although she suspected it was not a coincidence. She tried to pretend he wasn't there, but she sensed disapproval rolling off him in waves. The heavy silence led her to speak in a low whisper to the cop, turning her head slightly in his direction.

"You don't think I should be here."

"You're right. I don't."

"Because you believe I'm responsible for what happened to her." It was a statement, not a question.

Josh said, "No, that's not it at all. It's because you're upsetting yourself further by being here. It isn't necessary."

"Maybe you think it's unnecessary, but I disagree. I needed to do this."

"Why? What do you get out of seeing her family's grief?"

"I'm not sure. Closure? Perhaps, I just wanted to feel connected to her, and this was the way to do it. I didn't know her when she was alive, but her death is associated with me, so I had to take the next step."

Josh picked up on the most important part of her statement. "You're not responsible for her death."

Tierney glanced over her shoulder to ensure no one was eavesdropping before looking him in the eyes.

"I am, and you know it. If it wasn't for me, Jennifer would be alive. She'd be going about her life as usual, enjoying her family and friends, being a productive member of society. Now she's gone, and although I didn't know her, I feel the loss of her. I feel the loss for her family and for anyone else who may have cared for her. Look at all the people here today."

"Some are here out of curiosity."

"And what's your reason? Is it curiosity or sympathy? Or is it only professional?"

Josh's shoulders slumped. "I feel sympathy, but I didn't have to come here to experience it. I had enough of that when I spoke to the family and needed to ask them endless questions about Jennifer."

It hadn't occurred to Tierney that meeting with the family was part of Josh's duties, and she suffered a pang of remorse. She laid her hand on his arm. "I'm sorry. I should have thought of that. How horrible that must've been."

His eyes met hers, and she saw the anguish in them. "It wasn't pleasant, but it's part of my job. Someone has to tell them what's happened. Someone also has to find who killed her, and that means asking a lot of tough questions at a tough time."

"Did it help? Did you learn anything regarding the killer?"

Josh shook his head. The words of the priest reached their ears even though they stood at the back of the crowd. Everyone remained silent until they lowered the casket into the ground. The onlookers turned and made their way toward their cars, most of them mumbling among themselves.

Tierney and Josh walked side by side to the parking lot, but neither of them uttered a word until they reached Tierney's car.

"Look," Josh said, "If coming here today helped you, then I'm glad, but whatever you do, don't think you're responsible for what happened to Jennifer. Entire responsibility rests in the hands of the killer, and no one else."

Tierney slid into the car without looking at him, not wanting him to see the tears in her eyes.

CHAPTER 12

To top off her day, Tierney received a call from her mother, Irene. When they weren't in the RV, their home away from home, her parents were often on a cruise ship, as they were now.

"Ciao, darling!"

The high-pitched voice rang in Tierney's ear, and she picked up the sounds of music and laughter in the background

"Hello, Mom. I take it you're in Italy."

"We certainly are. I needed to check in and tell you it's absolutely divine here."

"Glad to hear it. How's Dad?"

"Your father is bene, very, very bene! He says ciao to you too."

"Great. Ciao back at him. Is the cruise as nice as you expected?"

"Oh, even better! We hit the jackpot this time. Everyone here is just like us. We couldn't have dreamed of a more perfect trip!"

Tierney could not have dreamed of anything more astounding. An entire cruise ship overflowing with people just like them? She had always considered them the unequaled two-of-their-kind on the face of the earth.

Although in their early sixties, her parents were as vivacious as a pair of twenty-year-olds. While at the end of that particular decade of their lives, they had taken an interest in the silver screen era and had immersed themselves in the trivia and gaiety. When their son was born, he became the namesake of Montgomery Clift. They baptized Tierney in the same manner, as they did every pet. They had a cat named Fred Astaire, a poodle by the name of Rock Hudson, and Lauren Bacall was a goldfish. Gary Cooper was the last of the pets to be so christened.

Despite this idiosyncrasy, or perhaps because of it, Tierney enjoyed her parents' company. She never tired of hearing stories of their trips, of which there were many. But today was an arduous day; she wasn't sure if she could handle her mother's frivolity.

"Oh, and sweetheart," Irene continued. "You wouldn't believe who we met. A man who looks exactly like Gregory Peck when he was in his prime. If it wasn't because I love your father dearly, who's as charming and handsome as Laurence Olivier himself, I may have run off with this other chap."

"That's nice, Mom." Tierney had heard similar stories from her mother on many occasions. Her parent often met someone who was the clone of a late, great movie star. Her spouse stood by her side with his usual affectionate amusement and blithely accepted his role as the much-loved but oblivious husband.

"So how are things at home, baby? Have you seen Monty?"

Tierney's relationship with her brother was complex. He was the older sibling by three years, and they sat at opposite ends of the scale. Monty's life revolved around money and status. As a financial consultant, he dealt with high rollers daily. He had a buxom, bejeweled, trophy wife and two children who were always required to be perfect.

In contrast, Tierney focused on what brought her pleasure rather than how much money it put in the bank. She dressed simply, drove an older model car, and lived in her childhood home. For friends, she chose quality over quantity.

Tierney rarely saw her brother, although he lived in downtown Ottawa, and they were both content with the arrangement.

"No. He's away at a convention," she said to her mother.

"Oh, yes, I remember something about that. And how's Gary?"

"Cooper's the same as usual." Irene insisted on calling the golden retriever by his first name, but Tierney thought 'Cooper' sounded somewhat less ridiculous for an animal than 'Gary'.

"So, there's nothing unusual happening at home?"

Tierney considered her mother's choice of words for a moment. Yes, there were unusual happenings. Too unusual, but she knew better than to mention the murder. Her parents might appear to be self-absorbed, but they would drop everything at a moment's notice if she needed them. She didn't want to ruin their perfect vacation and bring them rushing home to support her when there was nothing to do to change what had already happened.

"No, Mom, everything is the same here."

"Are you sure, love? You sound a bit off."

"I'm just tired, that's all. I've been wrapped up in my book." At least she had stuck to the same lie for everyone, she thought.

"Well, take a break. Oh, I have a glorious idea! Why don't you fly over and join us? Wouldn't that be fun? Why didn't I think of it before? Winston, isn't that a splendid plan?"

A shudder ran through Tierney at the prospect of joining a cruise ship loaded with eccentric movie buffs, having to fend off the eligible men her mother threw at her. She would rather clean the toilets in a federal prison.

"Mom!" she shouted, trying to snag her mother's attention over the phone lines.

"Your father agrees, Tierney. You have to come. There's the most gorgeous man who would be perfect for you. He's around your age. Well, he may be a bit older, but not too old, mind you."

"Not Gregory Peck, I hope."

"No, not him. This one's more like Gordon MacRae. You remember him, don't you? He was in *Oklahoma* with Shirley Jones."

"Thanks, Mom. I appreciate the thought, but I can't get away now. Next time, okay?"

"Oh, sweetheart, I'm so disappointed. It would have been such fun. We still have ten days on board, you know. And then another ten days visiting Spain. There's time for you to get here."

"Yes, but I have too many things lined up, and it's impossible for me to leave."

"I understand. As you said, maybe next time." Her mother sounded only mildly put off by Tierney's response. Doubtless, the next exciting activity on the ship's roster preoccupied her.

After a few more minutes of chatting, mother and daughter said goodbye and disconnected. Tierney suffered a twinge of remorse for not confiding in her parents. When they arrived home, they would discover what had happened during their absence, and there would be hell to pay.

Tierney would deal with that when the time came. She refused to allow her problems to disrupt the lives of the people she loved, and despite their eccentricities, she loved her parents dearly.

That didn't solve the problem of her restlessness. Tierney yearned to unload her troubles on someone, but she was so loaded down with guilt, the thought of telling anyone of her part in the death of an innocent woman tore her heart to shreds. Besides, she had been told to not discuss the case with anyone.

Even so, Tierney was tempted to give Faye a call just to change her mind and talk about things that did not involve murder. But, when she checked the calendar, she realized her friend was away with the kids, visiting her parents for a few days.

Instead, Tierney spent much of her time pacing the house and walking with Cooper in the deserted fields of farmland that surrounded her home. She neglected her laptop and her novel. Whenever she sat down to write, she stared into space, thinking of Jennifer Danvers.

Two days later, tired of waiting and feeling as if she might go mad with no news, Tierney dug out Detective Riddell's card and placed a call. After explaining to the receptionist her business with the cop, she was put through to his phone, and he answered on the first ring.

"Detective Riddell here."

"This is Tierney McGinnis speaking."

"Yes, Tierney." The cop's voice held a note of interest, and she pictured him sitting forward at his desk, concentrating on the phone call. "How can I help you?"

"I was wondering if you have any news." She hated the tremor in her voice and hoped he didn't notice.

There was a pause, and she realized he tried to decide how much to tell her. It bothered her that Josh felt the need to withhold information. Tierney understood the police always hesitated to reveal details of a case, but she believed, with her intimate link to this case, she deserved to be informed of everything.

"Not very much. The suspect left nothing in the way of trace evidence behind, except the items we already mentioned."

"Nothing new?"

He wavered. "Not very much."

"Did you find out how he got into the house?"

The sound of a deep sigh reached her ears. "Miss McGinnis...Tierney...I'm sorry, but I can't discuss the specifics of the case with you."

"Detective Riddell, you and your partner were kind enough to come to my home the other day and tell me my book was connected to this case. Therefore, by association, I am also connected to this case, and I'm entitled to information."

"I understand how you feel," he said. Tierney detected another sigh before he continued. "But, as a crime writer, you can appreciate the fact that we're not able to, nor are we required to divulge the details of an ongoing murder investigation."

"Don't patronize me, Detective." This time the tremor was caused less by nerves and more by anger.

"I suggest you not be high-handed with me, Miss McGinnis," he replied.

Tierney didn't know where to go from here.

"I'll let you get back to your work, Detective, and if something should come up that you can share with me, feel free to call." Tierney hung up the phone before he reacted to her attitude, and she felt a certain amount of satisfaction in the way she had handled the situation.

CHAPTER 13

"What was that about?" Clint stared at him from his position on the opposite side of Josh's desk.

"T.L. McGinnis is trying to push her weight around and find out what's happening with the case."

"And since she doesn't have much weight, literally or figuratively, you didn't tell her anything." Clint didn't look up from the report that lay before him.

"Other than what was purposely left, we don't have a lot to tell. No fingerprints. No trace evidence. The killer was spotless. We've got the novel and the heart, and she's already aware of them."

Forensics had determined the page cut from the book was in mint condition, with no suggestion of manipulation. The suspect had removed it from the paperback version that had only been available since the previous month. The experts said the person had likely held it with the left hand, and a very sharp utility knife had made the cut. That meant the killer was right-handed.

The detectives theorized that the murderer had read the hardcover copy of the book, planned the attack, and purchased a paperback for leaving clues. It would have taken time to find a blond-haired accountant named Jennifer, learn where she lived, and set the stage for her murder.

They made the small plastic heart in China, sold in batches of twenty-five and distributed through large chains of discount stores, making them impossible to trace.

A sweep of the databases had uncovered no murders using a similar MO in Canada within the last twenty years. They had hit a dead end.

"Did she ask how the suspect got in?" Clint said.

"Yeah. I won't tell her."

The investigators had discovered the lock of the back door had been picked. It was a regular door lock, not meant as heavy security. There had not been a deadbolt or an alarm system as added protection.

Josh felt a woman living alone should have better secured her home. He also didn't believe he needed to share any of that information with the writer. She dealt with enough guilt at the moment. No, he thought, with Ms. McGinnis he wanted to work on a need-to-know basis.

When Josh saw Clint's expression, he waited to see what words of wisdom would roll off his tongue. He didn't have long to wait.

"Josh, women have a boundless desire for information. Even if we think it's useless, it makes them feel better that we're sharing something with them. It makes them feel needed and useful."

Josh rolled his eyes. "So, what you're saying is we should tell her something, anything at all, even if it's not true."

"It always works for me."

"You're a snake, Clint. No wonder you go through women like a bag of potato chips."

"At least I see women. It's more than I can say for you."

• • •

Clint rolled his shoulders and tried to loosen up his muscles. He unbuttoned his dark navy sports jacket, only to button it again a few seconds later. His gaze swiveled up and down the street, uncertain from which direction she would arrive. Or if she would arrive. She may have had second thoughts. Lydia had agreed to go out with him, but she had insisted on meeting him at the restaurant instead of letting him pick her up at her place.

Que sera sera, he told himself, but a crushing disappointment followed. It was a foreign emotion for Clint where women were concerned. He had always been laid back in his relationships. Until now.

He yanked his phone from his coat pocket and checked the time. Again. One minute had passed since the last time he had looked, and she was just three minutes late, he reminded himself. He would give her ten more before he gave up and went home. Maybe twenty.

Clint spotted her from a distance. Her face was in the shadows, but he recognized her walk. She held herself straight, shoulders back, and chin raised. Her gray silk sheath dress draped her body, accentuating her curves and drawing the eye to her slim calves. A green and gray shawl protected her shoulders from the cool spring evening.

As he stepped forward to meet her, he searched for a sign of regret for her decision, but what he witnessed was a combination of shyness and pleasure. A relieved smile lit his face.

"Sorry, I'm late. I hope you weren't waiting long."

"Not at all. I just got here." He offered his arm and grinned as she slid her hand through the crook of his elbow to rest it on his forearm. "Have you ever been here before?" He gestured toward the massive wooden doors before them. He had chosen the upscale Restaurant e18hteen to prove his tastes weren't limited to noisy pubs.

Lydia acknowledged it was her first visit, and her enraptured gaze as she entered the establishment made it more than worth the price he would pay for their meal. Clint was lucky. His friend Dave worked as the sous-chef here, and he'd placed a call earlier in the day to tell him they had reservations at the restaurant. There was sure to be an impressive surprise ahead for them.

The hostess showed them to an intimate table for two. A window, deeply set in a wall of rustic gray bricks, gave them a view of the Byward Market from their corner location. The other wall housed an immense fireplace that dominated the room.

Lydia seemed impressed, if her avid scrutiny was any sign. Clint presumed he had earned a few points. It was important to impress this woman.

As they dined on Atlantic lobster and Angus Chateaubriand steak, Clint filled Lydia in on his background and family. At first, he placed as little emphasis as possible on his career, remembering her reaction to his revelation at The Laff. But, to his surprise, Lydia showed an interest in his career, particularly the cases he had worked in the homicide division.

While he shared as much as possible of his history with her, he wasn't having any luck with reciprocation. The most he learned was she was an interior decorator, both of her parents were dead, and she had been born and raised in Ottawa. A change of subject blocked any other attempts to gain information.

That didn't mean they didn't talk. They covered topics that ranged from politics to sports, carrying them from the appetizers to the *pièce de résistance*. Dave pulled through for Clint, preparing a dessert board for them and delivering it to their table himself.

Bite-sized portions of tarts, cheesecakes, and chocolate mousses lay amid scatterings of fresh fruit and a chocolate coulis. Clint wasn't normally a dessert person, but the presentation made his mouth water. The bottle of port that arrived at their table, compliments of the house, was the perfect accompaniment.

"That was wonderful," Lydia said, as Clint walked her to her car. "I haven't eaten so well in forever."

"It's nice to do something special once in a while."

"That was definitely special."

Clint almost said, "So are you", but he stopped himself just in time. It would have sounded too cheesy, and they hadn't reached that point in their relationship. Yet. With any luck, that would change. One thing of which he was certain was that he wanted to see more of this woman.

But he also knew not to push her. They'd had fun, and Lydia had been animated and cheerful throughout the evening, but there was something that told him he had to move at a pace uncommon for him. The story of the tortoise and the hare.

He stood beside her car, gave her a quick peck on the lips, and promised to call her in two days. As she drove away, he marveled at the power this woman had over him. He told himself to be careful, or he would find himself in deep water. Clint shrugged his shoulders and walked to his car. So be it, he thought with a smile.

CHAPTER 14

Josh was at home Saturday morning, making a cheese omelet, when his cell phone rang. It was Sara Evans at dispatch.

"There's a report of a suspected homicide on Birch Street. They need you there right away. I've called Weller."

Josh's blood froze. He got the exact directions, shut off the stove, and headed out of the apartment on an empty stomach.

• • • •

Once again, Josh stood with Clint by his side on a Saturday morning surveying the scene of a crime. This time, it was in a young woman's bathroom, and Josh's heart sat somewhere in the vicinity of the stomach he hadn't had a chance to fill.

"Jesus. I didn't want to see this."

"Spit it out. What are you not telling me?" Clint said.

Josh met his partner's gaze and witnessed the moment Clint realized something was wrong.

"What is it?" Clint's expression was grim.

"Another chapter."

Clint closed his eyes for a moment and heaved a sigh. "Our worst fear."

"Yeah, it is, but…" Josh faltered, "maybe I'm wrong. Let's hope so."

He wasn't wrong, no matter how much he wished to be. Once the crime scene team was set up in the bathroom, it took a few minutes for them to find three pages from *Murder by the Dozen* in the medicine cabinet. They appeared to have been removed from the book in the same manner as the page at Jennifer Danvers' house. Following Josh's instructions, they found a plastic heart in the back of the victim's mouth.

"What do you say?" Clint looked over Josh's shoulder at the bagged pages.

"I remember it, and at first glance, I'd say it matches. This vic is a brunette. She was strangled in her bathtub. Those details coincide with Tierney's fictional victim."

"Detectives?"

The two men turned to face Benson. The team had recently gained the junior detective as a member. "The victim's name is Penelope Morrison." She checked her notepad as she spoke.

"Penny," Josh said.

"What?"

Josh looked at Clint. "Penny is the name of the character in the book. It's short for Penelope."

"Where did she work?" Josh asked Detective Benson.

"She works in a women's clothing boutique."

Josh frowned. "No, that's not right. Unless I'm making a mistake, she should be a dental hygienist."

The female detective appeared confused. Clint gave her an apologetic shrug before addressing Josh. "The killer went off track this time."

"Possibly. I'll check my notes. And we'll dig into Ms. Morrison's background." He turned back to Benson. "I want you to talk to the people at her workplace. What's the name of the store?"

"Betsy's. It's at the Rideau Centre," Benson said, referring to the large shopping mall in downtown Ottawa.

Josh flinched.

"What's up?" Clint frowned at him.

"Nothing," Josh murmured. "Never mind."

The cops stood to the side while the experts scoured the apartment, swabbing, bagging, and dusting for fingerprints. They ran adhesive rollers over surfaces, trolling for trace evidence, and they photographed the victim and the crime scene before they moved her to the morgue. The medical examiner was once again on site to catalog his findings before performing the autopsy. When he finished with the preliminaries, he approached the detectives.

"What's your opinion, Chris?" Clint said.

"She didn't have time to put up a struggle. No visible signs of external injuries. Nothing under her fingernails that I observed with the naked eye. I'll see more when I get her in the lab."

"Time of death?" Josh said.

"Judging from the rigor, I'd say approximately twelve hours, which puts it at around nine or ten last night."

It was as Josh had guessed. That was the straightforward part. The rest was too scientific. A laboratory, an experienced coroner, and the proper equipment would nail down the details.

He checked in with the police officers who had gathered information from neighbors, but they were unsuccessful. Penelope lived in a small four-apartment building. There were no security cameras. The neighbors were friendly, but not nosy. No one had heard any unusual sounds during the night. They were scared and worried, wondering if they could be next.

Josh had reminded everyone to keep details to themselves. The standard response was that there was an active pursuit of the suspect, and they expected to have said suspect in custody soon. Josh wished that was the case. They had two murders, no clues, no witnesses, and no direction in which to turn.

"Josh?"

He turned at the sound of his partner's voice.

"Her brother's in the other room," Clint said. "He found the body."

Josh swore under his breath. "Okay, we'll do it together."

Phil Morrison sat in an armchair, his head in his hands, his shoulders slumped. He lifted his head when the two men entered the room and looked at them with shell-shocked, red-rimmed eyes.

The two detectives lowered themselves onto a couch across from the victim's brother. They expressed their sympathies and watched as the other man nodded, his expression numb.

"How about you start from the beginning, please?" Josh said. "Why were you here?"

"I had a few errands to run, and I stopped by to see Penny."

Josh and Clint exchanged a glance at the mention of the nickname.

"Was the door unlocked or open when you got here?" Josh said.

"No, it was locked, as usual. I have a key, so I let myself in."

"And then?"

"I wanted to surprise her, make her a nice pancake breakfast." The man's eyes filled with tears, and his voice broke. "She loved pancakes."

The detectives gave him a moment to compose himself before Clint continued with the questioning. "Where did you go after you entered the apartment?"

"To the kitchen." He gestured toward the other room. "I prepared the coffee and mixed the batter. I was sure she'd hear me and get out of bed." His voice faltered on his last words; his expression stricken.

"What did you do then, Mr. Morrison?" Josh said.

"I thought it was strange, so I went down the hallway to knock on the bedroom door. As I walked by the bathroom...the door was open, I looked in...I saw her. I didn't understand why she'd be taking a bath in the morning, and why she hadn't heard me come in. Something was wrong. I called her name. She didn't move. Oh, God!"

Phil covered his face with his hands, and his shoulders quaked.

"Can I get you something? A glass of water?" Clint asked.

The man shook his head and dragged himself back to the present.

"Did you touch her or any objects in the room?" Josh continued. "Did you see anyone? Hear an unusual noise?"

Again, the man shook his head, his gaze focused on the floor.

Josh's cell phone rang, and he stepped outside the room to take the call, knowing it was his boss, Lieutenant Helen Lowe, on the other end. Someone would have filled her in on the preliminary details of the murder. The lieutenant would want an in-depth rundown of the case, and Josh was sure his superior would not be happy regarding the lack of evidence.

He tried to put an optimistic spin on a dismal situation. "We're getting there, boss."

"You're getting where, Riddell? It doesn't seem as if you've gotten anywhere at all."

"We've interviewed the brother. He didn't have much to add, but we're waiting for the techs to finish doing their job. They might come up with something."

"What? You said yourself there didn't seem to be any trace. All we've got is the damn heart and those pages. Get back out there and talk to that McGinnis woman. She's got to tell you something. Two strangulations in two weeks will make the press suspicious. And if they create dialogue about a serial killer, we'll have problems."

"I get that. We're doing our best."

"I need you to do better than your best, and you're aware who the key to this whole thing is, aren't you?"

"Yeah, I am, and I'm on it."

CHAPTER 15

It was fascinating. The last time, the killer wasn't close enough to Jennifer Danvers' home to discover what went on inside. The girl hadn't been considerate; there were no concealing sheds or shrubbery on her property, and the police had kept the crowd too far away from the house.

This time, things had worked out much better. With a perfect view of the front door of the apartment building, it was easy to blend in with the curious onlookers. Everyone wanted to memorize the details and repeat them to their family and friends. It gave them a sense of importance. For the killer, the memories were private and to be savored. This was a personal moment of triumph.

True, the first killing had been perfect in its execution and also in the victim's selection. Everything coincided, but the thrill of watching and taking part in the aftermath had to be sacrificed.

The expressions on the faces of the law enforcement personnel who traipsed in and out of the apartment building were easily visible. The same two homicide detectives were on the premises along with many of the same crime scene investigators who had served on the Danvers' case. It was perfect.

It was exciting to imagine what they were doing inside the apartment, the evidence they hunted, the swabs and samples they removed from the body and from every surface in the vicinity. A pang of envy ripped through the killer, wanting to be among them, listening to their conversation, impressing them with wisdom.

Other police officers worked outside, scanning the walkway, the grass, the parking lot, looking for a clue to point them in a direction. Any direction was better than what they had, which was none. The desire to laugh and shout at them and tell them they were wasting their time pulsed through the criminal's body.

The murder had been planned with care, and no evidence was left behind.

It was important not to be recognized as a bystander from the other crime scene. That appeared too suspicious. Whether it was good fortune or not, the killer had lived a life as an invisible person, always blending into the crowd. How odd was it to be introduced to someone at work or at a party, and a week later, upon meeting the same person again, there would be no trace of recognition?

It was impossible to discern what it was about the killer that was so bland. That people saw no quality worth remembering was a constant irritant. As ironic as it seemed, the very thing that had been so annoying in the past now worked in the killer's favor.

It took a minimal disguise to render appearances even more forgettable; a cap, a pair of sunglasses, a turned-up collar, or a different manner of dress, and no one had any memory of a murderer among a crowd of people.

Here the killer stood, pretending to be a dismayed spectator, worried about what kind of horror lurked in the neighborhood. What monster took another life? Would it happen again? Was anyone safe? Concerned remarks were exchanged with a few of the nearby people, but it wasn't overdone. There was nothing to be gained by risking a memory.

Watching the aftermath was almost as much fun as the actual killing, the person thought. The only thing better would be standing next to those detectives while they studied the evidence, or lack thereof.

Moving a few paces to the left, nudging aside an old woman, the killer leaned forward and peered through the few inches of space between the curtains. At least four people stood in the center of the living room. The lead detectives were there. One of them talked on his cell phone while the partner discussed something with the other two people, in all likelihood, members of the forensic team. The conversation was predictable.

"*It's the same as the last time.*"

"*The same clues are left behind.*"

"*What do they mean?*"

"*I don't know, but we must figure it out soon, because one thing I'm sure of is there will be more murders.*"

"*It's someone smart, very smart. I'm thinking we'll never catch the person responsible.*"

"*We have to. Otherwise, you know what will happen? We'll have twelve dead bodies on our hands.*"

Yes, they were scratching their heads. *What did the plastic heart mean? Who would be the next victim? Was the author, T.L. McGinnis, involved?* It had triggered extensive hours of detective work, not to mention boundless discussions and speculations. A giggle itched to escape. It would not do to laugh out loud while standing near a murder scene. For once, the killer might become the center of attention, and now was not the time.

And the best part of all was that the police detectives would think the killer was falling apart, having trouble following the plan. Little did they know that not following the plan was the plan. The laugh that erupted was quickly turned into a cough for the benefit of the elderly woman with the worried glance.

CHAPTER 16

The scenery didn't interest Josh as he and Clint made a second trip to visit Tierney McGinnis. The detectives had gone over the particulars of the homicide at the crime scene. They had questioned the neighbors, the brother, and the medical examiner. They had examined the three pages taken from Tierney's book and left in the medicine cabinet. Another evidence bag held the red plastic heart.

They disagreed about what to do concerning the writer.

Josh's gut reaction was to not tell Tierney, at least not at once, though he was under orders to do so. His reasoning was that it would upset her more, and they would gain nothing.

Clint argued she would get it from another source. It would be on the television and radio news. He insisted it would be better for Tierney to learn of it from them than from elsewhere. Besides, their boss would have their hides if they didn't follow through on her orders. They also had to consider that Tierney was their closest tie to the murder investigation. Not meeting with her would be a monumental mistake.

Clint didn't have to put into words his opinion regarding the way Josh was dealing with this case. His tone reeked of disapproval, tempered with sympathy. And Josh realized his partner was right, understanding he was not handling the case to the best of his ability. He vowed to get his head together and do better.

Josh didn't look forward to the visit. They would compound Tierney's distress a hundredfold, and even though their last conversation had not ended on the best of terms, he had no desire to witness her pain. She would bend herself backward, trying to heap more blame onto her shoulders.

Josh pulled the car into the driveway of the farmhouse and parked it at the foot of the steps leading to the porch. As they climbed out of the car, there was no sign of Tierney, but Cooper sprawled beside the door, and his tail wagged in greeting.

Josh was the first to set his foot onto the wooden porch, and he had no sooner done so before the door swung open, and Tierney stepped outside. Her hair was again pulled back into a ponytail, and she wore a simple pair of capris and a T-shirt, her feet bare. Once more, her look of youth and innocence struck Josh.

Worry creased Tierney's face. She stopped in Josh's path and pinned him with her distressed gaze, not saying a word.

"Hello, Ms. McGinnis. Do you mind if we come in?" Josh fought to keep the sound of defeat out of his voice.

"You've found something, haven't you? I've had an unpleasant feeling all day. Did you catch him?" Her gaze shifted from one man to the other.

"Please, can we talk inside?"

With his words, Josh saw her face register the fact they had dreadful news to deliver. Tierney wavered for a second before swiveling and leading them into her home. Her shoulders and back were stiff with visible tension. Without a word, they went to the living room and took the same seats in which they had sat two weeks earlier. A sense of déjà vu washed over Josh.

"What is it?"

Josh heard the light tremor in Tierney's voice. Their grim expressions didn't allay the woman's concerns. He fixed her with a steady stare. "Tierney, I'm afraid there's been another murder."

"No. Please, no." Her skin paled, and her vision lost its focus.

"I'm sorry, but I'm afraid so."

"But are you sure, maybe it's not..." Tears shimmered in her eyes.

"It is. We found pages from the book again."

"Oh, no."

Tierney's head bowed, and her face dropped into her hands. Her shoulders trembled. Josh knew this had been her worst fear, but the visit was unavoidable, no matter how much he sought to convince himself otherwise.

Josh studied the grains of the wood floor while Tierney struggled to get control of her emotions. When her sobs decreased in intensity, she straightened and looked at Josh, her eyes red-rimmed and filled with anguish, her chest heaving.

"Tell me," she said.

"A young woman, twenty-five years old, by the name of Penelope Morrison, was found in her bathtub, apparently strangled."

"Oh, my God. A brunette? Her friends called her Penny?" she asked.

"Yes."

"The heart? Did you find one?"

"Yes, we did. The same as last time."

Tierney paused and seemed to rake her memory. "She was a dental hygienist, wasn't she?"

Josh hesitated and glanced at Clint. "No, she wasn't. She worked in a boutique."

He saw a mixture of relief and puzzlement cross Tierney's face.

"So, does that mean it's not the same killer?" Tierney stopped when Josh shook his head.

"We found the pages from the book, remember? And her boyfriend is a dentist."

"So, it's not precisely the same as in my novel." Her tone was hopeful. Josh didn't have the heart to burst her bubble.

"Did you ever meet the victim?" Clint pulled her attention to him.

"No...yes...I mean I never met the actual woman. I know the woman in my novel." Tierney leaned back on the sofa, her expression stunned. "Oh my God," she said again. "I can't believe this is happening."

Josh stared at her, powerless. He imagined the terrible thoughts that ran through her mind, and he was incapable of coming up with any words of wisdom to offer her comfort. All he could do was capture the monster. With this in mind, Josh moved to sit beside her on the couch.

"Tierney," he said. "It's highly likely we're dealing with a serial killer. And your book is a guide, for lack of a better word, for the killings. We need to move as fast as possible to stop the suspect before it happens again."

"How? How can I help? I can't come up with anything." Her eyes pleaded with him.

"You can think of people you've been in contact with. Or the people you work with."

"I have. I've thought incessantly about it. I don't know anyone capable of doing something like this. It's horrendous."

Josh didn't feel it was the time to mention the fact that the 'horrendousness' had come from her imagination, and she had put it onto paper.

"Why do you believe the killer is someone who knows me?" Tierney asked. "They distribute my books all over the country. Anyone can buy one. What makes you think I'm acquainted with the killer?"

Tierney directed her question to Josh, but Clint stepped in to answer.

"We're not certain it's someone you've met or someone who knows you, but it's something we have to explore. It's too big a coincidence for the murders to happen in your backyard, so to speak, when the book is available around the world. What are the chances? We have to check out any lead we can find, and for now, you're the only one."

Tierney looked at Clint with a desolate stare. Josh realized it wasn't pleasant to be told you're the sole lead in a murder investigation. Her gaze shifted to Josh as he leaned toward her.

"Let me ask you a few questions and you can think out loud." He paused and waited for her to focus on him before he continued. "Tell me, do you do any research for your books?"

Tierney took a deep breath and released it through clenched teeth, fighting to get on an even keel. Josh knew concentrating on something other than the actual murders would help clear the fog from her head.

"Yes, I research. The majority of what I write comes from my imagination, but there are a lot of things I need to learn. I strive to be as accurate as possible, so I consult people or google subjects on the Internet."

"Who are the people you'd consult?"

Tierney paused for a moment. "Well, for instance, there's a cop I'm acquainted with. He's helped me when I needed advice for weapons, if I wanted to get an impression of the inner workings of a police department, or the day-to-day routine of a police officer, that kind of thing."

"Great," Clint said, "What's this guy's name?" He took out his notebook.

"You don't believe he's involved in this, do you?"

"We know nothing yet, but we can't leave any stone unturned," Clint said. "Perhaps he noticed something you didn't. Maybe he can give us a clue to lead us in a new direction."

Tierney nodded. "His name's Lucas Bishop. He's with the City of Ottawa police. I have his phone number. I can get it for you."

"Why don't we wait until we've gone through our questions? Then you can get us the book, and we'll get the names of everyone we want to contact," Josh said. "Is there anyone else you can tell us about?"

"Yes, there's the medical examiner, Chris Abbott. I've often consulted him for various things."

"Such as?" asked Josh.

"Such as how the human body reacts to different methods of killing. How he does his job. How he deciphers the clues he finds in or around the body. What it's like to see death every day. How he deals with the lawyers and the cops. What it's like to testify in court and provide evidence in a murder trial. He has so much to offer."

"He does." It didn't surprise Josh that Tierney consulted Dr. Abbott for her research. He was well known in his field, and it was something he'd be happy to do.

"I don't understand how he does it, day in and day out, dealing with dead bodies," Tierney said, with a shake of her head.

"How often have you been to his office?"

"Quite a few times. I haven't counted. Sometimes, we meet for lunch, and he answers my questions. He's been here a few times."

"Did you meet any of the staff? Are they aware you're a writer?"

Tierney considered the question for a moment. "Yes, Chris introduced me to his team members, but I don't recall if he told them my reasons for being there. He may have said something afterward. I didn't swear him to secrecy."

"Why not? Didn't you want to keep your identity a secret?" Josh said.

"Not a secret, no. I just don't blatantly advertise it. I value my privacy, but I'm not obsessed with it."

"What about Bishop?" Clint asked, following Josh's reasoning. "Did he show you around the station, introduce you to his coworkers, his boss, that kind of thing?"

"Yes, he did. Not in a big way, but he explained my presence to his buddies, at least the ones that were there."

Clint made another note in his book while Josh continued his questioning.

"Who else do you consult?"

"The only other person I can think of is Jim, the husband of my best friend. He's a lawyer, mostly civil law, but he helps me with criminal law questions I have, sometimes from his own knowledge, or he'll talk to another lawyer with the firm. I never have too many questions. The Internet answers most of them."

"Speaking of which, did you go to any chat rooms, contact anyone over the Internet, either by e-mail or via messaging?" Clint said.

"No. Never. Whenever I couldn't get an answer from a website, I'd usually call one of the three people I just mentioned."

"And neighbors? Do any of them realize they're living near an author?"

"Sure, I guess most do, but it doesn't seem to make any difference to them. I don't socialize much. I've met a few casually, but I don't know many of them well, apart from Faye and Jim. They live a mile away."

"I wondered if there may be someone in particular who seems to be a little more interested in what you're doing than the others," Josh said.

"Jeff Lakefield, I suppose. He considers himself an amateur detective."

"How old is he? Does he live alone?" Clint continued.

"I'd say he's around thirty-five and single. He works as an actuary," she said with a grimace. "I think he's bored, and he's looking for something exciting to add a bit of interest to his day. Believe me, Jeff's the most harmless guy you can find. I could easily scare him off with a nasty look."

Josh sent Clint a glance before turning back to the writer. "What about friends and acquaintances?"

"I don't have any friends who have a sideline as serial killers, Detective Riddell," Tierney said.

Her defensiveness made him suppress a smile. "I'm sure you don't, Miss McGinnis. But your friends may have been talking to someone else regarding the fact they know a writer of murder mysteries. Is that possible?"

"It's possible, but I have no way of knowing who they talk to or what they say to other people, and it seems as if it'd be difficult to ask them to remember every conversation with everyone they've ever met."

"Then, I guess you'd say our jobs are difficult, because that's what we spend a large part of our time doing."

Tierney's shoulders sagged. "I know. I'm sorry for snapping at you. It's just that..." She paused, searching for words.

"We realize how hard this is for you, and we understand." Josh glanced at Clint before rising to his feet. "We have to leave now, but if you can think of anyone or anything else, please call us. If you could get us that contact information, I'd appreciate it."

"Of course." Tierney also stood. She went to her office and came back with a small, black book, which was dog-eared and well-worn. "I keep everything in here. Names, numbers, dates, notes, you name it, it's in here."

She sifted through the pages and recited the contact information of the police officer and lawyer to Clint.

His hand on the doorknob, Josh turned to Tierney. "Are you going to be okay? Is there anyone I can call for you?"

"No, I'm fine. I want to be alone and figure out how to digest this."

"Contact us if you need something."

Josh scratched Cooper behind the ears and gave Tierney a slight smile before taking his leave, Clint by his side.

CHAPTER 17

The unpleasantness of the day settled on Josh's shoulders as the detectives drove back to headquarters. He mentally sifted through information, trying to come up with another idea of where to poke around or who to approach to bring them a step closer to the killer. Clint cleared this throat and snagged his attention.

"I realize you won't like what I have to say, but I need to run something by you."

"First, why wouldn't I like it? If it helps the case, I'm happy to hear whatever you have. On the other hand, if it's about your lousy love life, we should wait until later," Josh said with a feeble smile.

"You won't like this."

"Try me." Josh turned onto the highway that led them to the downtown area.

"All right. What if the entire thing's a publicity stunt? What if Tierney McGinnis is behind this to promote her book?" Clint said.

Josh's hands jerked on the steering wheel. "A publicity stunt? What? The murders? Who would murder for publicity?"

"A desperate author, perhaps," Clint said.

"Are you crazy? You're telling me that woman murdered people to publicize her novel?"

"I understand it sounds far-fetched…"

"Far-fetched? You're not in the same hemisphere. For God's sake, listen to what you're saying. Didn't you see her? Can you imagine Tierney McGinnis with her hands around another woman's throat strangling her to death?"

"I admit it's difficult to picture her doing it herself, but she might have hired someone to do it."

"You've got to be joking." Clint had always had a good imagination, but Josh couldn't believe how far out he had gone with this one.

"Hear me out. She's an author, but she's not John Grisham, hauling in the big bucks with her writing. Tierney has to live in her parent's house to make ends meet. There are umpteen thousand writers out there, pumping out books every day, and she needs to draw attention to her work. Once word gets around that someone is using her book as a guide for a series of murders, it'll shoot to the top of the bestseller list."

"Come on, only a lunatic would do something so extreme, and don't tell me Tierney McGinnis comes off looking like a lunatic."

"She seems to be a very nice, normal person. But so was Ted Bundy." Clint said. "What I'm trying to say is we have to keep our options open, and, at the moment, Tierney is the one choice we have."

"Only because we haven't had the time or opportunity to find others," Josh said.

"Granted. I just want you to keep an open mind, without a preconceived certainty of Tierney's innocence to cloud your vision."

"I always keep an open mind. You know that."

"I do. I also know you're having a hard time with this case and one of the reasons is that you're attracted to Tierney. Perhaps you've compromised your professional detachment."

"That's not true," Josh said. "I'm neither attracted to Tierney nor have I set aside my ethics, for whatever reason. Yes, I believe she's innocent, but that's my instinct kicking in, nothing else. I'm capable of remaining detached."

"You're thinking of Andrea," Clint said in a low voice.

Josh sighed and ran his fingers through his hair. "Of course, I am. How could I not? That doesn't mean my judgment is clouded."

Clint held up his hands in defense. "All right. I believe you. I just wanted to have my say."

"Okay, you've had it, and it's duly noted, but there's no need to worry about me."

Clint snapped his fingers. "Wait a second. Betsy's. That's what bothered you today. Didn't Andrea work there?"

Josh winced. "Yeah. That's where she worked. Can we drop it now?"

"Consider it dropped," Clint said, but Josh caught the sympathetic look he shot him.

• • •

That evening, Josh warmed a frozen dinner in the microwave and crashed on the couch. He picked up the book written by Tierney McGinnis and stared at the cover without cheer.

It irked him that Clint questioned his ability to distance himself from the case. Josh admitted to himself the fact Clint had noticed rankled more than the possibility a certain amount of unprofessionalism existed. He prided himself on being a good detective, and he swore to be unbiased in this case.

Josh didn't believe Tierney was a suspect in the killings. His belief had nothing to do with any attraction he may or may not have for the woman, but with his instincts. They didn't often fail him.

The idea of Tierney orchestrating the murders as a promotional scheme was ludicrous, and if Clint wasn't a good friend as well as his partner, Josh may have caused him bodily harm. All anyone had to do was look in her eyes, and they'd see she did not have a mean or devious bone in her body.

Josh set the book aside and scraped his hands over his face. It had been an interminable day. The first day on which they discovered a murder was always difficult. There was so much to do as fast as possible.

But it wasn't just the discovery of the crime that bothered Josh, nor was it the volume of work. It was Tierney herself that disturbed him, and Clint's speculations were off base. Josh had an uneasy sensation about this case, and his unease concerned Tierney. He was certain she was in danger, but he didn't know where the danger lurked or when it would happen.

He stood and stared out the window at the quiet street in front of the apartment building. Not for the first time, Josh wished he had a crystal ball.

His job comprised catching killers after the fact. He preferred to prevent the crime from happening.

It was not Clint's mention of Andrea's name or the boutique where she worked that brought thoughts of her to the forefront of his mind. Memories of her had been there ever since the beginning of this case. There were tiny similarities that struck a chord and nagged him. Again, his instincts kicked in and led his thoughts down a rough road.

Josh sighed and opened the book to where he had left off the previous night. He'd had little opportunity to read in the past week, but he had made it to murder number four. He took a few minutes to flip through the pages he had already read to refresh his memory. Just as he had guessed, Jennifer Danvers' death matched that of the first murder, but Penelope Morrison's matched the third killing in the novel.

That might be good news. Perhaps the suspect didn't intend to kill twelve victims as described in *Murder by the Dozen*. Maybe the intention was not to kill them in the same order. Or it was too difficult to find victims that matched those in the novel to a T, a distinct possibility.

"Maybe the killer intends to kill the people he can match as closely as possible. Or maybe he had another system in mind." Josh mumbled to himself. "Not every victim in the book is female. Maybe he intends to kill just females, or maybe he's started with women, and intends to move onto the men later. Maybe the killer is a woman. Too many damn maybes." He tossed the book onto the coffee table.

No one understood what went through the perpetrator's mind, least of all him. Josh rubbed the back of his neck. The effects of fatigue had caught up to him. He couldn't concentrate when he was in this condition. He would read more of the novel and see if something lead him down a different path, but not tonight. Now, he had to get some rest.

CHAPTER 18

Josh woke early the next morning, considering it was a Sunday and his day off, but with a fresh homicide, downtime fell by the wayside. He needed to go to the morgue and talk to Chris Abbott regarding the victim. If he was lucky, the medical examiner had performed the autopsy. If he wasn't, he might have to wait until Monday.

Josh also needed to have a discussion with the forensics group to see if they had collected anything more of interest. If so, they might tell him how the killer had broken into Penny's apartment.

Josh took his coffee into the living room, sank onto the couch, and picked up *Murder by the Dozen*. He planned to read a few more chapters.

An hour later, Josh reached murder number six, and he took a break to review his notes. So far, Jennifer, the accountant, and Penny, the dental hygienist, were both crossed off the killer's list. Next, he needed to worry about Walter, a construction worker; Vivian, a waitress; Paula, a housewife; and Arthur, a musician. There were another six not yet revealed. Josh suspected the killer had the victims in sight, and it was just a matter of going through the list. The order in which he did it was a puzzle Josh hadn't yet solved.

Was it going to be one every second week? Would the killings always happen on a weekend? What was the game plan? Why had the killer skipped a character? Was it too difficult to find one who fit the mold? The second victim in the book was the musician. Josh knew it couldn't be easy to find a musician named Arthur. *Would it eventually happen? Was the killer's quest for victims still ongoing?*

There were too many questions, and Josh wasn't convinced they would ever piece together a pattern. Perhaps not soon enough to prevent another murder. He could not find and protect everyone who had a remote resemblance to the characters in Tierney's novel.

Was there a common thread between the first two victims? He didn't think so. They needed to study the files and search them for something that bound the women together.

Josh laid his head back, closed his eyes, and tried to put himself in the killer's shoes. *If he wanted to find people fitting a certain description, how would he do it?* The Internet was the obvious choice. It was fast and easy.

Josh pulled out his laptop and googled accounting firms in the area. Within a few minutes, he found the company where Jennifer Danvers had worked, and he discovered her name listed among the employees. That had been easy. Way too easy. However, there were no photographs to go with the name.

How had the killer known her age and physical characteristics? She could just as easily have been a sixty-year-old, gray-haired grandmother. Had the killer hunted by name first and matched physical descriptions next? It seemed like a laborious task.

Finding Penny would have been difficult. He checked on the web, but Josh couldn't find any dental clinics in the area with a Penelope or Penny among the staff members. No doubt, the killer had experienced the same problem. *How was the second victim found?*

He explored the website for the clinic where her boyfriend, Alex Friedman, worked and tried to find personal information hidden within it. There was nothing to show a connection between Alex and Penelope.

Josh repeated the exercise to locate a construction worker named Walter, but the results were staggering. There were so many construction companies with thousands of employees, it was impossible to comb through each one looking for the famous needle in the haystack. *Was that why Walter hadn't shown up in the morgue yet?*

Josh reached for the phone. A groggy voice answered on the third ring.

"What's up?" Clint said.

"Just checking in. I've been doing research on the Net."

"Do you know what time it is?"

Josh checked his watch and frowned. "It's mid-morning."

"Nine o'clock is not mid-morning, not in my books. Get a life."

"Didn't mean to disturb you, Bud. I just wanted to share my thoughts," Josh said.

"Share away. I'm awake now."

Josh filled him in on what he had read and researched so far, needing a sounding board. "I can't think of anything more to do. With the tiny amount of evidence we have, there's no way I can narrow a search for potential victims to a few people."

"Any news on the bookstores?"

Josh had delegated the task of canvassing the local bookstores to Benson. She had been diligent in her work, sending out teams, and transmitting the results back to Josh.

"Same problem. We've got people questioning the salespeople in the local stores, but no one can remember who purchased one book out of thousands. It's impossible."

"We had to try."

"What about the heart transplants?" Josh asked. That had been Clint's dossier.

"Two people died within the last year. One was a woman with no family. It's unlikely anyone avenged her death. The other was a man. We're looking at the family and close friends, but so far, nothing has popped."

"Keep looking," Josh said. "I just can't figure out Tierney's connection. She's the most obvious link to the killer, but is it random, or was it calculated?"

"We have to dig deeper into her background."

"We will, but I don't expect to find a lot there," Josh said. "I'm going to the morgue."

Josh wasn't surprised to find Chris at his desk on a Sunday morning, filling in forms in his usual diligent manner. At least, the coroner had conceded to the fact that it was the weekend by wearing jeans and a polo shirt instead of his usual businesslike suits. The doctor seemed equally unsurprised by Josh's visit on a day of rest. They were both aware that criminals didn't respect people's wishes for a normal working week.

Josh scanned the room with unease before dropping into a chair opposite the doctor's desk. The morgue always gave him the heebie-jeebies, with its stainless-steel sterility and the incessant reek of formaldehyde. It took a special person to work here, Josh thought.

"You're alone. I guess that means you didn't do the autopsy yet."

"Wrong. Nick was in." The coroner referred to his assistant. "We got it done, nice and early."

"Find anything?"

"Death by strangulation, as expected. But what you didn't know is the killer hadn't surprised her while she was having a bath. Penelope was killed in her bedroom, her clothes were removed, and she was placed in the tub."

Josh sat forward in his chair. "How do you know?"

"I discovered traces of fiber in her hair that matched the carpet in her bedroom. Quite a few of them, which means her head had to be pressed down firmly, as would be the case in strangulation."

"Any other signs of struggle? Did she put up a fight?"

"To an extent. I found material under her nails."

Josh's heart rate increased a notch. "What was it?"

"Tyvek," the doctor said with a grimace.

"Tyvek. Damn, the bases were covered, weren't they?" He paused for a moment, scouring his memory. "You didn't find any with Jennifer."

"No. Nothing."

Because the killer had surprised Jennifer in her sleep, Josh thought. She didn't have time to react or fight her aggressor. In Penny's case, she may have been awake and prepared to defend herself. That defense had left a tiny amount of evidence behind.

"Anything else about Penelope I should be aware of?"

"She'd been dead between ten to twelve hours. No sign of sexual assault. The killer was clean, Josh, and understands how to keep us from finding any helpful clues."

"Yeah. But eventually he or she will make a mistake. It has to happen."

"I hope so."

They always hoped, Josh thought, but they needed more than hope. They needed something to fall into their hands between now and the next time the killer tried to strike.

"Did you get any information from the boyfriend?" the doctor asked.

"Nothing. He's beside himself with grief.

"He's not a suspect?"

"No, he's clean," Josh said. "He has a rock-solid alibi. Besides, I don't think anyone could fake his emotions."

"I wish I had more," Chris said with an apologetic shrug.

"It's not your fault. We don't have much to work with. Maybe next time we'll be luckier. I hate to say that, because it means I expect a next time, but I'm afraid there isn't much I can do to prevent it. Not unless we have a miracle."

On that sour note, Josh left the coroner's office and headed to the station.

CHAPTER 19

Monday morning was not a pleasant one. First, Clint was late. Again. He arrived at headquarters looking as if he had slept in his clothes, carrying a cardboard cup of Starbucks coffee, a half-eaten muffin peeking out of his left pocket. Josh had called his partner at nine a.m. to tell him to get his ass to the station ASAP.

Josh, in contrast, had awoken surprisingly rested, ready to apply himself to the case. But his boss dragged him into her office as soon as he arrived and gave him a blistering dressing-down on the hazards of leaking information to the press.

By the time Clint sauntered in, Josh was at his desk after having suffered through a thirty-minute rant from his boss, a fifty-something, short, wiry woman who was tougher than she looked. According to Lieutenant Lowe, she had forwarded the lecture, word for word, from her own superior, Superintendent Rick Dunn.

"What's going on?" His partner looked around him with a frown. Despite Clint's laid-back attitude, he didn't miss a trick.

"Everyone's in an uproar, from Lowe all the way up."

"Nice pun, but why?" Clint lowered himself into the chair opposite Josh.

"The press wants confirmation that the two recent murders are the work of a serial killer using a locally written book as a basis for the crimes."

"Shit. Where did that come from?"

"I don't know, but as usual, your timing is impeccable. You missed out on the boss ripping me a new one."

Clint winced. "I owe you one."

"One? No, that was worth a few."

"Was it just a general reference to a serial killer and a novel?"

"No. That would have been bad enough. They referred to pages specifically removed from a book."

"That narrows down the pickings."

Josh realized only the people who worked the crime scene, or the technicians who analyzed the pages, could pass such knowledge on to the press. But he knew this team. They were professionals and would never be indiscreet.

"Whoever did it, for whatever reason, jeopardized the investigation," Josh said. "For the time being, the powers-that-be convinced the media to put a lid on it, but we know how reliable that is. We don't have much time before it'll be out, and we'll have more trouble weeding out the crazies. Anyone who's ever read a crime novel will call to tell us they can unmask the killer."

"Once again, you won't be happy with what I'll suggest, but..."

"You don't need to say it. I've already thought of that," Josh said with a scowl. Tierney was the most likely suspect for the leak. He remembered Clint mulling over the possibility the writer had organized the murders as a publicity stunt, and his stomach turned.

Was it possible he had been so wrong? Josh's instincts had always been dependable. *Were they skewed by a preconceived belief of Tierney's innocence? Had his past tainted his skills as a detective?*

•   •   •

"Can I speak to Mr. McGinnis please?"

"I'm sorry, he's away right now. Can I pass along a message for him?"

"Perhaps you can help me, Miss. I was wondering if he's the T.L. McGinnis who writes crime novels."

Tierney's shoulders tensed. "May I ask who's speaking please?"

"This is Bill Flaherty from The Record. I'd like to schedule an interview with him today or tomorrow. Just to discuss his novels. Do you expect him home soon?"

"I'm sorry, but I'm afraid you have the wrong Mr. McGinnis. My father is a retired plumber, not a writer."

The journalist was still talking as Tierney hung up the phone, but she wasn't interested in hearing any more. She was suspicious. *Why would a journalist call for an interview? She had never received such a request. Why now?* She just had time to consider the question when the phone rang again. Irritated, thinking the journalist was persistent to a fault, she answered with a too-brisk 'Hello'.

"Tierney?"

"Yes?" It wasn't the same voice, but she remained wary.

"It's Josh Riddell. I need to talk to you."

A rush of relief swept over her as she forced her mind to switch gears. "Do you have news? Have you arrested someone?"

Tierney heard Josh's sigh.

"No and no, but we still need to talk."

"What is it?" Tierney's heart chilled as she wondered what the detective needed to say.

"Did you speak to any reporters concerning the murders?" Josh asked.

The question surprised Tierney, right on the heels of the call from the journalist. "Why are you asking?"

"Did you talk to any reporters about the murders?" Josh repeated.

Tierney detected something in his tone. Was it tension? Anger? "I just got off the phone with a reporter."

"When?"

"Just now. A few minutes ago."

"Was that the first one?"

"Yes," Tierney said.

"Did you talk to anyone else? Anyone at all?"

"No. No one. What is this about?" Josh's urgent tone worried her.

"What did he ask you?"

"He wanted to interview me. Well, not really me. He asked if Mr. McGinnis at this phone number was the writer and, if so, he wanted to interview him."

"What did you say?"

"I told him he had the wrong Mr. McGinnis."

"That's it?"

"That's it."

"Are you sure?"

"Naturally, I'm sure," Irritation clung to Tierney's words. "I remember what I said. Are you accusing me of lying?"

"No. I'm just trying to understand. I need to sort this out."

"Sort what out? It might help if you shared it with me."

There was a pause, and Tierney pictured Josh weighing how much to tell her. Finally, he spoke.

"There's been a leak. To the press. They're looking for information about the serial killer who's leaving behind pages from a book."

"How would they know that? And how would they trace it to me?" Tierney paced the length of the kitchen and back, her mind racing.

"They seem to be aware it's a local writer. I guess they're doing their homework, the same way we did ours to find you."

"Yes, but at least you had a name and a title of the book."

"Granted, but with the internet and a few industrious journalists, it doesn't take long to track someone."

"I wish I could say the same for tracking a murderer." Tierney suffered through the heavy silence at the other end and realized how she had sounded. "I'm sorry. I understand you're doing the best you can. I only meant it'd be so much simpler if all we had to do was hit a few buttons to catch a criminal."

"I know what you mean, Tierney. I agree with you."

"Who could have given that information to the press?"

"I don't know, but I'll find out. I'll get back to you."

With that, Josh hung up, leaving Tierney to puzzle over another twist in the tale.

CHAPTER 20

Over the last ten days, Clint and Lydia had seen each other whenever his schedule permitted. Regardless of the fact Lydia seemed to enjoy his company and never refused a date, Clint tread with care. He sensed he shouldn't push for a deeper relationship even though, with each passing day, he was more and more certain it was what he wanted.

They met, sometimes on the run, to grab a bite together when Clint had a free hour. Once, they went to a movie, and, another time, they took a walk along the Rideau Canal, enjoying the view of historic buildings and the riot of color during the Canadian Tulip Festival, held every May.

"What's got into you?" Josh's gaze pierced his partner and dragged him back to the present. The detectives sat shoulder to shoulder on stools at a diner. They each had submarine sandwiches and fries on the counter in front of them.

Clint looked at him and shrugged. "Nothing."

"What's the smile for, if it's nothing?"

Clint glanced over his shoulder. He didn't want anyone to eavesdrop on a conversation concerning his love life. "I'm seeing Lydia tonight."

Josh's eyebrows shot upward. "Okay, so what's different from the other nights you've seen her?"

"She's coming to my place. For pizza and a movie."

"Ah." Josh grinned. "The old pizza and a movie ploy. You'll move in for the kill."

"Only if the opportunity presents itself."

"I have to say, Bud, you're showing an enormous amount of restraint. I'm impressed."

"Yeah, well, sooner or later, I need to get my game up where it used to be. I feel like an old man, like you." Clint was prepared for the swipe of Josh's arm to the back of his head and ducked just in time.

•   •   •

Clint and Lydia relaxed on the couch. The room was darkened except for the glow from the television. Clint had suggested a couple of movies to stream, and they had decided on a romantic comedy Lydia had wanted to see. He preferred action films, but when she suggested they watch one next time, he was more than happy to concede. It meant she was planning on a next time.

An empty pizza box sat on the coffee table before them, along with an unopened bottle of wine. They had both opted to drink beer with their pizza. As the movie started, they propped their feet on the table, and Clint laid his arm across Lydia's shoulders, tugging her unresisting body closer. He smiled with contentment. This was where he wanted to be.

Halfway through the film, the chirp of a cell phone shook him from his half-sleep. The unfamiliar ringtone confused him until Lydia leaped from the couch to grab her phone from the side pocket of her purse. She headed to the bathroom with the device held to her ear.

Meanwhile, alarm bells sounded in Clint's head. *Why the terrible need for privacy? Was it a husband? Was that the real reason for her apparent qualms when she first visited the Laff? Was that the little something he couldn't put his finger on?*

A few minutes later, Lydia came back to find Clint wide-awake and staring at her with raised brows. She smiled shyly and gathered her things together.

"Where are you going?" Clint asked, straightening. He grabbed the remote control and muted the volume on the TV.

"Since I'm up anyway, I'd better go home." Her eyes avoided his.

"There's no hurry."

"I know, but I have an early client to visit tomorrow, and I want to get home and have a good sleep."

"Was that your client on the phone?"

"Yeah, it was. It's a good thing she called to remind me. It may have slipped my mind altogether."

"That would have been upsetting," Clint remarked, his voice stilted. *Who called their interior decorator at this hour?*

Clint didn't know what to do at this point. Should he confront her and ask her if she's married? If she isn't, that was an excellent way to insult her and make her angry. He didn't feel secure enough in their relationship to risk a full-fledged argument.

If she was married, he had no intention of continuing the relationship. That's where he drew the line.

Clint decided to let it ride for now. He was a detective, for goodness' sake. If anyone could find out the truth, it would be him, wouldn't it?

He stood and slipped his hands into the back pockets of his jeans, hoping to appear casual and unconcerned. "Can we get together again sometime?" He knew he might be asking for trouble, but he was convinced this girl was worth it.

"Of course," she said. "Why would you even question it?" Lydia looked him in the eye, her expression sincere.

"It could be because of your hastiness to leave," he ventured.

Lydia's face fell. "I'm sorry, Clint." She stepped forward and wrapped her arms around him. He pulled her close and breathed in her scent.

"I need to go." Her breath was warm on his ear. The weight of remorse was in her tone, and he realized it wasn't the time to push her.

And her story regarding an early client the next day was bull.

With a guilty expression on her face, Lydia left behind a very concerned boyfriend.

CHAPTER 21

Tierney went to another funeral, held in a small Protestant chapel on a quiet, tree-lined street. The setting was different, but the grief was the same; the pain and confusion palpable. *How could something this horrible happen to someone so loved?*

Tierney sat on a scarred wooden pew at the back of the church, and, as if on cue, Detective Riddell slid in next to her. When she noticed the brief brush of his elbow against hers, it registered in her mind that she had expected him. Before Tierney had time to explore that notion further, the long and sorrowful service began, complete with heart-wrenching eulogies and hymns.

They followed the procession to the cemetery, led by a bagpiper playing "Amazing Grace". Tears clogged Tierney's throat as she stood beside Josh at the edge of the crowd and listened to the prayers while Penelope's casket descended into the grave.

On their way to the parking lot, Josh leaned closer to Tierney and spoke in a low voice. "We have to stop meeting this way." His comment earned a glare from Tierney. "Sorry, I'm not known for having the best jokes. Would you rather hear the same speech about how you shouldn't attend the funeral?"

"You could try." Tierney shrugged. "I wouldn't listen to you, anyway."

She swung around to face Josh when they reached her car.

"On top of everything else, I have to deal with what people are thinking of me. Whenever anyone glances in my direction, no matter how innocently, I wonder if they realize who I am and if they're silently accusing me of inciting murder."

"No one knows of your connection."

"Someone does, and now the press is onto it," Tierney said, her voice earnest. "I don't know how much more I can take. Will this be the last time we meet like this? Another day, another church, another funeral."

Josh didn't comment, but she saw the slump of his shoulders and understood the detective had nothing to say to relieve her suffering.

Tierney returned home to an empty house, a house that had never been lonely for her in the past. It had always seemed to burst with her mother's exuberance, even in her absence. Cooper picked up on Tierney's mood and remained tucked away in a corner after delivering his initial greeting.

Tierney would have liked to call someone, a friend to keep her company, but even that prospect was ruined. The detective had planted suspicions in her mind. Small little seeds, but like bad weeds, they grew and wound their way around her thoughts.

Tierney hadn't spoken to anyone of her connection to the two murders. But what if one of her friends had talked to someone, the killer, of her and her book? What if they had created the monster, or at least fed it? She couldn't get past the thought, and, rather than spend time with someone and have to analyze everything they said to each other, she decided she was better off alone.

Perhaps Tierney always wished to see the best in people, or maybe she was blind, but she didn't believe anyone she knew could commit such hideous crimes.

Yes, it was conceivable someone had mentioned her book to another person, but it was an avenue that seemed difficult to trace. Should she investigate everyone she had ever met? No. She would take it from another angle. But Tierney had not decided what that angle would be.

CHAPTER 22

Josh had a busy week, but he carved out a few more hours to put his nose in the book. By early Friday evening, he had made it to the ninth murder. As he read the details of the victim, a surge of heat rose within him. He wasn't sure if it was fear or anger or a combination of both. Josh didn't take the time to analyze it. He jumped from the couch, grabbed his coat and keys, and rushed to his car.

Josh knocked on the front door, with no response, until a bark came from the direction of the vegetable garden on the left-hand side of the house. His long strides took him around the corner before Tierney had a chance to get off her hands and knees. He closed the distance between them, his expression furious. Josh carried a paperback book, and as he got closer, he waved it in the air.

"Why didn't you tell me?" Josh said.

Tierney winced. The cop didn't give her the opportunity to answer him.

"Why the hell didn't you tell me?" he said, emphasizing each word.

Tierney focused on the novel in Josh's hand. "What chapter are you on?"

"Twelve," he growled.

"Oh, I see."

"'Oh, I see.' Is that all you can say? At least you might've warned me."

"Warned you of what?" she said, her voice intense. "I can't predict what'll happen. I don't know who he will kill. I don't even know *if* he'll kill again. Neither do you."

"Of course, I don't, but haven't you ever heard forewarned is forearmed?" Josh glared at her. "I can't believe you're not worried about this. It should terrify you."

"You're the cop around here. Aren't you supposed to be offering me platitudes instead of trying to scare me half to death?"

"If I'm scaring you half to death, you're doing a damn good job hiding it."

"I didn't say you were succeeding. I said you were trying to. There's a difference."

"I forgot," Josh said. "You're the expert in semantics."

"I guess I didn't mention it because I didn't want to overreact. If I spend my time thinking of it, I'll drive myself crazy, and frankly, I'm almost there. Besides, the writer in the book was named Theresa, not Tierney."

"Yeah, right, close enough."

Tierney turned her back to Josh, returning to the beauty of her garden.

"Look, we have to take this seriously." He followed behind her. "It isn't overreacting; it's being cautious. I've racked my brain trying to figure out a way to find and protect every prospective victim described in the book, even though I understand it's impossible. But in your case, we can do it."

"Only if you believe I'm a prospective victim, which I don't think is likely."

"Consider it. There are too many coincidences. If the murders had happened two thousand miles away, I'd agree with you. But they're too close for comfort. We can't leave you living here alone and unprotected."

"All right. What do you want me to do?" Tierney turned to face him, her hands on her hips.

"I don't know yet. I haven't had time to come up with a plan, but I'll discuss protection for you with my boss. In the meantime, you're coming with me."

"No, I'm not. I'm staying right here."

"Think of it. Two women have lost their lives. You fit the bill for another victim in the book. Why do you want to chance it? You could be the next one."

"I don't believe this guy even knows me. Like most people, he assumes I'm a man. I don't believe I'm in danger."

"Yeah. And what if you're wrong? What if he knows who you are and where you live? How will you protect yourself?"

Tierney opened her mouth to speak but seemed to change her mind. Instead, she concentrated on removing her gardening gloves.

"Did you hear me? What could you do here, living by yourself, with just an old dog for company, if this guy decides to kill you?"

Tierney's gaze lifted to his, her chin set.

"I refuse to live in fear. What kind of life is it to spend my time looking over my shoulder and jumping at every little sound? I'll be very careful, and I won't take any foolish chances. I'm also forewarned, not like those other two women. But I won't hide."

Josh rubbed the back of his neck, took a deep breath, and released it on the count of three.

"I'm not talking about the rest of your life. I'm referring to a temporary measure. Until we catch this guy, you could go somewhere else. When it's over, you can resume your life as usual."

"And when will it be over? How long will I have to wait? A week? Six weeks? Six months? What if you never catch him?"

"You realize I can't answer that, Tierney. We're doing the best we can." His tone was exasperated.

"I'm sorry. I didn't mean to sound as if I questioned your competence. It's just that no one knows. No one can predict what'll happen. I can't, and neither can you, no matter how much you may want to. I want time to go backward, but it can't. I'm not able to make it go forward either. I can't plan. God, I even have trouble concentrating. I'm in a daze most of the time."

"Let me help you. If I can get you into a quiet, safe environment, you'll be able to relax and move forward."

CHAPTER 23

Josh and Tierney argued for several long minutes before the cop seemed to accept the fact she did not want a bodyguard. As he lowered himself into his car, Tierney suspected he wanted to give her the impression he had given in, but he would be back to convince her to leave her home and hide out until the police captured the perpetrator.

Was she wrong to stay at home alone? If the killer intended to find her, and if he was as smart as everyone thinks he is, he would find her no matter where she hid, wouldn't he? Especially if it's someone she's acquainted with, as the police seem to believe. But she risked putting someone else in his path. Was she willing to sacrifice the safety of one of her friends?

No, they were no more prepared or experienced than she was. She wouldn't risk it. She would do her best to protect herself.

Tierney closed her eyes and lifted her face to the sky. The warmth of the sun and the smell of the flowers made her appreciate her home all the more. This was her security blanket, her comfort zone. She looked at Cooper, lying on the grass, soaking up the same comfort.

"Oh, to have a dog's life. What do you think, Cooper? Is Josh right? Should we pack up and leave?"

The dog opened one eye to peer at her but did not seem to have an opinion.

"I tell you what. Faye's away for a few days. When she gets back, I'll see if I can stay with Jim and her for a while, but it might mean telling them what's happening. I'm not certain our fine detective will be okay with that or not."

Having made that decision, Tierney had the sense she had lifted a weight off her chest.

"Is it a good time to prune those rose bushes?" The dog showed little interest in her question. "I've been putting it off long enough. Bloody fingers might take my mind off things."

If the thump of his tail was any sign, Cooper agreed.

"Need any help?"

Tierney dropped her clippers and swung around, her hand at her throat.

"I'm sorry. Did I frighten you?" Jeff Lakefield was Tierney's nearest neighbor and often dropped by when she worked in the garden.

Tierney laughed uneasily. She was more skittish than she wished to admit. "No, I'm fine. I just didn't hear you. I guess I was too absorbed in my work."

"You're always like that, no matter what it is." An indulgent smile lit his face. "What's new, Tierney? How's the next book coming along?"

Tierney had expected the question. Jeff loved to dig for information regarding her current work-in-progress, but she insisted on keeping it private until they published it. The only other people who had any insight into her books before their release were her agent and editor.

"It's going well."

"Is it a sequel?"

"No, it isn't."

"Why not? Why don't you arrange for the killer to escape from prison, move to another part of the country, and start killing again?" he asked.

This wasn't the first time Jeff had made such a suggestion, but Tierney didn't do sequels. She enjoyed starting fresh, with a whole new storyline and cast of characters.

"I've already explained it to you. It doesn't interest me."

"I could help you." The pleading in his voice made Tierney uncomfortable. "If you have a mental block, I can help you through it. You wouldn't even have to give me credit for it. I'd do it for fun."

"You've already made that offer. Why don't you take up writing if it interests you so much?" Tierney picked up her clippers and clenched them in her hand, wishing the conversation would end.

"I don't think I can do it, and I'd be afraid to put time and effort into something that may be a failure. But I could work as a collaborator. You know, with another author." His eyes were bright, his tone hopeful.

Tierney and Jeff had had this conversation many times before. In normal times, she indulged him and gave him a gentle letdown, but her nerves were frayed, and she couldn't soften the edge in her voice.

"I've told you before that I work alone. I can't do it any other way."

The words had just escaped her mouth, and Tierney wished to pull them back. A wounded look settled on her neighbor's face. Although he didn't move, Jeff appeared to shrink into himself.

Tierney wanted to groan out loud. He was a lonely person with a severe lack of self-confidence. One of the few joys in his life was reading murder mysteries and discussing them with Tierney. In all honesty, she often enjoyed doing the same with him, but recent events had taken the shine off her work, making her doubt the merit of putting effort into something that could be used to take someone's life.

"I'm sorry," Tierney said. "I didn't mean to sound so bitchy. I've got a splitting headache, and I need at least five bandages on my fingers at this point."

Part of the hurt evaporated from Jeff's face, and he shrugged. "It's all right. I understand. Everyone has lousy days."

"Thanks. You're a real friend." Tierney forced a smile. She wasn't in the mood for soothing stung feelings when her own were so battered, but she wouldn't feel better until she made peace with her neighbor.

"No problem." He glanced toward his house. "I guess I should be going. I got things to do at home."

Tierney was convinced the man had nothing to do, but she didn't have the strength to amuse him for the rest of the evening. He trod away, taking the shortcut through the grove of apple trees that acted as a boundary between their respective properties.

When he disappeared from view, she set about her gardening once more, but her heart was no longer in it. She stabbed the small spade into the ground and rose to her feet. As she turned toward the house, she thought she saw a movement in the vicinity of the treeline. She stared through narrowed eyes but decided she must have been mistaken.

CHAPTER 24

"Clint!"

"What?"

"Did you pay the slightest bit of attention to what I said?"

"No, not really. Was I supposed to?"

Josh raised his hands in frustration. "We're working on a case here, if you haven't noticed. Remember? The guy who's strangling people? Could you help me out a bit?"

Police headquarters was quiet. It was late on a Tuesday and the detectives pored over forensic reports from the most recent murder. The lack of results had them both on edge. In Clint's case, he had other issues that preyed on his mind.

"Yeah, you can have a few hours," he conceded grudgingly.

"Okay, give. What's going on?" Josh set down his pen and crossed his arms.

"Nothing."

"Yeah, right. The nothing that means everything." Josh glared at his friend. "Let me guess. It must be a woman, and the only woman I've heard of is Lydia. So what happened? Did you screw it up somehow?"

"Why do you assume I screwed it up?" A pained look crossed Clint's face.

"From what I've heard, she's perfect, so how could she screw it up? Besides, I've learned from years of personal experience that you are far less than perfect, therefore..."

"Okay. Okay. I get the drift. At any rate, for your information, nothing is screwed up between us. Everything is just hunky-dory."

"Cut the crap. If that was the case, you wouldn't be going around with that battered puppy dog look on your face."

"It's not that bad."

"It's worse." Josh leaned back in his chair and joined his hands across his stomach.

"Look who's talking." Clint had long ago learned that the best defense is a good offense.

"What do you mean?"

"Following Tierney around like a lovesick puppy."

"That's not true." Josh sat forward and jiggled his computer mouse, fixing his attention on the screen.

"It is. You've got it bad."

"What I've got is a firm sense of responsibility. Something that you used to have, but you lost it somewhere near Lydia."

Clint stared at his partner long and hard. "I hate to say it, but it looks as if you've set aside a few of your high and mighty standards for Tierney. You're not able to keep your head on straight around her."

Josh flushed and opened his mouth to shout out an argument, Clint was sure of it, but he watched in surprise as his partner's shoulders slumped and his head bent forward to stare at his keyboard.

"You may be right," Josh said in a low voice. "It's not just Tierney, it's this entire case. Like it or not, it's reviving a lot of awful memories. Those young women being murdered, Tierney standing in harm's way. I'm doing my best, but it's not easy."

Silence fell between them. Clint sympathized with his friend. Cops were human too, and often that was forgotten. Everyone expected them to be emotionless, and it wasn't the way it worked.

Clint shook his head. "There's something I can't put my finger on with Lydia."

"Like what?" Josh shifted his attention to the other detective.

"I'm not sure. A certain cautiousness. I mean, I can understand a woman being cautious with a man she just met, but it's been weeks and she still seems to be holding back. I'll catch her staring at me with an odd look on her face, but as soon as she sees me looking, she'll either glance away or change her expression.

"And she keeps getting these phone calls. She always goes to another room so she can talk in private, and, if I ask who she's talking to, it's always her sister or her mother or a client. I'm not sure. There's just something up, that's all."

Josh took a second to let the information sink in. Once Clint decided he wanted to talk, he didn't hold back. Josh had a concern he wanted to voice, and even though he hesitated to do it, he reminded himself this was his best friend. "You think she's married?"

"That's why I'm worried," Clint said. "Either that or she has a boyfriend somewhere in the picture."

"It doesn't sound good."

"I know." Clint nodded, his expression bleak.

"You want me to look into it for you?"

"No, it's up to me. I planned to do it. It's just that I put it off too many times. I guess I'm afraid what the answer will be."

"Yeah. I get it." Josh appreciated the doubts that assailed a man when he tried to second-guess a woman.

• • •

When he had a few minutes available, Clint did a quick background check on Lydia. Guilt swamped him as he did it. He had never investigated a woman he dated, always relying on his instincts, and it galled him to resort to methods at his disposal to get to know someone better.

He rationalized his decision by telling himself Lydia wasn't being open with him. She forced him to go this route, and more men would do it if they had the means available, he reasoned. Those thoughts did nothing to remove the bitter taste from his mouth.

His guilt was further reinforced and only exceeded by his relief when he discovered Lydia had nothing more than a minor traffic violation committed twelve years earlier to besmirch her otherwise perfect record. He also found out she had never been married, never bore any children, and was indeed an interior decorator. *So what the hell was up? Why the secrecy? Why didn't she confide in him?*

His friends and colleagues considered him an easy-going guy, Clint mused. Lots of people confided in him. *Was it him? Was it his career? If so, why did she have anything to do with him? Why hadn't she dumped him?* He had too many questions and not enough answers.

Clint grimaced. The next step was arguably worse than doing a background check. He needed to follow her.

Two days later, Clint took a few hours away from the case. As a rule, on a day off, he rested or hung out with friends. Or he hopped on his motorcycle and headed for the open road. This day, he used his bike, but he never left the confines of the city.

In black jeans, a black leather jacket, with a black helmet on his head, he would be unrecognizable to Lydia. He'd told her he owned a motorbike, but she had never seen it, so he was certain he could remain incognito while he monitored her movements.

Clint set up his surveillance a discreet distance from her shop, allowing a view of the building and parking area. Her car sat in the lot along with one other. Lydia had told him a girl worked for her part-time. Since she often visited other people's homes, someone needed to mind the store when she was out.

As Clint sat on his bike, waiting for activity, he decided Lydia had a good setup. He had been inside the store, Ins and Outs, once. She offered a wide assortment of decorations and services available for either the interior or exterior of people's homes or places of business.

Clint, a man who was much more at home in a hardware or electronics store, cringed at having to choose a color for a bathroom or a fabric to recover a chair. But he appreciated her talent and the amount of effort she put into her chosen career. It made him more determined to find out what hindered their relationship, so they could get on with the business of living as a couple.

The morning dragged on with little activity. It turned out the other car belonged to a female customer. She left after an hour with an enormous bag in her hand, smiling widely, pleased with whatever doodad she had purchased. A few other women entered and left the shop during the same period. At one point, a man went in. He was there for a few minutes and left empty-handed. Lydia never came out.

Early afternoon, another car parked in the lot, and a young woman entered the building. Ten minutes later, Lydia came out and got into her car. Clint waited until she pulled onto the street and two other cars separated them before he started his motorcycle and followed.

His heart pounded in his chest, whether it was with hope or fear, he wasn't sure. What he knew was Lydia was not headed toward her apartment. *Was she going to the grocery store? Did she have a decorating job to visit? Or did she have a date with someone else?*

When she took a left onto Debra Avenue, Clint worried. A lot. *What the hell was she doing here? This was hardly a district where people hired interior decorators. They were more likely to call exterminators, or the cops. How many times were the police sent to this street for domestic violence or reports of gunfire?*

When she pulled up in front of a rundown row-house, Clint parked in a nearby alleyway. He unzipped his leather jacket to give him easier access to his weapon. His fear was not for himself, but for Lydia. This was not an area in which a young, attractive woman should hang out.

She climbed the few steps of the building and pulled open an old metal door. It bent dangerously on hinges that hung on by what seemed to be a miracle. Lydia didn't appear concerned. In fact, she seemed at ease, as if she had been here hundreds of times.

The door slammed behind her, and, through the dirty window, Clint caught sight of her climbing stairs that looked perilously unstable.

Clint gnawed on his lower lip. He worried for her safety. He didn't understand what she was doing in this neighborhood. He knew what kind of person lurked in those buildings.

He was tempted to say to hell with subterfuge and follow her into the row-house, but something made him resist the impulse. He'd give her twenty minutes. If she didn't come out by that time, he would go in after her.

It was the longest twenty minutes of his life. When Lydia's allotted time was up, he climbed off his bike but stopped when he saw her come down the stairs. She seemed unharmed as she climbed into her car and drove away.

Clint followed at a reasonable distance until she reached her apartment in the trendy Glebe area and entered the upscale building. Later, when he was at home, he realized no one near the row-house had seemed surprised to see a sleek, well-dressed woman like Lydia walking into that place.

CHAPTER 25

Two weeks after Penelope's murder, everyone involved in the investigation, including Tierney, braced for another death, but the weekend passed without incident, as did the following week. They began to hope there would be no other murders, but on Saturday, a call came in reporting the discovery of a body in a small, downtown, performing venue.

The deceased was a man, and they had found his corpse in a dark corner of the backstage area. The murder warranted a visit from Lieutenant Lowe. Whether she was there to get a first-hand look at the victim or to add weight to the investigation, Josh wasn't sure, but her presence added another layer of somberness to an already grim occasion.

"What do you have, Riddell?" The lieutenant interrupted Josh's conversation with a patrol officer.

"His name's Art Landon. He's a drummer for an alternative rock band by the name of River Peace." His expression told her what she wanted to know.

"Would you mind excusing us please?" Lowe addressed the other policeman. The man didn't seem disappointed to leave their company.

"Does it fit?" She spoke to Josh in a lowered voice.

"Yeah, a musician named Arthur. The second murder in the novel."

"Did they find the pages?"

"Inside his jacket pocket." Josh wanted to shout with frustration, but he held onto his emotions with a tight rein.

"How closely does it match?"

"He was garroted with a rope, as described in the book."

"Any variations from the novel?"

"Yeah. The fictional victim was murdered at home, in his kitchen."

The lieutenant's gaze roamed the area. "It'd be easier for a killer to get in here and hide in plain sight, waiting for the right opportunity."

"I agree." The thought had occurred to Josh.

"Time of death?"

"Dr. Abbott has set it at around 8 hours, which coincides with the closing-up for the night. The victim often stayed behind and stowed away the equipment."

"Was there a large crowd?"

Josh grimaced. "Full house."

He scanned the backstage area. He was familiar with this venue. Andrea had been a fan of both amateur theatre and music, and she had invited him to a couple of shows here. But Josh had only ever seen the stage from the front.

"Lots of witnesses to sift through." His boss looked at him with lowered brows.

"It'll take time." Josh felt the weight of that time on his shoulders.

"Get a team together and put Benson in charge of doing a first run through the witnesses. You have someone else you need to talk to." Lowe sent him a meaningful glare. "She's got to be aware of something that can help us."

Without another word, the woman spun away from him and marched toward the crime scene, presumably to accost the coroner.

"Better him than me," Josh mumbled.

"What's up?" Clint appeared behind him.

"Another case of impeccable timing. How do you do it?"

"It's one of my better qualities." Clint flashed him a smile.

Josh filled his partner in on the name and profession of the deceased. "I don't remember seeing either the band or the drummer in my searches." Josh's voice shook with anger. "If I had, I could have prevented it. Now, we have another victim on our hands."

"And we need to face Tierney with the news," Clint added.

The CSI people did their jobs but made little progress. Once again, they dropped a small red heart into a plastic bag for testing, but Josh didn't cherish any hope it would give them any fresh information to help them.

They had three murders so far, and nine left to go. In Josh's mind, the murderer was one step closer to adding Tierney to his list of victims.

CHAPTER 26

Tierney could not settle into any one task in particular. She did laundry, only to forget it in the washing machine. She pulled the vacuum cleaner out of the closet, planning to rid the house of the endless supply of blond dog hairs, and left it lying untouched on the floor. She went into the bathroom to scour the bathtub, only to sit on the floor with a bottle of disinfecting cleaner in one hand and a sponge in the other, staring into space.

Tierney's mind jumped from one thought to another, most of them running the gamut from disturbing to downright alarming, with nothing positive in between.

The visit from Josh and Clint didn't go well. When she saw the car pull into the driveway, Tierney had known. She met them outside on the porch steps.

"Which one?" Her heart was wedged in her throat.

"Arthur," Josh said, sympathy clear in his expression.

Tierney nodded with misery. *Yes, she remembered Arthur.*

She did not comprehend how the killer's mind worked. From her point of view, he didn't follow a pattern. She hoped he had made a mistake, or someone smarter than her would figure him out.

Nothing the detectives said put her at ease. The three of them seemed to sense the hopelessness of trying. The same empty clichés sounded hollow to everyone, filling the painful silence.

To set aside her brooding, she got to her feet and moved to the bookcase in the living room. Tierney lifted her hand toward the novel and waffled for a moment before pulling it from the shelf. She carried it to the sofa, as if it was a bomb set to explode in her hands. She sat, staring at it, reading the title over and over. *Murder by the Dozen. Could it be? Or would it be?*

Tierney opened the book and flipped to chapter ten. She scanned the words, remembering them, remembering the act of putting them to paper. She pictured Art Landon in her mind, the same vision that had been there when she had described the murder of his fictional counterpart. The short, honey-brown hair, the blue eyes, his smile; everything was so familiar, as if she had known him her entire life.

The need to understand was too powerful. She could not stay in this house, picturing him, leaving so many questions unanswered. She had done it with the first two murders, and the anguish had almost been her undoing, but she would not put herself through it a third time.

Tierney grabbed her purse and pulled her car keys from the rack by the door. She had her hand on the doorknob when she realized she looked too disheveled to be scurrying around in public. She didn't want people to think she was a madwoman.

Tierney dumped her purse and keys on the kitchen table and headed for her bedroom. A few minutes later, she looked better. At least she had clean clothes and freshly brushed hair, and she had applied blush and lip gloss.

She pulled into the familiar parking lot outside the government building, found an unoccupied spot, and turned off the engine. Tierney took several deep breaths before straightening her shoulders and leaving the car. She didn't consider herself much of an actress, but she promised to give it her all.

Part of her tension fled when she spotted Ben at the security desk. The guard's round face broke out in a grin when he saw her, and he circled around from behind the desk to give her a light hug.

"Hey, it's been a while since you've been here. How's it going?"

Tierney's own smile was natural; she was comfortable with the friendly guard. On the occasions she had been here, they had spent a substantial amount of time talking. Ben was aware she was a writer and had endless questions regarding the process. In return, he filled her in on life as a security guard, which she assured him she would use in one of her future books.

"It's going great, but I'm afraid I don't have much time today to stay and chat. Is he in?"

"He sure is. He may be busy right now, but if you want to check, go ahead."

"Thanks. I won't keep him long."

Tierney walked along the corridor and hesitated at the gray, windowless, steel door. During the drive downtown, she had imagined how to play this and realized she needed to work hard if she wanted to succeed. She straightened her shoulders, pushed the door open, and went into the large office.

There were three desks in the room and a handful of computers, printers, microscopes, and other technical equipment. There were no people. Tierney knew where to find them. With a fluttering in her stomach, she looked toward the door across the room and imagined what was on the opposite side. There was a tiny window, but from this distance, she couldn't make out anything.

She crept closer, forcing herself to put one foot in front of the other. Now that she was here, where she had so urgently needed to be, she wanted to turn around and leave. It wasn't too late, but it had taken so much emotional effort to make it this far, she vowed not to let it go to waste.

As she reached the door, she peered through the tiny window, and what she saw confirmed her suspicions. Chris Abbott, dressed in his lab coat, worked on a body that lay on the table in front of him. The doctor faced the door, his head bent over the corpse. Blood and God only knew what else smeared his white coat.

Standing across from him was his assistant, Nick. Slim and of medium height, he didn't take up a lot of space, but he blocked Tierney's view of the dead person's face. Within her sight were long, bare, masculine legs stretched out on the gurney.

Tierney didn't move, but Chris must have somehow sensed her presence. His head snapped up, and his gaze connected with hers. A dismayed expression crossed his face. Tierney was unsure how to interpret it. *Was he upset because Tierney had interrupted his work, or did he suspect she had an ulterior motive for being here?* Tierney hoped it was the former. She had a better chance of achieving her goal if it was.

Dr. Abbott spoke to his assistant before he set aside his tools and strode toward the door. She noted the grim look on the doctor's face and fixed a not-too-bright-but-friendly smile on her face. When the door swung open, she was ready with her prepared greeting.

"Hi, Chris. I hope I'm not bothering you at an inconvenient time."

Tierney was proud of how normal her voice sounded to her own ears.

"What brings you here?" Something in his tone did not bode well for Tierney.

"I'm sorry for dropping in unannounced this way, but I was putting in a few hours on my book, and I came up against a block. I need your expertise, and I guess my timing is perfect. If I sat in on this one, I'm sure it'll answer a lot of my questions, and I won't have to take too much of your time."

The doctor looked at Tierney for several moments, his expression inscrutable. She marveled at how good he was at controlling his expressions. It was important in his job to stay composed and unemotional, even when faced with the most horrific sights.

But she was worried Chris saw through her own forced pleasantness.

"What are you doing here?" The medical examiner's glare seemed to peer into her soul.

"I told you. I have a few questions I need resolved for my book and..."

"Go home. This will not help you," he said, not without sympathy. Tierney witnessed the look in his eyes and realized she hadn't gotten away with her ploy. It was obvious Detectives Riddell and Weller had kept the doctor informed of the case as it unfolded. Tierney now had to fall back on Plan B: begging and pleading.

"Chris, I need to understand. I truly need to see him."

"It won't do any good."

"I think I can be the judge of what's good for me."

"You're not in any state to be a judge of anything."

"There's nothing worse for me than not knowing. I have to see him. I'll lose my mind if I don't. Please. Just let me have a glimpse."

The medical examiner pulled his gaze away from Tierney's imploring eyes and stared at a computer screen a few feet away, the screensaver swirling with images of tropical vistas morphing one into the other.

He clearly weighed the advantages and disadvantages of giving into Tierney's plea, putting himself in her place and trying to decide whether he might experience a similar need under the circumstances. Chris swung his gaze back to Tierney, a hard look in his eyes, like a father admonishing his child.

"All right, but just for a minute. You look at his face only. Then you have to leave."

"I will. Thank you." Tierney let out a pent-up breath.

"You know the rules. Put on a gown, mask, and gloves. I can't have you contaminating my victim. Now, give me a second."

As Tierney grabbed the required materials from the closet and rushed to pull them on, Chris opened the door to the lab and hurried to the corpse. His assistant stood beside the victim, looking uncertain.

The doctor pulled the sheet over the body, leaving the face exposed, before gesturing to Tierney to come forward.

She walked the fifteen feet needed to reach the gurney, but didn't acknowledge either of the two men, her eyes fixed on the victim lying on the steel table. She stared at the gray face, her brow transforming her expression into a puzzled frown.

"It isn't him," she whispered.

"What?" The doctor leaned closer.

"It isn't him. He's not the right man."

The medical examiner looked from her face to the astonished expression on his assistant's face and back again. "Did you know him? Have you seen this man?"

"No. No, you don't understand. This isn't the same man as in my book. They look nothing alike."

To her own ears, Tierney realized she sounded crazy. She was sure she looked crazy, but no one else grasped the way she connected with her characters. The body of the man before her was nothing like the person from her imagination.

Before anyone said anything more, the sound of the door banging against the wall interrupted them. Chris glanced over his shoulder, and his patience snapped.

"Oh, for God's sake, what does everyone think this is, Grand Central Station? This is an examining room. We have protocol to follow, and I won't allow people to come traipsing through here willy-nilly."

"Then what the hell is she doing here?" Josh Riddell demanded, pointing an angry finger at Tierney.

"That's my business." The doctor would not accept any nonsense from Josh either.

"It's my business, too. This is my case, and she shouldn't be here."

The raised voices shook Tierney out of her daze. She swung toward Josh.

"How dare you say that! This is as much my business as yours. He was my creation. He came from my imagination, and he's dead because of me."

"Stop it, Tierney!" Josh said. "That's not true, and you know it. He's here because of a creep with a sick mind, and you're just making things worse for yourself."

Tierney turned back toward the corpse and shook her head.

"No, I'm not. I had to do this, and I'm glad I did. One thing I've discovered is the monster didn't make it inside my head. This is not the right guy. This is not the guy from my book."

CHAPTER 27

Tierney drove straight home. She needed to be alone to analyze her impressions and figure out why they conflicted.

She was relieved to see the victim differed from her own mental image of him. Tierney felt less involved in the person's violent death. Yet, because the man was so different, it left her with the strange sensation she was disconnected in a way. *But disconnected from whom? The deceased? The killer? Did she want to be connected? Why would she?* It confused her, but one thing was certain; she was better off after having seen Art Landon than she had been before.

As Tierney drove into her driveway, she glanced in the rear-view mirror and caught sight of a familiar blue car pulling in behind her. He had followed her home. Uninvited. She gritted her teeth, sensing she was in for another lecture, and she was not in the mood. But that didn't matter to the thick-skulled detective. Well, Tierney decided, he could follow her, but it did not mean she had to let him into the house, and she didn't need to listen to him.

Tierney slammed the car door and marched toward the house, ignoring the cop who did the same behind her. She fumbled to find her house key amid the others on the ring and cursed the fact she couldn't move faster and get into the house before he stepped onto the porch. Josh's boots hit the step as she slid the key into the lock, seconds too late.

"Ms. McGinnis, I'd like a word with you, please."

"I'm afraid I don't have time, Detective Riddell." Tierney imitated his formal address.

"You need to make the time."

She had unlocked the door, and her hand gripped the doorknob. A faint, unthreatening bark came from inside; Cooper, the vicious guard dog.

Tierney swung around, forcing Josh to take a step backward.

"No, not for you and not for anyone else. The only person I have to make time for is myself. I don't care if you want me to or not. So, if you please, Detective, I'd like you to leave."

"I realize you're upset. So am I. But we need to talk about this. And I don't mean the fact you were at the morgue this afternoon. I've gotten over that. I want to discuss the victim, Landon. It's important for me to get your take on this."

Josh's words threw Tierney off guard. She had expected a dressing-down, not a request for help. She hesitated, still yearning for time alone, yet unable to give a flat-out no to such an appeal.

Tierney looked at her hand wrapped around the doorknob and watched as the appendage decided for her. Her wrist turned, the door opened, and she walked in, leaving it open behind her.

"Hey, Cooper, how're you doing?" Josh scratched the grateful dog's ears.

Tierney circled to the opposite side of the kitchen table before turning to face the detective. Josh straightened and looked at her, waiting for her to make the first move. Tierney stared back. Just because she had let him in the house, he shouldn't assume she would cooperate. She was still wary, expecting a lecture from him, one she was sure he intended to give.

"Can I get you something? Water, a beer, a soft drink?" Tierney's innate politeness came to the fore.

"Nothing, thanks."

She pulled out a kitchen chair and sat, resting her elbows on the table, linking her fingers together. Josh did the same.

"What do you want from me?" Tierney asked.

"I want you to spell out what you meant when you said he wasn't the same man."

Tierney sighed. She had expected the question, but she didn't fathom how to explain it. "The victim differed from the man in my imagination."

She looked at Josh to see if he understood. When he stared at her silently, she continued. "I have a picture in my mind of my characters and know exactly how they look, including Arthur. I went into the morgue convinced I would see a familiar face. It was a complete shock when I looked at the man on the table. It was as if I'd walked into the wrong room. I realize it makes no sense, but it's the way I feel."

Tierney stared at Josh with raised brows, hoping for a response. He rewarded her with a slight nod.

"I can't remember how well you described the character in chapter ten," Josh said. "Did you use details, or did you portray him in general terms?"

"I described features such as height, build, eye color, that kind of thing. That's what I cover, unless there are specific elements relevant to the story. In my mind, the details are much sharper. But the killer didn't get that. He didn't get any of it. He's not in my head, Josh. He may want to be, but he isn't. I guess that was what had me the most worried. That he'd get into my head, and it wouldn't be my own anymore. I understand it sounds silly to you, but I can't help it."

"It isn't silly," he said. "Did you have the same experience with the other victims?"

"I never saw the others." Tierney stood and filled the kettle with water.

"You must have seen pictures in the papers or on TV."

"I did, but they were grainy photographs in a newspaper. I found Jennifer had a striking resemblance to the girl in the novel. Penny, less so, but the picture wasn't a very good quality, so that made a difference." She held up a tin of tea with a questioning look. When Josh shook his head, she placed a scoop of leaves into a strainer. "Honestly, I wonder if I wasn't afraid to see them. I think I didn't want to feel too close to the victims."

"Yet today, you wanted to look at the actual body," Josh stated, sounding baffled.

"I don't get it either. What I know is that I need to move forward. I have to face my demons or let them drive me crazy."

"I admit it was a brave thing to do. Not something I recommend, but...," he said with a shrug.

Tierney sat down and wrapped her hands around the mug. "From your perspective, it may have seemed naïve, but from mine, it was necessary."

"Do you feel better now, after having seen Arthur?"

"I do. Yeah, I guess I do."

"You guess?" He leaned back in the chair and cocked his head to one side.

"I'm not sure. I suppose I thought if the killer had made it into my head, it'd be easier for me to help you find him. But now I realize I don't sense any connection to him. I don't know if that's good or bad."

"It's good, Tierney. It has to be. No one wants a freak like him inside their head."

"I feel even less capable of helping the police find him. I've taken a few steps back, and I'm now on the outside looking in."

"Being on the outside, both physically and emotionally, is the best place for you to be."

Josh's stare grew intense, as if trying to come to a decision. He leaned forward and took her hand, sandwiching it between his.

"Tierney, would it bother you to look at good-quality pictures of the other two victims? I have them in the car. It's important to get your impressions, but if it's too much for you to handle in one day, we won't do it. You can consider it and tell me your decision when you're ready."

Tierney didn't waver. "I'd like to see them. After having seen that body in the morgue today, looking at pictures couldn't be any worse. Besides, now you've piqued my curiosity. I want to learn more details of the actual victims and compare them to mine."

Josh retrieved two five-by-seven photographs of Jennifer Danvers and Penelope Morrison from his car and set them on the kitchen table. They were pictures the police had gotten from the families, and they portrayed two young, lovely women at their most healthy, rather than the gruesome images captured by the crime scene specialists.

Tierney squirmed under Josh's watchful expression as she studied the faces in the photos before her.

"No," she said.

"No? What do you mean by no?"

"I mean, no, it's not them."

"You're sure?"

"Yes. As I said, there are similarities, particularly with Jennifer. In the hair and eye color, but that's as far as it goes. They don't fit."

"But you never described the characters in detail?"

Tierney considered for a moment before answering. "Not vividly. For instance, I might have described them as tall or petite or somewhere in between. I'd refer to a body type, such as thin, plump, curvaceous. If someone has a distinguishing characteristic, such as an overbite or a disfiguring mole, I'd mention it. I'd need to go back and review what I wrote regarding these two women, but I can tell you with certainty these images were not born inside of me."

"Good." His smile was genuine.

"How? What difference can it make whether the victims match the imprints I have in my head?"

"It may not make any difference, but sometimes it takes several minor things that, on the surface, don't seem important, but together lead us to something very significant. Maybe the killer wants to be you. Perhaps he or she wants to have those pictures inside their head, and they want to think the same as you. But today, we found out they can't.

"Maybe that means zilch for solving this case, or maybe it does. But, if nothing else, at least you realize the killer wasn't able to get inside you, and that alone made today a success. We'll get this person, no matter what. He'll make a mistake, and we'll have him."

Tierney tried to smile, but the tears welled in her eyes, and she fought to regain control of her emotions.

"I hope so. I truly do. I'm not sure I can handle another death," she said.

Josh took her hand and cradled it between his own once again.

CHAPTER 28

The next day, Tierney woke disgruntled, an unusual occurrence. The image of the body lying on the gurney in Chris Abbott's autopsy room haunted her sleep and waking hours. It hadn't been the first post-mortem the writer had attended, but it had been the most upsetting, even though she had simply viewed the victim's face for a few minutes.

A black cloud hovered over the morning. When she stepped outside with her cup of coffee, Tierney noticed something was not right in the garden. As she moved closer, she saw a groundhog or raccoon had helped themselves to her vegetables. She paced, fuming and plotting revenge.

Tierney's frustration mounted further as she tried to start her car, and nothing happened. Not only would she not make it to the hardware store to buy fencing, but she would, in all probability, have to get the car towed to a garage.

She popped open the hood and stared at the engine as if a hard glare would solve the problem, but it looked the same as it did any other day of the week. She was no wiser and far from happier.

Tierney returned to the house, more than a little miffed, and searched online for a repair shop. She picked up the handset to place the call and was startled when the phone rang in her hand.

"That was quick. Were you waiting for my call?" she heard Josh's voice reply.

"That's ridiculous. How was I supposed to expect you?" Tierney said. A brief silence hung on the line before Josh responded.

"Who peed in your cornflakes this morning?"

"I figure it was a groundhog or a raccoon." The words came out in a grumble.

"What?"

"Never mind. Let's just say I'm not having a marvelous day. And something tells me you're not calling to make it any better," Tierney said.

"Wrong. I was wondering how you were doing."

"Oh." The black cloud dissipated a little.

"So? How are you doing?"

"Apart from the fact something invaded my garden and my car won't start, I guess I'm doing all right."

"What's wrong with your car?"

Tierney noticed Josh didn't seem to care about her garden. "I have no idea. I was trying to find a mechanic."

"Let me look at it first. It may be something simple."

"No," she said, contrite. "I can't ask you to do that. I'll find a repairman."

"I have a few hours off work. I'll drop by. Dollars to doughnuts, it's your battery. If it's too complicated, I have a talented mechanic who can take care of it for you. I was going to be in your area this morning anyway," Josh added before she protested any further.

"But, Josh..."

"I'll be there in half an hour."

The cop ended the call before she responded.

True to his word, Josh was on her doorstep in the allotted time and insisted on looking at the vehicle right away.

"Why are you so worried about it?" Tierney led the way to a garage converted from an old barn.

"It's important to have a car, especially when you live alone out here."

"Sometimes I go for days without driving anywhere. It doesn't make that big a difference."

"Everyone needs wheels in case of an emergency."

"Oh, I see. In case the killer comes after me." Tierney crossed her arms over her chest.

"It's something to consider." Josh climbed into the disabled vehicle and turned the switch. "Yeah, just as I thought, a dead battery."

"That's not so bad. Dad has a charger in here somewhere."

The garage wasn't wide, but it was high. It was equipped with a loft that had stored hay in its life as a working farm, but Tierney's father had organized it with racks to hold tools and other equipment.

Tierney squinted and pointed to one of the shelves.

"Yeah, there it is. I'm sure that's it, don't you think? There's a ladder in the corner." She returned to peer under the hood of the car. Tierney had never charged a car battery before and wasn't sure how to set it up but assumed Josh would know. When she turned around, the detective hadn't moved and stared up at the loft.

"What's the matter? You don't think that's it?"

"Yeah, that looks like a charger," he said.

"What's wrong?"

Josh had a strange expression on his face. "Nothing."

Josh arranged the ladder against the wall, checking to make sure it was secure. Tierney watched as he took a deep breath and climbed to the loft. When he reached the top, he crawled to the shelving before pulling himself upright. The detective clutched the battery charger with two hands and turned to stare down at Tierney, his face chalk white.

"Are you okay?" This was the first time she had seen the cop less than self-assured.

"Fine." The word came out like a bullet.

"Are you afraid of heights, by any chance?"

His Adam's apple jumped.

"Why didn't you tell me? I would have gone up," she said.

"I'm okay. I got this. The worst part is coming down."

"I can't carry you down. The best I can do is hold the ladder. Take your time, and you won't have to worry. Leave the charger in the loft. I'll get it after."

Josh made his way down the ladder, one slow step at a time. His breath left him in a rush when his feet connected with the cement floor of the garage. The detective glanced at Tierney, his face red.

"You're laughing? It isn't funny," he said.

"I know it's not." Tierney couldn't suppress the giggles any longer. "I can't help it. The big, tough cop. I thought you'd make a mess in your pants."

"It's a thing, okay. It's a phobia of mine. Lots of people have them."

"You're right," she said. "I'm sorry. I'll stop."

But, as she sprinted up the ladder to retrieve the battery charger, Tierney couldn't resist one more giggle.

Josh took the apparatus from her hands with a glare that could curdle milk. A few minutes later, it was hooked up to the battery. "That should do the trick, but you'll need a new one as soon as possible."

"Sure," Tierney said.

"I mean it," Josh said. "You can't be stuck out here without a car. It's bad enough you insist on staying here alone."

"All right. I got it," Tierney said. "You don't have to get in a snit over everything."

"I just want you to be extra cautious, that's all."

"Yep. I got it." Tierney's tone made it clear the subject was closed.

"I have news for you. No, don't get your hopes up." Josh raised his hands. "I got a phone call from headquarters on my way over here. We have approval for a profiler. He'll analyze the crimes and the way they were committed to develop a list of possible characteristics of the killer. Are you familiar with the process?"

"I'm aware of it. I'm a crime writer, but I've never met a profiler."

"It took me a while to get it cleared through the proper channels. And he's one of the best. He'll be able to help us, but he has to meet with you."

"I'll do whatever I can. You know that."

"I do. I just want to prepare you for it."

• • •

The next day dawned sunny and warm, in sharp contrast to Tierney's mood, which had returned to black and dismal. Her expression grim, she put aside her negative thoughts and concentrated on her manuscript. The writer had received yet another e-mail from her editor wondering how the book was coming along, and she had learned the man's patience only lasted so long before the messages became more and more demanding.

Tierney poured a cup of coffee, retrieved her laptop, and made her way to the sunroom on the south side of the house, her favorite spot. Through the floor-to-ceiling windows, her desk gave her a view of the flower gardens, planted among a collection of apple, maple, and mountain ash trees.

Tierney was a country girl. She rarely spent more than a few hours in the city before she was ready to come home, and it was in this room that she most appreciated what she had.

Several hours passed as she struggled through a few paragraphs. The result was disjointed and unsatisfying. Tierney laid her head against the back of the chair and heaved a sigh of frustration. She straightened when a knock sounded on her front door. Her surprise increased when she spied the man who stood on the other side.

It had been several months since Tierney had last seen Adam. They had spoken on the phone twice following their breakup the previous fall. The couple hadn't parted on bad terms. Quite the opposite. They had suffered a bout of mutual disinterest and decided to each go their own way, while remaining friends.

But the friendship seemed to fall by the wayside as both of them reveled in their newfound freedom and resumed their busy lives. Theirs had not been a passionate, all-consuming love, but something resembling the relationship of two old men meeting in a park every afternoon to play chess. Comforting and dependable, but not heart-palpitating.

Tierney was happy to see Adam. The comfort and dependability that had seemed stale and uninteresting in the past took on a new value now that Tierney's life had turned topsy-turvy. The sight of him grounded her.

Adam took a small step back when Tierney threw open the door with unusual enthusiasm.

"What a wonderful surprise," she said. "What are you doing here?"

Adam chuckled. "It sounds like a cliché, but I was in the neighborhood and thought I'd drop by."

"I'm so glad. You look great." Tierney's house was at least a thirty-minute drive for Adam. His career as a paramedic obliged him to be close to the city and available to answer emergencies. Her insistence on living in the country had been a point of contention between them in the past. But today she would not question his unexpected presence. Tierney led him into the kitchen and gestured toward a chair while she put on the kettle.

"So do you," he said.

Tierney recognized a lie when she heard one. Lack of sleep and too much worry made her haggard looking, but she didn't call him on it. He meant well. Adam had always been a kind person; unassuming to the point of being boring, but kind.

"What have you been up to?" His gaze scanned the kitchen, as if snooping for a reason for her odd appearance.

"Nothing out of the ordinary." Tierney avoided his gaze as she prepared two cups of tea. She couldn't lie as smoothly as him.

"Is something wrong?" Adam took her by the elbow and turned her to face him.

"No. Why should there be?" She kept her gaze fixed on the collar of his shirt.

"You seem a little tired. Is everything all right around here? Your parents, how are they?"

Tierney's spirits lifted. She didn't need to lie about this subject.

"They haven't changed. You remember how they are. They're away on another cruise, having the time of their lives." She laughed. "No doubt, my mother has everyone dancing to her tune. I'm sure she's commandeered the ship by now."

"If she has, no one will complain. They'll be enjoying themselves too much." Adam shot her a warm smile. "How's Monty?"

For a reason she didn't comprehend, Adam had gotten along well with her brother, but they mustn't have kept in touch, she thought.

"Busy. I see little of him. He's flitting from one business trip to another, but he doesn't seem to mind. I only see him when Mom and Dad are here, and that's a rare occasion."

"They must be pleased you're keeping the home fires burning. You're still writing?"

"Yes," Tierney said, after a moment's hesitation.

"Is it not going well?" Adam picked up on her uncertainty. "Can I help?"

"No, thanks. I'm just going through a period of writer's block."

She couldn't meet his gaze. Tierney understood she wasn't authorized to discuss the case with anyone, but the temptation to spill out her story of woe to Adam was almost too much. Whatever their differences, he had always been a sympathetic listener, and he had a solid shoulder to cry on, in both a literal and figurative sense.

In that way, he reminded her of Josh, but even though she trusted the police detective to work in her best interests, she realized it was difficult for him to remain objective. A cop's top priority was catching a criminal, and she didn't feel as if she should distract him from that job.

A firm hand touched her arm.

"You and I haven't been in contact very much in the last little while, but I hope you understand that if you need anything, I'm here to help you."

Tierney looked into his warm brown eyes and knew Adam was sincere. "I appreciate that."

An expectant silence hung between them.

"I can't talk about it right now," Tierney continued, "But, maybe another time, I'll take you up on your offer."

Adam hesitated for a moment before shrugging his shoulders, but the worry lines remained etched on his face.

"Now, enough of that." Tierney stood and headed for the kettle. "I'll get us both a tea, and you can bring me up to date on what's going on in your life."

CHAPTER 29

Tuesday morning, Tierney stared at the computer screen and tried to move forward with the manuscript when the trilling of the phone broke her concentration. Clint's voice greeted her.

"Could you come to headquarters this afternoon at one o'clock? The profiler would like to speak with you."

"Today? I guess so." Tierney experienced a now-familiar churning in her stomach.

She wondered at her uneasiness in having to talk to the expert and, stopping to analyze her emotions, Tierney realized she was afraid of what conclusions he might reach. *Would he point his finger in her direction? Would he affirm her guilt in the murders? Would he say her book was the cause, not the means?*

She stewed over the upcoming meeting all morning, once again setting aside her writing to pace the floor. Tierney arrived at police headquarters half an hour ahead of the scheduled time, torn between curiosity and wanting to put the experience behind her.

The young woman at the front desk directed her to the interview room on the second floor of the building. Tierney took the stairs instead of the elevator, wanting to use the time to prepare, but she regretted her decision when Josh met her in the hallway to find her slightly out of breath.

"Are you okay?" he said.

His gaze swept over her, and Tierney felt a moment of self-consciousness. Although her attire was far from formal, she wore a pair of pale blue dress pants and a white blouse. Her hair hung loose on her shoulders, and a light coating of gloss adorned her lips.

"Yes, I'm fine. Why wouldn't I be?"

"I thought you might be nervous."

"No. There's no reason to be." *If she said it aloud, did it make it true?*

Josh shrugged, pulled open the door, and ushered her into the room.

It was more crowded than Tierney had expected. The harsh fluorescent lighting and the stuffiness of the room did little to put her at ease.

Josh took care of the introductions. The forensic psychologist, Dr. George Ackerman, was a tall, distinguished-looking man in his mid-fifties. He stood and smiled as he shook Tierney's hand. He appeared relaxed, even after what seemed to have been a busy morning, judging by the number of empty cardboard coffee cups littering the table.

There were two other members of the task force present, Brian Kenyon and Linda Benson. The four detectives wore a harried look. It occurred to Tierney she may look as bad as they did, if not worse.

"We've spent the morning studying the specific points of the cases with George," Josh said. "He's done preliminary work. Now, he wants to review elements with you, getting your take on them."

Tierney nodded her understanding and faced the profiler, who again graced her with a reassuring smile before speaking.

"Ms. McGinnis, I've studied the three crimes from two perspectives. First, I went over the case notes for each of the homicides. I've read the crime scene and forensic reports, and I've scrutinized the photographs. Second, I've read your book to better evaluate how the killings tie in. I realize the detectives have questioned you, and you're unable to come up with a suspect from your list of friends or acquaintances. Is that right?"

"It is. There isn't anybody I'm acquainted with capable of committing these murders."

"All right. That's natural. For most of us, murder is beyond our comprehension. We can't commit the crime, and we have a tough time imagining why anyone else would, least of all someone we know or believe that we know.

"But, in your case, we have an exceptional situation. You're a crime writer. You write of murders for a living. To do so, you put yourself in the killer's shoes. You imagine how he is thinking, what strategies he's using, and how he reacts. It's much the same as what I do. I need to put myself in the killer's mindset. I must reason the way he reasons. The difference is I'm dealing with real life, and you're dealing with fiction. Writers can manipulate the conclusion to their liking. I can't. I can try, but I'm just a minor part of a team. Often the ending is not the one we prefer."

Tierney realized the doctor said this to put her at ease. He wanted to make her think of herself as part of the team to which he referred. In an odd way, she had felt left out of the investigation, like a spare player sitting on the bench, being informed of the score once in a while but not taken seriously enough to take part in the game.

George didn't wait for Tierney to respond.

"I've had experience with serial killers. Many of them share common characteristics. Yet, most of them possess something different that makes them stand out from the others. I often study a case and see a pattern, a method that tells me the type of individual for which we're searching. I hope I don't sound conceited or self-important. That's not my way. I'm not the only person who can do this. I just want you to comprehend that usually my services help, especially if I'm working with people willing to use what I can give them."

"I understand," Tierney said. Her gaze never left that of the profiler. She focused solely on him and every word he spoke.

"Good, because I want to tell you what my impressions are of the criminal we're dealing with." Ackerman paused and took a long sip of water. "First, I believe he's masculine. It takes a certain amount of physical strength to overpower and strangle someone. A strong athletic woman could commit these crimes, but men carry out the large majority of murders by strangulation."

The profiler paused and seemed to expect Tierney to react. She nodded her agreement.

"He's young enough," Dr. Ackerman continued. "I'd say in his late twenties, early thirties. This is possibly his first experience with murder. Often, it's something they've been considering for years. It may have occurred to him once as a whim, and then he forgot about it for a lengthy period, perhaps several months, until the idea reappeared again. Then the killer would have researched the possibilities, may have used a novel as a blueprint. I'd guess he's an avid reader of mysteries and crime fiction.

"He's very organized. That he's using your book leads me to believe he enjoys following a pattern, much like a person who can only cook if he or she has a recipe to follow, or someone that can only get things done by making a to-do list and checking off each item as it's completed. His thought process is very linear. He may have excelled in math or science in school. The suspect chose your book. If it hadn't been yours, he would've used another work, perhaps a movie or a TV show.

"This individual may have been abused, either physically or emotionally as a child. It's often the case with serial killers. He has low self-esteem and wants to prove himself. The killer's not trying to hide what he's doing. He's proud of it, showing us the pages from the book, demonstrating how clever he is. He wants us to realize he's smart and especially that he's smarter than you and the authorities. One can assume he wants to build it to a climax, reach a better conclusion than you did. When he's captured, he'll most likely brag of his accomplishments. What do you think, Tierney? Does it make sense to you?"

"Yes," she answered, nodding, "It does. It seems logical when you put it like that."

"Is there anyone you can think of who fits that description?" Josh leaned forward in his chair.

Tierney glanced at the detective, her mind racing with what the expert had revealed. She tried to fit one of her acquaintances into a slot that had those attributes. "I don't think so." She turned to face Dr. Ackerman. "Is there more?"

"Well, like a lot of serial killers, this person is doubtless very nondescript. He presumably has unremarkable features, neither overly handsome nor terribly ugly. He may have spent his life blending in to where sometimes he feels invisible. People wouldn't recognize him on a second meeting, or they'd forget his name. This may anger him and make him want to prove to the world he can do something no one will forget. Yet, because of this characteristic, he goes unnoticed in a crowd. He may be a bystander at the crime scene, or at the funeral."

The profiler addressed these last remarks to the detectives sitting around the table, although the significance was nothing new. They were very much aware that killers often attended the funerals of the victims. That's why the police always made it a point to attend those events; hoping to see a face that didn't belong, or one they had seen somewhere else.

"What about the way he's doing this?" Tierney asked. "The first victim, Jennifer, was right on the mark. Everything matched. The next two didn't quite match. Do you believe he's doing that on purpose?"

"He may be, but I think it's just too difficult to sustain a perfect match every time. I think it was just luck, if you want to call it that, when the first victim fell into place, the way you had set it out in the book. He must have been very proud of himself. After that, he may have had to settle for whoever he found to fit the bill as closely as possible."

"What of the sequence? He's not following the chronological order of the novel. Is there a reason for that?"

"Possibly. He may want to keep us on our toes. The killer doesn't want us to expect who the next victim will be. Perhaps he's having trouble finding the right victims at the right time. That can work two ways for us. It could cause a problem, or it might make things easier."

"I don't understand."

"He might escalate. He'll become frustrated with the inefficiency and sense he's not fulfilling his dream the way he was meant to. This means he may get desperate and start killing more quickly or indiscriminately. It means he might make mistakes, and that's excellent news for us. Because the more mistakes he makes and the more clues he leaves, the easier it will be for us to catch him."

"What you're saying, though, is it will take more victims before we'll be able to catch him, aren't you?"

The profiler grimaced. "Possibly, yes. Unless we're able to find a suspect before then using the information I'm giving you today."

"Dr. Ackerman, why do you think he chose my book?"

The doctor didn't blink. "As I mentioned, I presume he's a fan of crime fiction. As likely as not, he's been reading the genre his entire life. The suspect reads a work by a local author and gets the crazy idea that he'll turn fiction into reality. He wants to show up the resident celebrity and have his fifteen minutes of fame."

There was a moment's pause while Tierney absorbed this information. "Do you think he knows me?"

George Ackerman's gaze didn't waver from her face, but Tierney sensed the brain waves being transmitted from Josh to the profiler, willing him to say what the detective wanted Tierney to hear.

"My sense is that he does. He's thorough, and he's done his research. The suspect may not have met you, but he knows who you are, and he possesses a lot of information regarding you. Tierney, I read the book. I know one victim is an author. I think you should be very careful. If I were you, I'd find someplace to hide for a while until they've caught this guy."

Tierney turned an accusing stare at Josh. He just lifted a shoulder in an I-told-you-so shrug.

CHAPTER 30

Tierney drove home without remembering the drive. She mentally kicked herself for leaving her digital recorder behind. It would have helped to bring it with her, and she wouldn't have worried about forgetting things the doctor had shared. A fresh sense of purpose motivated her.

Once in the house, Tierney recorded her impressions of Dr. Ackerman, his opinion of the suspect, and her own reflections on the interview.

It was the latter part she found the most difficult. Tierney's reactions were mixed. The doctor's conclusions were logical, a combination of experience, learning, and good common sense. He could have been describing the antagonists in her books. Tierney experienced a closeness to the profile the doctor had outlined.

The problem was she couldn't imagine knowing someone the profiler described and not realizing it. But she wouldn't let that deter her. Tierney would do the exercise, if not for the benefit of the investigation, at least for her peace of mind.

Tierney pulled out her laptop and mulled over her method while waiting for it to boot up. Once a blank spreadsheet appeared, she made a list of every friend, relative, and acquaintance she recalled. Columns followed for their occupations, relationship to her, and how long she had known them.

Once completed, she reviewed her work to make sure she forgot no one. Tierney even added the names of the librarians who helped her with her research. She included the men she had dated since college, shopkeepers she spoke with on a regular basis, and anyone with whom she dealt to publish her books. This took into account her agent, editor, publicist, and webpage designer. Afterwards, she began the process of elimination.

Tierney tried not to be biased. She ruled a certain number out because they were out of town at the time of the murders, or they were not strong enough to strangle two women and a man. The first cut eliminated the women, along with her father and brother. That still left a healthy portion of males listed as possible suspects.

With the next scan, she removed the people over fifty years of age. Dr. Ackerman had suggested a man in his late twenties or early thirties, but Tierney planned to be more generous with the range of ages.

The following step was more difficult. Tierney needed to analyze the remaining names to decide which fell into the profile the expert had given her. It surprised her how little she knew of the backgrounds of most of the people on the list.

She had a limited knowledge of their childhood. They may have spent their childhood torturing the family pet, and there was no way for her to be aware of it. There were a few she disregarded because she didn't consider them loners or capable of blending into a crowd. There remained an uncomfortable number Tierney couldn't cut without asking further questions.

The phone rang as she skimmed the file another time. A shiver danced along her spine when Josh told her the reason for his call.

"Can you put together a list of people you know?"

"That's what I was just working on," Tierney said, surprised by his perfect timing.

"Great. What have you gotten so far?"

"To be honest, I'm not sure. I eliminated the obvious, but now I'm left with the not-so-obvious, and I don't understand what to do next."

"That's where I come in. I'm on my way."

Josh hung up the phone as Tierney racked her brain for an excuse to stall him. She felt protective of her minor effort, as if it were a child who was small for its age, and she was afraid the larger, more powerfully developed kid would subject it to ridicule.

Josh arrived, and without preliminaries, asked to see her list. Tierney swallowed her reservations and showed it to him. She scrutinized the cop's face as he studied the computer screen.

Josh surprised her by saying, "Good. This is good, Tierney."

"You mean it?"

"Yeah." He raised his head and stared at her with narrowed eyes. "You don't think so?"

"I guess so. It's just I've never done work like this before, and now I'm stumped. I have to narrow it down."

"I'd like to go over each one with you. Ask you a few questions. We'll see if we can't write off a few of them. After that, it means Clint and I will need to pay them a visit and see what we can find."

"You heard what Dr. Ackerman said. This person may not have ever met me. Which would mean he's not even on this list."

"He said maybe he didn't know you. But maybe he does. Look, it's what we have so far. There's no other bank of suspects to choose from. We've had people working on this for weeks now. They've combed every database of criminals available to law enforcement. We've found no known offender who fits this profile, who isn't incarcerated or has a solid alibi for at least one of the murders. We need a lead." Josh pointed at the laptop. "And this may be it."

"I hope so, but to be honest, there's no one on the list I believe capable of committing those crimes."

"I'm sure if you knew someone capable of murder you wouldn't have associated with him. That's just it. A murderer won't advertise the fact. He'll do everything possible to conceal his identity and his character from everyone. What we need to do is take the information given to us by the profiler and use it to narrow down the list of suspects."

"That's what I've been trying to do," Tierney insisted, "but it's difficult. There are fifteen people on this list who possess at least one characteristic Dr. Ackerman mentioned. Several have more than one. My problem is I don't know most of these guys well enough to be sure if they have more."

"You don't need to. Tell us as much as you can, and we'll do the rest. That's what we're here for."

CHAPTER 31

The next week passed without incident. Tierney continued to struggle with her writing. She spoke to her parents every few days, never indicating that something was amiss in her life. One sunny Tuesday, she accepted an invitation from Dr. Abbott to meet him for coffee.

"How's it going?" Concern creased the coroner's face.

"Not that good." Tierney avoided his gaze. "It's been hell. I feel so helpless."

"I can imagine."

"There's got to be a way to catch this guy." She looked up from her mug, her eyes pleading.

"I didn't invite you here to discuss these crimes. I had hoped to take your mind off your problems."

"I know. I'm sorry. It's just that it preoccupies my thoughts twenty-four/seven."

"Then, let's get it out of the way. If you want my opinion, the guy is smart. He knows how to cover his tracks. But this isn't news for you. I'm sure you've heard it before. They'll catch him. So far, he's executing his plan perfectly, but it can't go on forever."

"So, you believe he's an expert?"

The doctor shrugged. "He's knowledgeable. Where he gained that knowledge is anyone's guess. He may even be in the medical profession," Chris said with a wry smile.

"Could it be an acquaintance of yours?" Tierney's tone was hopeful.

"I know a lot of people. Believe me, if I suspected anyone, I'd have mentioned something by now."

•   •   •

Tierney settled into a routine, similar to the one before the murders, albeit with a dismal fog hanging over it. When Josh and Clint pulled into the driveway on a warm Saturday afternoon, it shook her routine to the core.

Tierney kneeled in the shrubs, her pruning shears in her hand, and her heart thumped against her ribcage as she saw the detectives climb out of the car. They had those expressions on their faces she recognized as the 'bad news' looks. And, in a cop's profession, bad news often meant death. Her knees trembled as she rose to her feet and squared her shoulders. Tierney looked Josh in the eye when he approached her.

"Who is it?" she asked, as he stopped in front of her.

"Let's go inside."

"Who is it?" Tierney said, her tone stronger as she tried to control the telltale tremor in her voice.

Josh sighed and exchanged a helpless glance with Clint. "It's a man. His name's William Marsden. Chapter nine."

Tierney shook her head in confusion. "I don't remember..."

"In the novel, his name was Bill. The character in your book strangled him in his home while the victim watched TV," Clint said.

"Yes, of course." A disturbing sensation crept over her as she realized she had reached the point where she could discuss a real-life murder while she stood among her roses.

"Except it didn't happen that way," Josh added.

"It didn't? What? How?" Her gaze probed his face, needing to understand what was different this time.

"They found the victim in his car in the garage of his home. The pages from the book were stuffed into his shirt pocket."

"And Mr. Marsden was a manager of a construction company, not an electrician," Clint said. "But I guess the killer's not splitting hairs anymore."

"No. No, he isn't." Tierney peered up at Josh. "Can I see him?"

"I was sure you'd say that. No, you can't. But I tell you what. I'll get you a picture, so you can satisfy your curiosity. How would that be?" Josh didn't hide his frustration, but Tierney was too dazed to care.

"Okay. That'll be fine."

Contrite, Josh said, "We'll get him."

"You keep telling me that."

"We're doing our best, but this guy is clean. Like the profiler said, he's smart, but he'll screw up."

The three of them stood in silence for several long minutes until Josh spoke. "Tierney, I need you to leave here. Go somewhere safe. I'm worried about you."

"I'll be okay."

"The murders are in this area. The guy is around here. He knows you. You could be next on the list."

"I'm not that well known."

"All it takes is one person to mention their friend who's a crime writer to someone with a sick mind, and he gets a brilliant idea to become a serial killer."

"My friends respect my privacy." Worry and frustration darkened Tierney's face.

"Clint and I found you. The journalist did too, didn't he? How did that happen?"

"I don't know. But I'm sure it wasn't one of my friends."

"Okay, so it wasn't a friend. How about a neighbor or an acquaintance? Maybe it was the guy who sells bananas at the fruit stand. My point is, word gets out. Sometimes with the most innocent of intentions. And it reaches the most dangerous ears. We can't take any chances. We're talking about your life."

"You work with death every day, and you see shadows in every corner. That's not how I want to live. I can't."

Josh's face clouded over with anger as he turned toward the car, but he didn't leave without having the last word.

"I'll be back. I won't let this go."

CHAPTER 32

At this moment, the police detectives were talking to her, informing her of the latest murder. She'd be upset. *Was her level of distress increasing with each new victim? Or was it possible she was complacent regarding the entire affair?*

The killer didn't think so. She seemed to be a compassionate person. Possibly, this very minute, she sobbed and wailed and wondered when it would end. It would be great to have her take on it. Perhaps she would see how well the original version had been enhanced.

"1 mean, for goodness' sake, it's more challenging and daring to kill a man in his car than in a chair in his living room. Anyone could have looked into the garage and seen what was happening." No one heard the words as they echoed through the empty room.

Today's event had been enjoyable, with a glorious spot on the street to observe the comings and goings. The detectives and other people working the crime scene appeared bleak today. An air of futility emanated from them.

The killer was too smart for them, not leaving any evidence behind. Only a stupid person would do that. A successful mission called for intelligence and care. Even though the script had been tweaked, it didn't mean the research hadn't been exhaustive.

Another door from the garage had opened onto the darkened back yard. No one had seen anyone leave that way. If they had, what description could they give? Someone in a white Tyvek suit? Yes, the killer, but unrecognizable.

It was too easy. The police were less competent than expected. A third of the victims were killed without them having a clue where to look.

The mission had always been two-pronged: to improve the plot and to relay an important message. *Perhaps the relaying of the message was too subtle. Yes, that could be it.*

The time had come to up the ante, make everyone frantic. A little confusion could be thrown in. They needed to realize who controlled the plot.

CHAPTER 33

Tierney paced the floor, dragging her hands through her hair. She wasn't sure how much more of this she could take. She felt helpless, useless, and frustrated. *How was it possible to evade an entire police force? Was he a wizard? The killer threw around clues, teasing and taunting them, showing his superiority. Why couldn't the authorities catch him?*

Her thoughts turned to Josh and his stark warnings. She fought to put on a brave front, but when she was alone, she gave in to her fears and anxieties. She thought she might go mad, jumping at every noise and movement. But the thought of exposing her friends to the same dangers and fears was unimaginable.

Tierney hated isolating herself. Work was impossible. Preparing a meal, weeding a garden, or sweeping a floor took more concentration than she had to give.

She needed to talk to a friend and the sooner the better. If ever she craved someone to hold her hand, it was now. To hell with not discussing the case with anyone, Tierney wanted a confidante, and she decided Adam was the best candidate for the position.

Seconds later, Tierney had him on the other end of the line. Her ex-boyfriend didn't question her request to come over to her house. He said he would be there within thirty minutes and hung up the phone.

Adam kept his promise, even though the half hour had seemed like several hours as Tierney checked the driveway every few seconds. He took the steps two at a time to reach her door.

"What is it? Is it your parents? Are they okay?"

"They're fine. I...I just." Tierney broke off, torn between telling him the whole dreadful story, or keeping it to herself as the police had instructed her to do.

"What is it?" Adam said again. "What's so terrible? I've never seen you like this before. Whatever it is, you can tell me. It can't be that bad."

Tierney looked into his eyes, saw the sincerity in them, and almost stepped over the precipice. But, at the last moment, her integrity stopped her. She had made a promise, and the police had already experienced a problem with leaked information. She had to draw comfort from her friend's presence without revealing information concerning the case.

"It's the burden." She scrambled for an explanation. "It's the pressure I'm getting from Ron and the publisher. I don't think I'll make it."

"That's what this is about, your manuscript?"

"My writing is important, Adam. I take it seriously." She didn't have to fake her hurt sensibilities. Neither Adam nor her brother had ever fully supported her chosen career. Monty had always made it clear he considered it a hobby and a waste of time. Adam hadn't been heartless enough to say it aloud, but Tierney sensed his thoughts coincided with her brother's.

"Of course, you do," he said, his expression apologetic. "I can't be much help as far as writing, but I can give you a hug, if it helps."

Tierney offered him a feeble smile. "It would help."

His arms came around her and pulled her in for a fierce hug.

"Look, you're fine, and your family is okay. Those are the most important things. We can deal with the rest."

"You're right," she mumbled against his chest. Tierney wanted to breathe an enormous sigh of relief. She had come close to exposing confidential information to Adam and might have threatened the investigation.

An idea occurred to her. Tierney leaned back and gazed at her friend. "You *can* help me."

"How?"

"I need a sounding board. If I told you the story, you might give me a few ideas, help me get around my block."

Adam appeared doubtful. "I'll try, I guess."

Tierney guided him to the couch and took a place by his side. She wrung her hands, wondering where to start.

"Okay," she said. "The plot concerns a serial killer who uses a book as a blueprint for his murders."

Tierney studied Adam as his brows lowered into a frown.

"Let me get this right," he said. "The killer buys a book about murder? That doesn't sound realistic. I doubt they'd allow anyone to write a how-to book for homicide. No one would publish it."

"It's not a how-to book. It's fiction."

"Which one? Yours, or the other one?"

"Both."

"Yes, but is the other one fiction because you made it up in your book, or is it fiction within fiction, or is in non-fiction within fiction?"

"Adam, you're making this complicated." Tierney's exasperation was apparent in her tone, but it couldn't be helped.

"I'm sorry, but I don't understand."

"I can see that. Let me start again." Tierney regretted her experiment. She stared at the ceiling, trying to figure out how to explain it in terms he could follow. "My book, my fiction novel, is about a serial killer who uses another fiction novel about a serial killer to create a series of copycat murders."

Adam sat with his elbows resting on his knees, eyes narrowed in concentration. "Okay," he drawled. "I get it. That's a brilliant idea."

He still sounded doubtful. "So, what's your problem, and how do you think I can fix it?" Adam said.

Tierney sighed. "I'm not sure anymore."

"I'm sorry. I guess I'm not good at this sort of thing," he said with a wry grimace.

"Not at all. You've been a big help. I'm inspired."

"You think so?" He gave her a wide smile.

"Yes, I truly do."

After Adam left, with a promise to return soon, Tierney made herself a cup of tea and took it into the solarium. With her feet propped on the ottoman, she held the mug in both hands and stared out the windows. A light drizzle sent tiny drops down the long panes of glass as she thought of the visit with her ex-boyfriend.

Tierney was proud of the way she had pulled back from the brink and turned a conversation with a potential for disaster into a test of Adam's innocence. She had never considered Adam a suspect in the murders, but he was on the detectives' list. And she had eliminated him as a person of interest in the investigation.

Adam's reaction to her story had been sincere. She knew him so well, his guilt would have been evident if it existed. The hard part would be convincing Josh of the same.

CHAPTER 34

Two days after the fourth murder, Tierney received a phone call from Chris Abbott. "I won't ask how you're feeling because I realize it mustn't be good."

"No, it isn't," she said. "What can we do? We're sitting with our hands tied, not able to stop him."

"That's how it seems, but it isn't the case. They're working hard to sort this out. Josh and Clint have become regulars in my office, poring over the reports and asking questions. We've discovered nothing, and neither has the CSI crew."

"I've heard that, but it doesn't mean it's any easier to accept. The poor man's wife found the body. He had two teenage daughters, a good job, and didn't bother anybody. Why did he deserve to die?"

"He didn't. No one does. We have to hang in there, Tierney. He'll make a mistake."

"Yeah, I've heard that before too. I just hope it happens soon and with no one else having to die."

Disconnecting the call, Tierney fell back on the couch, her right arm thrown across her eyes, and contemplated the conversation with the medical examiner. Something occurred to her, and she grabbed the cordless phone in one hand, while she dredged her purse for Josh Riddell's business card.

Within moments, a monotone voice told her to leave a message. Tierney did as instructed and disconnected with a grunt of frustration. She paced the living room, and, four lengths later, the phone rang. She snatched it up and didn't have time to say hello before Josh fired questions at her.

"What's wrong? Are you hurt? Did something happen?"

Tierney's head flinched. "No, I'm fine. Why would you think I'm hurt?"

"Because your voice sounded urgent on the phone, that's why."

"It is urgent, but only because I had an idea."

A lengthy breath reached her ears before Josh spoke again. "Okay, what's your idea?"

"I talked to Chris Abbott today, and he mentioned how careful this guy is, and how he left no evidence behind. It occurred to me the killer's knowledge had to come from somewhere, and who has the most insight about how not to leave evidence behind?"

Tierney waited for his answer.

"A cop?" Josh said.

"Right. Or someone involved in law enforcement."

"Okay."

"You don't sound enthusiastic." She had expected more from him.

"It's not that I'm not excited. We've considered the possibility. We started with your cop friend and came up with nothing."

"Oh."

"But look, it's great you're thinking of these things."

Tierney's excitement deflated. "Yeah, right. Well, I'll try to come up with something original another time."

"That's the attitude."

The dial tone buzzed in her ear, and she scowled at the phone, hoping Josh sensed her reaction. She wasn't a hot-shot detective, but if she put her mind to it, she could play a role. She had made headway with her questioning of Adam. She reminded herself she had yet to tell Josh of it, so she couldn't blame him for doubting her abilities.

A smile lit her face as another idea occurred to her.

Tierney sat at her computer and pulled up her list. Thirty minutes later, she walked out the door, armed with a pad and pen.

Tierney rarely sought out her neighbor. It was often the other way around, but it wasn't so unheard of it would create suspicion. At least, she hoped not. Jeff wasn't outside, so she couldn't make it appear as if she had spotted him and come over for a chat. Instead, she had to knock on the door to talk to him.

"Tierney, what a surprise!"

Jeff was dressed in his usual neat style, with perfectly combed hair. As a rule, Tierney only wore t-shirts and sweats, with her hair pulled back and her face bare of makeup. She had learned from experience that wasn't the case with her neighbor.

In high school, Jeff would be the guy who wore a buttoned-up creaseless shirt, perhaps even a tie, while the other guys ambled around in torn jeans and baggy t-shirts. They'd have teased him as the class geek. *That could have affected his self-esteem, couldn't it? Was he now thinking he had something to prove?*

"Hi Jeff. How's it going?" Tierney plastered a smile on her face and hoped it looked sincere.

"Wonderful. Please come in. It isn't often that you stop by to visit." He pulled a chair out from the kitchen table and motioned for her to sit. He grabbed another chair and perched on the edge of the seat, bubbling with eagerness. Tierney swept her gaze around the room. It was the same as on the few other occasions she had been in the house. Everything was tidy, the small appliances on the countertop lined up like soldiers waiting for inspection. Nothing had changed or been rearranged.

"It's not that I don't want to drop by. I've been very busy. I'm working hard on my latest book, and the publisher's getting antsy."

Tierney knew how to get to Jeff. He had an abundance of interest in her writing. In fact, it was the only subject he ever wanted to discuss with her.

"Do you have writer's block?" Excitement lit his face.

"That might be it. I'm not sure. I can't figure out where to go with it."

"Maybe I can help."

"You realize how I hate asking other people for help, but I may be at that stage now." Tierney strived to appear humble.

"What's it about? Fill me in." Jeff forced a look of concentration onto his face, but it wasn't possible for him to disguise his elation. Tierney guessed his thoughts. *I'm a consultant for a manuscript. My ideas may appear in print!*

"It's about a copycat serial killer," she said.

"You mean a killer who's copying the MO of another killer?"

"Not quite. He's copying the MO of a fictional killer. A character from a novel."

Tierney studied Jeff's facial expressions and pretended an interest in what he might contribute to the plot of her manuscript. Surprise, understanding, and admiration crossed his features, but it was what she didn't see that was most telling. There was no guilt or fear.

"Wow, that's a marvelous idea!" her neighbor said. "So, what's the problem?"

Tierney had never thought Jeff capable of murder. Even though, according to the profiler, he fit the bill; he was guileless. Planning and executing a murderous plan were outside his reach. She saw it in his eyes. After her exchange with him today, she would remove Jeff from the list of suspects with a clear conscience. Now, she was eager to end this visit and go home.

"I can't figure out how to bring it together and catch him," she said.

"If you showed me what you have so far, I could give you a hand. I'd have to get a real feel for the story first."

"Yeah, that might be the solution." Tierney stood and moved the chair to its original position, tucked under the table.

"I'll come to your house and look at it right away." He stood and bounced from one foot to the other.

"Oh, Jeff, I'm sorry. I can't do it. The contract with the publisher prohibits me from showing my work to anyone without written permission from them." It was a blatant lie, but Tierney had no intention of inviting him in to read her manuscript, especially since the plot she had discussed with him did not exist. This was a runaway train she had to bring to a grinding halt.

Disappointment fell across Jeff's face. "Will you be able to get approval from them?"

"I'll do my best." Tierney walked toward the door, and she sensed his presence close behind her.

"When will you get back to me?"

"As soon as I can. I'll call you. If you don't hear from me, it means I couldn't get anywhere with them."

It was Tierney's version of 'don't call me, I'll call you.'

At home, she went to unearth her list and put a firm line through Jeff's name. Tierney thought of Josh and Clint, and how tedious the business of tracking suspects must be. The encounter with Jeff was enough for one day.

Tierney took the phone off the hook and settled into writing. Her efforts were unsuccessful, and she tossed the papers aside in favor of a lengthy walk in the fields behind her home with Cooper.

She didn't turn back until she noticed the dog's enthusiasm flag, and she worried he might give up on her. The last thing she needed was to drag a seventy-pound animal home. Woman and dog returned to the house, Tierney dumped herself into bed at an early hour, and left the rest of the people on the list for another day.

CHAPTER 35

The detectives were in the car, on their way to Bill Marsden's employer's location. They had set up interviews with coworkers to gain insight into his movements or any meetings they may have seen him have with a stranger. The drive took them past majestic Parliament Hill, poised on the bank of the Ottawa River, with the Centennial Flame eternally burning in front of the Centre Block.

Clint normally enjoyed the view, but his mind dwelled upon his problems with Lydia.

If anything, the situation had worsened. The mysterious phone calls seemed to increase, and each time Clint questioned Lydia, her answers were hazier.

"What's up? Still have problems with your love life?" Josh interrupted his thoughts, but he was on point for the subject matter.

Clint caught the trace of humor in Josh's voice, but he needed a sounding board, and his partner was a good one. "I can't figure out what to do."

"Why don't you just come right out and ask her what's going on?" Josh glared at him; his eyebrows squished together.

"I've tried to bring up the subject. In a roundabout, indirect way."

"Maybe it's time to go at it in a straight, direct way."

"I don't want to hurt her." Clint's shoulders slumped.

"I understand, but you need to figure this out. It's driving you crazy."

"Don't I know it." Clint sighed. "I've convinced myself she's not having an affair with another man."

"Yeah? How's that?"

"I just don't think she'd be able to do it, string two guys along at the same time. It doesn't seem like the Lydia I know."

"Okay, let's say for the purpose of argument, she's not having an affair, what are the other possibilities?"

"I don't know. I've followed her a couple of times now. Believe me, I hate doing it, and she always goes to the same place. She isn't usually there more than half an hour, goes in alone, comes out alone. And everybody around acts as if it's normal to see her there, as if she's been there often, and it isn't unusual. I don't get it. I just don't get it."

"Have you checked out the residents of the building?"

"I've looked into it, but nothing pops. The next step is to question each one, but if she has a connection with one of them, word could get back to her."

"Look, you've done everything you can." Josh pulled into the parking lot, found a spot, and turned to face his partner. "The best option is to confront her. Tell her how you feel and give her a chance to explain."

"Yeah, but how do I explain the fact I've been investigating her and following her around?"

Josh punched him on his bicep and smiled. "That, my friend, is your problem. I don't know how to solve that one."

"Thanks, Bud, you're a prince among men."

"Anytime." Josh opened the door and climbed out of the car.

●   ●   ●

The moment had arrived at last. Clint couldn't go on any longer living with suspicion and guilt. The suspicion was directed at Lydia, and the guilt was directed at himself for having suspicions in the first place. But enough was enough. It had reached the point he had trouble looking her in the eye. At times, he considered calling it off between them, but something stopped him, made him think she was worth the fight. What he had to do was build up the courage to confront her and get to the bottom of the problem.

The time came after an enjoyable dinner for two in his apartment, prepared by Lydia, when they had settled on the couch to digest their meal.

"Honey?" Clint said.

"Hmmm." Lydia snuggled closer to him.

Clint rolled his eyes and reminded himself to put on his big boy pants. "I have to talk to you."

"Go ahead. Talk."

"I have a strange sense you're leading a double life." As he said this, he watched her reaction. She stiffened and her eyes popped open wide to stare at him.

"What are you talking about?"

"Look, I'm a cop, right? A detective. I notice things for a living. And I noticed you receive a lot of strange phone calls at odd times, and afterwards you seem kind of secretive or guilty."

"I do not!" She straightened and swiveled to face him.

"You don't what? Receive strange calls or look guilty."

"Either. Both."

"Sweetheart, I don't mean to sound accusatory." Clint used his most charming smile to defuse the tension. "What I want to say is, if you have a problem, any kind of problem, I can help. I'm here for you."

Lydia shut down. She sat on the edge of the couch, no longer drowsy and relaxed. Her shoulders rigid, her back ramrod straight, she stared ahead, as if concentrating on the wilting plant in the corner of the room. With her lips pressed together, Clint was convinced she wouldn't let any words escape through them.

He leaned close to her and slid his arm around those oh-so-stiff shoulders. "Hey, what's wrong? I just want to help you."

"You believe I'm doing something dishonest."

Her voice trembled, but Clint couldn't tell if it was from sadness or anger. "No. Never."

It was clear by the glance she slid his way she didn't believe him.

"What is it you think I've done? Robbed a bank? Cheated on my tax return? Am I harboring your famous serial killer? Or better yet, I could be the famous serial killer!"

Clint had never seen her so distraught. He had known a confrontation would upset her, but he had imagined them discussing it in a calm manner.

"Lydia, I never said those things. I thought you were in trouble, that's all." He didn't dare mention he had suspected her of sleeping with another man.

Clint noticed a slight relaxation of her posture, so he pushed his advantage. "You understand you can tell me anything. I won't judge you." He winced when he saw her reaction. It had been the wrong thing to say.

"Judge! I don't care about being judged. I'm my own person, and it shouldn't matter what other people think of me."

"You're right. Perhaps judge was too strong a word. I meant I wouldn't think badly of you."

His remark didn't seem to help. Lydia jumped to her feet and gathered her things. "I'm going now."

"There's no hurry. Let's talk this through." Clint stood and tried to put his arms around her, but she shrugged him off.

"I won't do any more talking, Clint. If you find getting a few phone calls from my family offensive, then we have a problem with this relationship."

"It's not about getting phone calls from your family. It was that I didn't believe..." Too late, he realized he had made things worse once more. She didn't respond, but her eyes flashed in anger before she stormed out of the apartment.

CHAPTER 36

Tierney phoned her website developer, Andy Scarret, to find out if he was available to see her. Having no plans, he agreed.

Tierney had a deep admiration for Andy's computer wizardry. Her own skills were at beginner level, so she was more than willing to leave technical matters in his capable hands. Since her site was up and running with few problems, and she needed no changes, they hadn't interacted of late.

"Hey, Andy," she said, when the young man opened the door to his apartment, which also served as his office.

The reception she received was neither warm nor rude. She would describe it as a non-greeting, a miniscule twitching of the lips and a grunted 'Hello'. Tierney understood the lack of enthusiasm was an inherent part of his character. Andy didn't show emotion one way or the other, and it was why he was a hard person to read. She would do her best.

The webmaster was of medium height, with a build bordering on the thin side. His hair was long and unkempt, and his beard grew in uneven lengths. Andy's clothes hung loosely on him; his feet were bare. He didn't go overboard to impress his clients, she mused.

As with Jeff, Tierney had serious doubts Andy was capable of violence, but she couldn't eliminate him from the list without testing him in person. He left her with a strong impression of a man who spent much of his time alone in his small, nondescript apartment. He was very smart but didn't possess any characteristics that made him stand out in a crowd either physically or in terms of his personality. Not aware of any details of his childhood, Tierney wasn't able to come to any conclusions regarding him fitting that part of the profile laid out by Dr. Ackerman.

The young man didn't ask her reason for visiting him. Instead, Andy waited with an expectant expression on his face. Tierney realized the floor was hers. She sat before him with papers and a pen.

"I've been considering changing the website."

"Okay," Andy said.

"I toyed with the idea of including an excerpt from the next book, like a teaser to build interest."

"All right." He appeared bored; his eyelids heavy. No doubt, he wondered why they couldn't have taken care of their business by e-mail.

"Could we add in another tab for that?"

"Sure." His shoulders twitched in a minuscule shrug, as if anything more was too much effort.

"I put together the text I'd want to have posted to the site."

Tierney had spent an hour that morning composing a phony teaser. She handed the printed document to Andy and waited for him to read it. She was disappointed, but not surprised, when he set it on the desk beside him without looking at it. He turned back to her as if he expected her to either speak or leave.

"Don't you want to hear about the story?" she asked.

"I'm not much of a reader. I design web pages. Whatever you put in there is all right with me."

Tierney reached over and grabbed the paper from the desk, hoping she didn't appear too desperate.

"That may be, but I'm a writer, and writers are always going through periods where they second-guess themselves. I'm in the middle of such a period, and I need a sounding board. You wouldn't mind filling the part, would you?"

Tierney gave him her sweetest smile. She took his shrug as a positive sign and launched into a recitation of her text. As she narrated an excerpt from the nonexistent book about a killer taking his instructions from a novel, she flicked glances at Andy's face, looking for signs of anxiety or guilt. Instead, he stared at his feet with half-lidded eyes.

When she finished, Tierney waited for the young man to respond. He lifted his head and returned her expectant look, in all probability hoping the nutcase writer would leave him in peace, hopefully soon. She was at a loss. Her expertise with interviewing suspects only went so deep. She left him, taking the paper with her, explaining she would rework it, and he could hold off on changing the website.

The visit with Andy may not have given her any enlightenment as far as the murders were concerned, but it gave her inspiration for her current work-in-progress. Tierney worked for two solid hours and would have done more if the sound of car tires crunching on the gravel driveway hadn't interrupted her.

Josh's face appeared in the doorway, and a shiver of fear marched down Tierney's spine. His expression was somber, his eyebrows lowered. In the past, Clint had always been with him when he delivered news of another murder, so perhaps it wasn't the reason for Josh's visit, she thought. Maybe he was just in a nasty mood.

"What are you up to today?" Josh settled into a kitchen chair and declined her offer of a cup of coffee. His upbeat tone of voice was at odds with the tightness of his expression.

"I'm working on my book." This is a test, Tierney reflected. She trod with caution, wondering where he was headed.

"I saw your neighbor, Jeff, this afternoon."

Tierney vacillated for a moment. The way she looked at it, she had three choices. First, she could play dumb, pretending to have no clue what he meant. Second, she could confess, let him vent, and get it done. Last, she could defend herself from the get-go.

Tierney understood the first choice was a delay mechanism. Eventually, she had to face the music. The second left her open for verbal abuse, and her system was ill-equipped to handle it these days. The third seemed the wisest option.

"I can tell from your tone of voice you're not pleased with me."

"That's an understatement," Josh said. The fake upbeat tone was gone, replaced with a vibrating rage. "What the hell are you doing talking to suspects?"

"First, I don't consider Jeff a suspect, and..."

"You put him on the list." This was uttered through gritted teeth.

"...second, why can't I talk to my neighbor whenever I want to?" Tierney continued.

"You don't see a problem? What if he's the killer?"

"Come on. You met him. Jeff's just a bit taller than I am. He's the guy who would have gone through high school wearing a necktie and pants that were too short for him."

"Right. A geek. A guy who blended into the crowd so much no one ever noticed him. Someone with a lot of pent-up frustration because nobody takes him seriously. Is this starting to sound familiar to you? Do you recall Dr. Ackerman discussing this with us not too long ago?"

Tierney opened her mouth to protest, but Josh was on a roll and wouldn't stop for anyone.

"Just so you're aware of it, we've been looking into the background of your wonderful neighbor, Mr. Lakefield, and there are a few mysterious holes in his past. He's moving up on the list of prime suspects."

Josh looked at her with wide eyes, as if she hadn't already gotten his point. "And then, I get a call from Clint, who's just finished an interview with Adam Pendleton. What does he tell me? You met with the guy. You're out there trying to do our job for us? Are we supposed to thank you, Tierney? Are we supposed to be happy you're saving us so much trouble?"

Josh abandoned the chair and stood with his hands on his hips, a furious glare on his face, and waited for Tierney's answer. She wondered how to get out of this one without digging herself in deeper.

"I don't expect you to understand and, no, I'm not looking for appreciation, but I had to do something."

"Why?"

Cooper lifted his head to stare at the cop, not accustomed to shouting in this otherwise peaceful house.

"Because I'm going insane waiting." Tierney reined in her temper with great difficulty, standing to face him. "You don't get what it's like. You get up in the morning and go to work as if it's just another day. If you're lucky, you'll find a clue that'll bring you a step closer to solving the case. If you're not, oh well, there's always tomorrow. You can go home at night with your conscience clear, knowing you've done your best, and it's just a job you have to do. It'll still be there the next day. It's not like that for me. It's..."

"Stop it." Josh gripped Tierney by the shoulders. "You're wrong. It's not just a job for me. I care about what's happening. I care about the fact the killer is still out there and we have to stop him. I care about you."

The detective paused and faltered before he continued. "I care about the victims and their families. Do you think it's easy for me to talk to those people? Do you think I don't lie awake at night reliving their horror and grief? This is real to me, Tierney. Maybe you're suffering through it in a different way, but don't assume I'm not experiencing it too."

Tierney's shoulders relaxed under his hands, and her forehead slumped against his chest. He put his arms around her and pulled her against him.

"I feel so useless, that's all." Tierney mumbled against his shirt. "I wanted to help. I thought I might eliminate a few suspects for you." She paused a moment. "I saw nothing on Jeff's face. He's as innocent as the day is long. And you don't understand about Adam. I'm positive he's not involved. I know him. He couldn't fake it."

Josh wrinkled his nose like there was a bad smell in the room. "Adam will stay on the suspect list the same as everyone else until we check out his alibi."

"It bothers me that everyone's life is picked apart. The cops study innocent people under a magnifying glass. Meanwhile, I'm sitting here, twiddling my thumbs, wondering what's going on and driving myself crazy," Tierney said. "Besides, I didn't have the opportunity with Adam, but I have proof Jeff is uninvolved."

"Really." He pressed his lips into a fine line.

"Yes. Give me a second." Tierney went into her office and returned with a pen and her laptop. She set them on the kitchen table.

"I taped it. With this pen." She displayed the device with pride. "My parents gave it to me as a Christmas present. They thought I'd find it handy when I go to writer's conferences or meetings. It records video and audio. I downloaded it onto my computer."

Josh's expression held a dose of admiration. He watched the interview with interest.

"Could you...?"

"Yes, I'll e-mail it to you. No problem."

"That'll be great," Josh said. "If it helps, I understand why you want to become involved, but please, leave it to us. Just the idea of you alone with a murder suspect, untrained and unarmed, is scary. We're the professionals here. Even if, from your perspective, the police look like floundering incompetents, we still have a certain amount of experience."

"You're right." Tierney moved across the kitchen to turn on the coffeemaker, more for something to do with her hands than a genuine desire for caffeine. Without turning to see his reaction, she tossed over her shoulder, "I wouldn't bother talking to Andy Scarret either. I met him this afternoon, and he has nothing to do with the murders. I'll send you that one too."

She braced herself for the angry shout she was sure would follow, but all she heard was an anguished groan.

CHAPTER 37

After a lonely and unappetizing supper, Tierney breathed in fresh air as she sat on the porch swing, hoping to clear her head. Her quarrel with Josh had drained her mentally and physically. They had reached a cautious impasse, which appeared to be the way with them.

Even though the argument had seemed to clear the air, Tierney felt deflated. She glanced at Cooper. He lay so close to her feet she couldn't move the swing without kicking him. She might have insisted he change spots, but she knew the glare she would get if she tried, and it wasn't worth the trouble.

"I need to relax," Tierney said. Cooper opened one eye and stared at her, seemingly in agreement. "I'll take a nice, hot bath. That should do it."

She stood and stretched her arms over her head, reveling in the pull of muscles. Her hands fell to her sides when a noise emanated from the area of the pine trees. Tierney was certain she hadn't imagined it when Cooper's head popped up and swung in the same direction.

They both waited, unmoving, to see if something emerged, be it animal or human, but nothing happened. Tierney considered investigating, but creeping through the woods, alone, in the dark, was a move even she wouldn't make. She went into the house, casting one last look over her shoulder before locking and bolting the door behind her.

Tierney ran a bath, lit lavender-scented candles around the tub, and poured a glass of white wine, doing everything possible to make herself relax. After drying off, she crawled into bed and fell fast asleep as soon as her head hit the pillow.

The next morning, coffee cup in hand, she sat on the step, enjoying the warmth of the sun on her face as Cooper trudged over to the tree line to relieve himself. Tierney gazed at the old dog with affection. He was so predictable and stuck in his pattern, she could set her watch by him.

Her brows pulled together when the golden retriever broke from his routine and took an aggressive stance. Cooper was the least hostile animal she had ever known, and she could count on one hand the number of times he had worked up a growl. As she watched, the hair on the back of the dog's neck stood on end, and he barked in a frenzy.

Tierney ran into the house and fumbled in the kitchen drawers for a weapon, a memory of the noise the previous night flitting through her brain. She found a carving knife, the only weapon she had.

Cooper's barks grew more frantic, or so her imagination made them seem. A sense of urgency told her to get outside as soon as possible, but common sense told her to find the cell phone and be prepared to call an emergency number.

"Cooper, it's okay. I'm here." Tierney hurried toward him. Her gaze swiveled from side to side, looking for a source of danger. She suspected it was a groundhog or a porcupine that had set the dog off, but she couldn't eliminate the possibility it was something more sinister.

The dog's attention centered on a particular section of trees. Tierney wondered how foolish it was to march in there armed with nothing more than a knife and a cell phone. But Cooper's barking got to her. Tierney had never seen him so upset, and the more he barked, the more critical the situation seemed.

"Okay, I'm going. Stay close."

The trees were so thick they blocked the view of Jeff's house, and Tierney had no idea what she might encounter on the other side. She held onto the knife with a firm grip and used her other arm to shove the branches aside as she pushed her way through the foliage.

Tierney kept her gaze trained on the ground, expecting to find a dead or wounded animal in her path, and the last thing she wanted to do was step on it.

As Tierney emerged on Jeff's side of the trees, Cooper crashed through the shrubbery behind her and took up his barking once again. She glanced at the dog and shifted her gaze to align with his.

Tierney screamed and dropped the knife.

CHAPTER 38

Tierney cradled her head in her hands, the table hard beneath her elbows. Cooper was curled at her feet, his fur warm against her legs. A police officer stood a few feet away with her back to the kitchen door, her hands clasped behind her. Tierney wasn't certain if she protected her from someone trying to get in, or if her job was to ensure the writer didn't have a maniacal episode and run screaming out of the house.

The latter was a definite possibility. Tierney wanted to scream. She wanted to rant like a madwoman, but she couldn't move or think straight.

There was one image pictured in her mind, and she worried it would never leave. She needed to close her eyes and fall into a deep sleep where everything was rosy and nothing dreadful happened to anyone.

Instead, Tierney stared at a scratch on the kitchen table, caused by a mishap with a knife, leaving a permanent scar. *How many scars on her soul would she have before this nightmare ended?*

Heavy thuds followed by a familiar voice penetrated her stupor.

"Tierney."

She lifted her head and met Josh's gaze. He sat on a chair next to her, their knees close. His expressive eyes showed concern. Tierney suspected his protective instincts had increased tenfold now. Things had taken a turn for the worst.

"I guess there's no need to ask...is he...?" Her voice a whisper.

"Yes, he is."

"I don't remember which one he is. Did they find...?"

"Not yet. They'll tell us soon."

"It makes no sense." She turned her head to stare out the window, unable to appreciate the verdant landscape surrounding her home, her mind traveling elsewhere.

"I know."

A movement to her left snagged Tierney's attention. Clint had nudged past the police officer, his expression sympathetic. "I'm sorry. That must have been rough."

Tierney gave him a weak smile, but her bottom lip quivered.

"Anything?" Josh asked his partner.

"No. Still looking."

"It doesn't make sense!" Three pairs of eyes turned toward Tierney, all of them surprised, two of them worried. She clenched her hands into fists. She wanted to run through the patch of trees again, and find the answers to her questions, but she couldn't stomach it. Once had been horrible enough.

Josh's pocket buzzed. He exchanged a glance with Clint and strode to the corner of the room, his back to them, to take the call. Tierney kept her gaze on that back, wanting to analyze every word, movement, and twitch. She hoped whoever was on the line had answers.

"Okay...yeah...when?...all right, I'll wait to hear from you." The phone disappeared into Josh's back pocket before he turned.

"And?" Tierney's gaze bore into his.

"That was Chris. The results aren't conclusive."

"What? Jeff's dead, isn't he?"

"Yes, but the coroner hasn't determined if it's murder or suicide." A wince accompanied Josh's words.

"Oh God." Tierney's hand slid to her throat. "I never considered suicide. I assumed..."

"Yeah, we all did," Josh said. "But when you think of it, it's possible. There's no sign yet of a heart or pages from the book."

Tierney tuned out the other people in the room. In her mind's eye, she saw herself coming out on the other side of the copse of trees, concentrating on the ground, afraid of stepping on an animal. She raised her head and saw Jeff Lakefield dressed in his usual crisp shirt and cotton slacks, lounging on a chair in the middle of his immaculately groomed lawn, legs sprawled out in front of him.

His face was distorted, eyes bulging, lips blue. Something, she wasn't sure what, was tied around his throat. Attached to a branch of the tree behind him was the other end.

Tierney remembered screaming. She recalled taking a few steps toward the body, before turning and running as fast as possible through the trees and to her house. From there, she made two phone calls, one to 9-1-1 and the other to Josh.

Her memory was fuzzy. Tierney didn't recall her conversations, but she was certain she babbled like an idiot. She paced and cried; she may have whimpered and was relieved when Josh appeared in the doorway.

The detective held her as she sobbed. Tierney tried to explain what had happened, but she was incoherent. He left her with the female police officer while he went to check out the crime scene.

Now, the authorities weren't sure if it was suicide or murder. But Tierney was convinced the killer had struck again. She couldn't grasp which fictional character he had chosen or the connection they would find. The reasoning behind it confused her, but she was certain they would locate the pages and the heart.

"There's a lot going on, and we both have to be a part of it. Is there someone we can contact for you?" Clint spoke to Tierney, while tossing a meaningful glance in Josh's direction.

"I'll call Faye. She lives nearby," Tierney said. She didn't want to monopolize Josh's time, but she had to find a way to explain this to her friend.

The decision was taken out of her hands. Faye accosted a police officer in the yard and learned what had taken place before she set foot in the house.

"God, how awful! Is it true you found the body?" The woman shot the question at her friend as soon as she entered the kitchen.

Tierney burst into tears.

"Oh, honey, tell me what happened." Faye kneeled beside her chair and wrapped her arms around her.

Tierney repeated the same tale she had told the police. She explained how Cooper had alerted her to something, and how she had investigated and discovered the corpse. She didn't share the background behind the story, keeping her promise to withhold the information on her involvement in the other homicides.

"You shouldn't have gone over there," Faye said. "After the rash of murders around here lately, you can't take chances like that."

"I didn't expect to find a dead body. I thought it might be an animal."

"You're very brave, stupid but brave."

"Yes, I've heard that before."

"Why don't you stay at our house tonight? The kids will spoil Cooper, and we can have a couple of glasses of wine."

"That's a brilliant idea." A voice came from behind them.

Recognizing it, Tierney's back stiffened. A sharp retort jumped to the edge of her lips, but she caught the range of expressions on Faye's face and stopped short. It started with surprise, followed by a gleam of admiration, and finished with a dash of curiosity. Tierney didn't want to fan that fire, so she kept her mouth shut.

"You must be Faye." Josh held out his hand. "Tierney's friend."

"I am. And you are?" Faye stood and slid her palm into his.

"Detective Josh Riddell."

"And you're acquainted with Tierney? You've met before?" A speculative glimmer lit Faye's eyes.

"Yes," Tierney said. "Through my books."

"A consultant," the other woman said, with a knowing nod.

Tierney responded with a faint smile. It wasn't a lie. It was a non-correction of an assumption.

"Pack a bag," Josh said. "You can leave with Faye right away."

"Don't you think you may need me to hang around a while longer? In case you have more questions?" Tierney realized Josh was being protective, but she wanted to be here when they found the pages. She needed to understand what the murderer's reasoning had been. Once again, the detective wanted to shut her out of the investigation, and she didn't appreciate it.

"You can give me Faye's address, and if something comes up, we'll contact you."

"I'll gather Cooper's things while you go pack," Faye offered.

Tierney had no choice but to agree. If she made a fuss, Faye's suspicious nature would rear its head.

CHAPTER 39

"Are the police looking at you as a suspect?"

"No. Why would they?"

"You found the body, and you live next door. It's possible you'd be on their list until they eliminated you. I'm not a criminal lawyer, but I could have represented you. You should have called," Jim said. The counselor in Faye's husband looked at the incident from a professional angle.

"I don't sense the police consider me a suspect. But if it ever comes to that, I'll call you." Tierney was not at liberty to give Jim the reason for her lack of concern. That the police thought her more of a victim than a suspect needed to stay a secret.

She was ensconced in Faye and Jim's home, safe and sound. Brandon and Jessica, ages four and two respectively, entertained Cooper, and she had a glass of wine in her hand, even though the clock had yet to strike five.

"They have to find out whether the death was suicide or murder. It might take a while for the coroner to determine the cause," Jim said.

Tierney didn't think it would take long. Once they brought to light the evidence they needed, they would announce the cause of death. Tierney's fingers itched to call Josh. She was sure the detective held out on her. She pictured Josh and Clint standing at the crime scene with a handful of other people, discussing what the pages they had discovered signified.

"What's wrong?" Faye said. "You look as if you want to rip someone apart."

"Do I?" Tierney searched for an excuse for her bad-tempered expression. It wasn't difficult to find one that was no less true. "I'm angry for Jeff. I mean, he was harmless. He didn't deserve to die that way."

"Of course, he didn't." Faye waved her arm in a dismissive gesture. "No one does."

"I need to understand what happened. I can't stand this waiting." Tierney paced the living room, twirling the wineglass between her hands.

"Understand what?" Jim said. "How he died?"

"Yes." Tierney held out her arms. "Was it suicide? Was it murder? It's important."

"The cops may never find the cause of death. It's easy to make a murder appear to be a suicide. Any killer worthy of the name can do it."

Tierney frowned, wanting him to explain his statement, but Faye interrupted them.

"Why don't you sit and relax? You'll wear a hole in the floor," her friend said. "Besides you shouldn't worry about this. It's not as if the guy will come after you. You're not an eyewitness. You found the body, but you didn't see who did it. It was just rotten luck for it to happen to your neighbor."

Tierney set her glass down, closed her eyes, and took a deep breath. Frustration would get her nowhere. Josh would contact her, she decided.

On the heels of that thought, her cell phone rang. Seeing Josh's name on the screen, she punched the button and headed for the door. Tierney wanted to be away from her friends' curious eyes when he told her the news.

"Yes?" Her voice crackled with anxiety.

"Nothing."

"How could there be nothing?" Tierney's mind raced. "It was suicide?"

"No, it was murder, but there are no clues linking the death to your book," Josh said, his voice hollow.

"How could that be? Someone else murdered him?" Tierney's heart thudded.

"Perhaps. I doubt it."

"Why do you say that?"

"What are the chances? Jeff's your next-door neighbor."

"The others had pages and a heart. I don't get it. I was sure you'd tell me you found pages. Did you find any other evidence?"

"Nothing. It was clean."

"Like the others." Tierney leaned her forehead against a doorframe and closed her eyes. Her body couldn't sort out the conflicting emotions that coursed through it.

"Yes."

"What's next?"

"We'll treat it as part of the same case, unless we find something that tells us otherwise. My theory is the killer sent you an obvious message. He's getting closer to you, and he wants you to know it."

"That's a stretch." Her words were bold, but her voice didn't hold much conviction.

"He murdered your neighbor. How much closer can he get?"

Neither spoke. Tierney was aware of the answer to that question.

Tierney's spirits sank further. Jeff had lost his life because of a madman. What drove the monster, she did not understand. It was too big a coincidence for her neighbor to be murdered and for her to have no connection to the case. *Why wasn't the murder set up the same as the others? If it was the same killer, why had he deviated?* The urge to solve the mystery overwhelmed her. Tierney wanted to help, but she couldn't fathom how. And as more time passed, they could lose more lives.

CHAPTER 40

Tierney spent two nights at Faye and Jim's house. Though she loved her friends, she needed to get home. Living in a house with two active children, along with two other adults, took Tierney far from her usual comfort zone. Even Cooper showed signs of wear and tear. When Tierney found him hiding under a bed, trying to rest, she got the message. It was time to return home.

Her decision entailed reassuring Faye and Jim she was safe in her own house. The one way to do so was to find a roommate/bodyguard who suited her lifestyle. Adam fit the bill.

The tough part was explaining the need for his company without overemphasizing that need. Adam had learned of the death on the news channels but hadn't realized it was Tierney's neighbor who had been murdered. Tierney downplayed the danger for herself, not wanting to add another overprotective male to the mix.

To that end, Adam heard the same story as Faye. Tierney's neighbor had been murdered, and she had been unfortunate enough to find the body. The other neighbors were in the same position of taking extra precautions. As far as her friends were concerned, it was a random act of violence, and Tierney needed their company to help her feel protected.

"It's temporary until the cops come up with a suspect." Tierney felt the need to reassure him further. "They've warned everyone in the neighborhood to keep their doors locked and not stay alone. I'm no different. I'm just sorry to take you away from your life."

Adam accepted Tierney's explanation at face value. "There's no problem, Tierney. I told you to call whenever you want."

Neither of them discussed the specifics of the word 'temporary'. Tierney knew Josh wanted her to stay with someone until they caught the killer. She was open to have Adam stay for a few days. After that, Tierney would find another solution.

She was certain Josh wouldn't approve of her choice of Adam as a roommate, but what he didn't know wouldn't hurt him. As far as the cop was concerned, she was still at Faye's house, and she would let him live with that misconception until telling him was unavoidable.

Adam's shifts allowed him three days off one week and four the next. He was at the start of a four-day weekend, which, Tierney hoped, would be enough time for the cops to end the need for a babysitter.

Unfortunately, Adam became restless at Tierney's house. She settled herself in the sunroom with earbuds, laptop, and notebooks, while her roommate flipped channels on the television. At his home in Orleans, Adam had a brief walk to the gym, shops, restaurants, and most of his friends.

"Why don't we go to my place instead?" he suggested. "You can write there just as easily as here?"

"What about Cooper?" Tierney said.

Adam grimaced. His apartment didn't allow pets. "Maybe Faye and Jim could take him."

Tierney grimaced in turn. She had saved the old dog from the excitement of two young children. Taking him back to that environment wasn't her favorite option. Yet, she understood Adam. He was bored, and she wasn't a delightful companion. "Give me until tomorrow, okay? I'll try to come up with a plan."

Adam, in his usual good-natured manner, agreed.

That evening, Adam's boredom ended. Despite having time off, the city kept the paramedics on call in case of an emergency where they found themselves short-handed. After their meal, as they tidied the kitchen, Adam's pager emitted a shrill alarm. He snatched it from his belt and checked the code on the display.

"I've got to go. Something's up." He turned to head for the door but swiveled back when he realized he was derelict in his duties as a babysitter. "Are you going to be okay for a bit?"

"I'll be fine." Tierney turned him around and shoved him toward the door. "Whatever it is, it's important, or they wouldn't call."

"Lock the doors and be careful. Call Faye and ask her to come over, or you go there." Adam dashed to his car.

Tierney watched him pull out of the driveway, but she didn't want to phone Faye. She decided she'd be fine tonight, and Adam would get back as soon as they resolved the emergency.

During his absence, Tierney breathed easier. She hadn't realized how much of an introvert she had become since she started writing full time. She enjoyed the peace and serenity of her little corner on earth. Though Adam was quiet and tried not to bother her, she was aware of his presence, and the guilt of not being an entertaining hostess weighed on her.

Tierney took the necessary safety measures. She locked and bolted the doors and secured the windows. Adam had keys to all the locks; she didn't have to worry about him. Her last safety measure involved putting a carving knife under the pillow. She had prepared herself, unlike the earlier victims.

Despite the safeguards, sleep did not come with ease. Tierney's mind replayed the discovery of Jeff's body. Seeing a corpse on an autopsy table was horrible, but to see one *in situ* was a unique and terrifying experience. She recalled her neighbor's puppy-dog-like enthusiasm when discussing her writing, and she regretted not including him in the process, at least enough to give him something enjoyable to remember.

Tierney finally fell asleep, but a few short hours later, a noise woke her. At first, she wasn't sure what it was until she recognized Cooper's bark. She couldn't remember the last time he had barked during the night. She threw back the covers, grabbed a sweater from a chair, and set off to see what bothered the dog. She had taken a few steps before she did an about-face and returned to grab the knife from under the pillow.

Cooper's tail hit the floor in a pounding expression of relief when he saw her. The dog faced the front door, alternating between looking at her and the doorknob.

"What's the matter, Cooper? Do you have to pee?"

The dog's tail thumped louder and harder at the sound of her voice. He stood and whimpered. Tierney bent over the elderly dog to scratch him under the chin.

"Poor old Coop. You having a hard time holding it in these days?"

Tierney straightened, reached out to grasp the door handle, and stopped, frozen. There was a piece of paper taped to the window with the writing facing toward the inside. The few words were written in block letters with a thick, black marker.

It took a few seconds for the significance of the message to register in her brain. Her heart pounded in her chest. Tierney stepped back one slow step at a time and reached for the phone. Her gaze darted around the room, trying to peer out the windows into the darkness.

Her hand skimmed the hard plastic of the portable phone and she grasped it in her left hand. She held the knife in her right and scurried to the bathroom, calling for Cooper to follow. The dog reacted to the urgency in her voice. Tierney slammed the door and locked it behind him as soon as his tail cleared the doorframe. She crouched on the floor underneath the window and dialed 9-1-1.

CHAPTER 41

Josh's arm reached out as the cell phone jangled next to his head. It wasn't unusual to receive a call in the middle of the night, and his heart didn't kick into overdrive until he heard the voice.

"Josh?"

"What's wrong?" Josh jumped out of bed and pulled one leg into his jeans while struggling to hold on to the phone.

"He was here."

She spoke the words in a monotone, displaying no hint of emotion, which proved more worrisome to Josh than if she had been in a frenzy. Tierney's reference to 'he' was obvious, and disturbing images darted through his brain.

"Are you alone?" He fought to keep his voice calm, not wanting to further alarm her.

"Yes."

Josh didn't understand why she was by herself, but he would deal with it later. "Are you hurt?"

"No."

Something about the way Tierney uttered the word did not sound right. She sounded catatonic. He wasn't sure if he believed her. Josh ran out the door, carrying his t-shirt in one hand, along with his gun, keys, and wallet.

His other hand held the cell phone to his ear. "Listen to me. Call 9-1-1. Where are you now? Are you safe?"

"I'm in the bathroom. I've already called them."

"Good girl. I'm on my way. I won't hang up the phone. I'll text Clint, and I'll get in my car and head out there. The line will stay open. Don't move."

"I'm not going anywhere."

"Hold on a second." Josh texted Clint, told him what had happened, asked him to contact Benson, and switched back to Tierney. She insisted she was safe.

By this time, Josh was beside the car, fumbling with the lock while he juggled his belongings and pulled on his shirt. He tried to convince himself that Tierney being able to carry on a conversation was a good sign, but that didn't keep him from barreling out of the city as fast as possible.

"Do you hear him? Can you see him?" he asked. Josh headed toward Navan at full speed, aided by the late hour and the lack of traffic.

"No. It's quiet."

"All right. Tell me what happened. Did he break into the house?"

Tierney surfaced from her daze and told him what had taken place. She didn't stop until she reached the point where she had called him.

"Good. You did the right thing. You didn't..." Josh broke off when a squeal resonated through the phone line. "What is it? Do you hear something?"

"Someone's banging on the door." A voice filled with panic replaced Tierney's monotone.

Josh heard shuffling and intended to tell her to stay where she was when she spoke again.

"It's the police!"

"Okay. Now listen to me, Tierney. Walk toward the door, but don't stand in front of it. Stay to the side. Ask whoever it is to show you identification. Tell me what he says."

"All right. Hang on."

The rustle of movement reached Josh's ears. He strained to pick up something unusual or ominous. In all likelihood, it was the police at the door, but he couldn't take a chance in case the killer used a ruse to flush the writer out of her hiding place. He was within a mile of her house by now.

Tierney would not have to delay them long before Josh faced the visitors in person.

He heard muffled voices through the phone line until Tierney returned to tell him the officer had identified himself as Tony Geraldo.

The name was unfamiliar to Josh, but it wasn't surprising. They were from a local police station, and he didn't have a handle on their names. Fortunately, he didn't have to.

Josh pulled into the driveway to see two uniformed police officers standing on Tierney's porch, visible in the light. They both looked toward him as he parked his car behind the cruiser. One spoke to the other, before striding in Josh's direction, a gun clenched by his side.

Josh understood the protocol. He grabbed his ID, flipped open the case, and snatched his gun out of the holster he hadn't put on in his haste. Before the uniformed officer spoke, Josh showed him his ID, explaining he was a friend of Tierney's, and she had called him to come over.

As the cop examined his credentials under the beam of a flashlight, Josh told him Tierney was an interested party in a murder investigation, and it was possible she was in significant danger. Those words produced the hoped-for reaction. Using the radio attached to his vest, the officer contacted his partner, who still waited for Tierney to open the door. Josh saw the other cop draw his weapon and look with unease into the shadows surrounding the house.

This was his opening. Josh bounded to Tierney's door and hammered on it.

"It's Josh. Open the door."

Within seconds, the locks popped open. An instant later, Josh held a trembling woman in his arms and tried to sooth her tattered nerves as the other two officers checked the downstairs for signs of an intruder.

When Tierney's breathing returned to normal, Josh led her over to the kitchen table and gently lowered her into a chair. The detective leaned down until his face was level with hers, grasped her by the chin, and lifted her gaze to meet his.

"Are you hurt?" he said.

Tierney shook her head. "No, just scared."

"Can I get you a drink of water?"

Again, she shook her head.

"Where's the note?" Josh needed to see what it revealed.

"It was outside the door, taped to the window, but the cop pulled it off."

"Damn!" Josh swung around to face the local police officers. "Did you guys pull a note off the door?"

"Yeah, I did," Geraldo replied. "I've got it here." He removed the folded paper from his shirt pocket.

"Jesus! What the hell did you do that for? This is evidence. Don't you know what that is?"

"I didn't realize it was important. I'm sorry." The young patrol cop looked as if he wanted the floor to open and swallow him.

Josh shook his head, not trusting himself to speak without losing his temper. "Anybody have gloves?"

One cop pulled a pair of blue latex gloves from his pocket and handed them to Josh while the other one went to the car to get a plastic evidence bag. What Josh saw when he unfolded the paper elicited another curse. He looked at Tierney, understanding what had caused her terror.

CHAPTER 42

Josh sat in the chair opposite his boss and struggled to appear relaxed. His right leg jiggled, and he placed his hand on his knee to control it, while Lieutenant Lowe took her time looking over the report.

Periodically, she glanced at the note the cops had removed from Tierney's door. Several times, Josh wanted to interrupt her examination but had learned from experience it would get him nowhere. His boss was nothing if not thorough.

They had shut the door to the outer office, muffling the sounds of a busy police station, and the silence weighed on Josh. At last, Lowe set the report on the desk and folded her hands on top of it, returning her full attention to her subordinate.

"I'm not sure," the lieutenant said. "Yes, it's obvious there's a tie-in with the book as far as the murders are concerned. We've gone over this before. We have to follow that lead as much as possible. Both you and Clint need to familiarize yourselves with the details outlined in the novel, and you need to understand it inside and out. I've told you many times Miss McGinnis is a key witness in the investigation, but as for your assumption she's on the killer's hit list, I'm not sure I can justify it."

Josh sat forward in his chair. "He taped a threatening note to her door. Tierney has the same profession as a victim in the book. Those are two excellent reasons for her to be on his hit list, not to mention the fact someone murdered her neighbor."

"So far, Jeff Lakefield's murder appears to be unrelated to the others."

"He lived next door! I'd say it's very much related." Josh did not believe what he was hearing.

"There was no plastic heart, nor were there pages from the novel." The lieutenant's tone was challenging.

"I admit the MO is different. But the note could only come from the killer. No one else outside the people directly involved in the investigation would have that information."

"You seem to have forgotten the leak to the media," his boss added. "It isn't as much of a secret as you believe."

Both of their gazes fell to the slip of paper, protected by clear plastic.

"*Coming soon! Chapter Twelve!*" Jeff said. "It scared the shit out of her."

"I sympathize," Lieutenant Howe said. "From what I heard, there are eight other prospective victims to come. Are you saying I should offer protection for the brown-haired writers, redheaded truck drivers, and God knows who else?"

"I wouldn't exaggerate, but I'm worried for Tierney. I believe she's in danger, and after last night, I think she realizes it."

"Well, I can't change the way you feel, but I don't have the budget or the manpower to authorize protection for Miss McGinnis. I'm sorry. I'd love to have the latitude. I'm already having trouble finding personnel to cover our active cases. You can arrange for her to leave town for a while, go visit a friend or relative, if possible."

"Yeah." Josh's voice held no conviction. Tierney had given him a hard time in the past, insisting she didn't need protection, but he wouldn't give up. He had an awful sense regarding this case, and he didn't want to have her blood on his hands. Josh couldn't live through it another time.

"Try it."

"I'll see what I can do." Josh stood to leave.

"I'm truly sorry, but you know the trouble we have getting money from the top, and most of the time we have more to go on than what you've given me."

"Yeah, I do."

Josh was aware of the eternal budget problem. He had run into similar roadblocks before, but it was harder to accept this time around. His fear for Tierney outweighed the restrictions he would normally have accepted as par for the course.

CHAPTER 43

The car idled in the parking lot, but Josh didn't seem inclined to go anywhere. He sat with his hands on the steering wheel, apparently deep in thought, glowering out the front windshield. Tierney was in the passenger seat, staring at him, wondering if her force of will might make him speak.

After his meeting, Josh had taken a moment to introduce her to his boss. The occasion had been stilted and awkward, rank with an atmosphere Tierney could not interpret. Josh seemed angry, or at the very least annoyed, and the woman appeared embarrassed to shake Tierney's hand and say she was pleased to meet her.

The detective had not spoken to Tierney since, and from the grim look on his face, she wasn't sure she wanted to find out what had transpired in Lowe's office.

Tierney jumped when Josh finally spoke. "All right. I've got a plan."

"A plan? For what?"

"For you."

"Why are you making plans for me? I'll take care of myself."

Josh swiveled in his seat to face her. "What happened last night? Someone made it to your door and left you a little love note. What if he had broken into the house? What if he had a gun? Or a knife? Would you have been able to take care of yourself?"

Tierney swallowed hard and shifted her gaze toward the side window. She didn't enjoy being reminded of how vulnerable she had been the previous night. After enduring the invasion of the CSI team with their cameras and fingerprint powder, she had been left shaken and with an eerie sense of violation. Without being asked to stay, Josh sat beside her on the couch after the last law enforcement worker had departed, put his arm around her, and held her until she fell asleep.

It mortified Tierney to wake in the morning and find herself sprawled inelegantly beside the cop. She acknowledged it was perhaps for that reason she was, once again, giving Josh a hard time for trying to make her give up her home.

"Listen to me," he said. "I won't leave you alone in an isolated house."

"What did your boss say?"

Josh pressed his lips together in a fine line and remained silent.

"What did she say?" Tierney insisted.

"Lowe's not sure there's a connection." He spoke in a scarcely audible voice.

"Really?"

Josh glanced at her as he maneuvered the car out of the parking lot. "Don't jump to any conclusions. Lowe's vision is clouded by her budget, or lack thereof. The department won't offer protection, but that doesn't mean I can't make my own arrangements."

Josh swung the car onto the street.

"Where are we going?" Tierney asked.

"To your place."

"I thought you said I shouldn't go there."

"Pack a few things and I'll make a phone call or two. Besides, we have to get Cooper, don't we?"

"I don't want to go anywhere. I like my home. It's quiet there, and I can work in peace. I'll take extra precautions. I'll find someone to stay with me."

"Are you going to get a gun?"

"Perhaps." The idea had never occurred to her until now.

"Have you ever used one?"

"No, but how hard can it be."

"Hard enough that the rest of us mere mortals have to train for months and practice constantly, so we don't shoot the wrong person or ourselves by accident." Josh clenched his jaw.

"I don't enjoy living like this. I had the perfect, peaceful life, and I want it back." She wrapped her arms around herself.

"I have an idea, and if it works out, you may enjoy it."

Tierney didn't answer. She no longer wanted to argue with him, but she doubted Josh would find something preferable to staying in her own home.

When they arrived at the farmhouse, Josh instructed Tierney to pack enough clothes for at least a week and asked her what she needed for Cooper.

Tierney glared at him for a long moment. "Where are you taking me?"

"For tonight, to my place. Tomorrow, I'll make other arrangements."

Tierney shook her head, sighed, and trudged down the hallway to her room.

"It's for your own good." He followed and leaned against the doorjamb.

"It doesn't mean I have to be happy about it."

Tierney had her back to Josh as she removed clothes from the drawers and packed them into a suitcase. When the sound of a low laugh reached her ears, she swung around to confront him.

"You're laughing? You're amused by the fact my life is upside down?"

The smile disappeared from Josh's face, and he raised his hands in defense.

"It's just funny to see you sulking."

Tierney slammed the suitcase shut, brushed past him, and headed to the kitchen. She sensed Josh's presence behind her. Grabbing a large bag, she shoved Cooper's bowl into it, along with a package of dog food.

Neither of them noticed the vehicle entering the yard nor heard the slamming of car doors. Before they could react, the sound of a high-pitched female voice approached.

CHAPTER 44

"Sweetheart, we're home!"

"Oh no, not now," Tierney groaned, rolling her eyes.

Josh opened his mouth to question her and closed it abruptly when the door swung wide. Through it glided a redheaded woman wearing a tight-fitting, fuchsia pink dress with a low neckline that displayed impressive cleavage. On her feet, she sported a pair of matching, spike-heeled, open-toed sandals. A tall gentleman with striking blond hair and a dark tan, dressed in white, including his belt and wing-tipped shoes, followed her. They both beamed, and without seeming to notice Josh, rushed to sweep Tierney into a three-person hug.

"Oh, my baby, we missed you so much. It's so good to be home," gushed the glamorous redhead.

Josh stood to the side, having guessed the identity of the couple, but their appearance took him aback. They were so far removed from how he had pictured Tierney's parents; they could have been from outer space.

He assumed they were in their mid to late fifties, but they were very well-preserved, perhaps with chemical or surgical help. Mrs. McGinnis spotted Josh and interrupted the detective's examination of them.

"Oh my, who is this? Tierney, honey, you never mentioned *him*! He's absolutely *gorgeous*!" Tierney's mother grasped Josh's arm in a bear hug and the move made him fear for her modesty. The more she pressed against him, the more her breasts strained against the fabric of her dress. Still, his delight helped him overcome his worry. A middle-aged vamp had never accosted him, and a glimpse of Tierney's horrified expression was enough to bring a wide grin to his face, leaving no need for him to say a word. Josh decided to play along and enjoy.

True to her nature, the woman barely took a breath before continuing her assault. With one hand massaging Josh's chest, Irene McGinnis spoke over a pink-clad shoulder to a blissfully unconcerned husband.

"Isn't he, though, Win? Doesn't he put you in mind of Errol Flynn? Your name isn't Errol, is it? No, it'd be too much of a coincidence. But, Tierney, why didn't you mention him? Oh, I know, you wanted it to be a surprise, didn't you?"

"Mom, please..."

"Oh, we didn't interrupt you, did we? You both have your clothes on, so it should be all right, shouldn't it?"

"Mom!" Tierney's face had taken on an interesting red glow, and her eyes were both pleading and annoyed, but her mother continued on her rampage like a steamroller without a driver.

"What do you think, Win?"

Once his wife paused, Mr. McGinnis had an opening to speak, but instead of coming to Tierney's rescue as Josh had expected, he added fuel to the already raging fire.

"He looks much better than that other chap. What was his name? Phil or Sam? That one didn't do you any good, did he, dear?"

He directed this last question to an almost apoplectic Tierney, but the pink steamroller flattened any opportunity to respond.

"Oh, that was years ago. She hasn't had a decent man since then, apart from that Adam fellow, and he hardly counts. I dare say, it's time we saw a fresh face around here. I worried you'd never find anyone, but I can see now he was worth the wait. What's your name, honey?"

Before he answered, Tierney, humiliated beyond belief, found her voice.

"His name is Josh Riddell. Detective Josh Riddell. He's not my boyfriend. He's a cop, and he's investigating a series of recent murders."

CHAPTER 45

Introductions were made, and everyone regained a degree of calm. Irene McGinnis was no longer the scatterbrained, flighty temptress. Instead, she was very much in charge, leading Tierney through a series of well-honed questions whose answers detailed the events of the past several weeks.

Josh had explained to the couple the importance of not sharing information about the case with anyone. The details had to be closely guarded within the police department, and the one exception that could be made was with Tierney and her immediate family. He prayed his decision wouldn't come back to bite him.

Winston, or Win, as his wife called him, would, on occasion, insert a question of his own, but it was often one someone had already answered. Josh had the impression of a man content to remain in the flamboyant shadow of his spouse, following along behind, admiring the view. The straight man in a comedic duo. That quiet, self-contained Tierney was the product of these two colorful personalities amazed Josh.

"Tierney, you must comprehend you're not responsible for the deaths of these people," Winston said. Josh had dismissed the man as clueless but was surprised to hear him expressing the words Josh himself had tried to hammer into Tierney's skull. He was grateful to have found an ally who might have more influence over her than he did. Josh intended to take advantage of any help he could gain through this couple.

"I realize it, Dad, but sometimes I believe if I hadn't written the book those people would still be alive."

"If it wasn't your book, it would have been someone else's, or if not a novel, then a movie, or a TV show. This person is sick and just looking for something to help him with his game. You have to remember that." Her father was emphatic.

As he listened to Win McGinnis, Josh had the uncomfortable sensation of being watched. With a glance to his left, he met the gaze of Tierney's mother. Her scrutiny was a sharp contrast to the way she had looked at him earlier.

"Surely, you don't consider my daughter a suspect." Irene's tone of voice implied she would deal with such a consideration briskly and painfully, and the detective should think twice before entertaining the idea.

"No, Mrs. McGinnis. She's not implicated in the murders; however, we do..."

"The police want my input because of the book," Tierney said.

"That's true," Josh added, "but we also believe ..."

"They believe I can help. Now, Mom, you haven't told me about your trip yet. How was it?"

At Tierney's invitation, Irene switched back into her alter ego and gushed over the wonderful cruise from which they had just returned.

Tierney was good, and she was fast, Josh thought. She was aware of which button to push to distract her mother and prevent the detective from warning her parents of the danger for their daughter. Despite her grudging semblance of cooperation, Josh could see removing Tierney from her home, and keeping her away from it, would be an uphill battle.

Josh glanced at Winston to find him gazing back with a speculative expression. The man was aware of something more going on, and Josh planned to get time alone with him. For the next little while, he relaxed and listened to the discussion taking place around him. He ignored the occasional warning glare coming from Tierney's direction.

The next several minutes were diverting. It seemed the McGinnis' fascination with the movies of the forties extended into many facets of their lives. The cruise they had taken was aimed at people with their particular interest. There were movie showings and activities geared around the same theme, and the couple were convinced they were in heaven.

They planned to leave for Boston the next day to join another movie-buff couple they had met on the sailing. Irene was giddy at the thought.

When Winston rose to go to the kitchen for a drink, Josh caught his almost imperceptible nod and stood to follow. The cop didn't look at Tierney, but hoped her mother's incessant chatter kept her glued to her chair for a few more minutes. Her father must have wished for the same thing, because he wasted no time speaking of his concerns when Josh stepped into the room behind him.

"Will she be all right?" the older man said.

"I'll make sure of it, sir."

"If she's in any kind of danger, whatsoever, we won't leave."

This was his chance. Josh could ambush Tierney, bring her parents onside, and get them to bully her into cooperating with him. If anyone could get her way with persuasion, it had to be Tierney's mother.

Yet Josh hesitated to do it. It looked as if Tierney would concede of her own free will. Her bags were already packed. She would view the use of her parents' influence as underhanded, and he didn't want to alienate her.

"I know," Josh said. "You don't need to worry." *But I do.*

"Good." Winston laid a hand on Josh's shoulder. "I can tell you're a fine person, and I trust you to take care of her."

"No problem, sir." Josh endured the weight of responsibility bestowed on him by that hand.

Returning to the living room, Josh saw the worried glance Tierney sent him. He assumed she wondered how much he had told her father. He, in turn, wondered if her parents had even read her book. If they had, they would have remembered the part describing the murder of an author and would have been as concerned as him. *Was he the only one who saw the connection? Was Tierney right when she accused him of overreacting?*

A half-hour later, when Josh bid goodbye to Irene and Winston and turned to do the same to their daughter, Tierney raised her palm to stop him. "I'll walk you to your car."

Tierney's suggestion didn't surprise him. Josh knew she had itched to speak to him ever since he had returned from the kitchen with her father. They had just stepped off the porch when she began her line of questioning.

"What did you tell him? Did you mention to him your theory about me being stalked by the killer? I swear to God, if you did anything to upset them and make them cancel their trip, I'll…I'll…"

"What will you do, Tierney? Hit me? Strangle me? Report me to the police?" he said, arms outstretched on each side.

"I'll think of something. What did you say to him?"

"You want to hear what I said? That he didn't need to worry."

"You did?" She stopped and stared at him, her eyes wide.

He turned to face her. "Yes. But I also told him I'd look out for you. And I will, but you have to cooperate with me."

"I am cooperating." Tierney's pained expression revealed how much effort it took to offer that cooperation.

"Yes, you are. And if you give me a hard time, I'll fill your parents in on what I suspect. How do you expect them to react?"

Tierney shuddered at the thought. They would smother her to within an inch of her life.

"I'm serious, Tierney. I have the information I need to contact your parents when they're away, and I won't hesitate to do it." It was a lie, but Josh's qualms about using her parents' influence to persuade her didn't reach as far as blackmail. "They'll come back here right away. Is that what you want?"

"You're a cruel, scheming person. I don't appreciate it."

Josh was convinced he had gained ground and was poised to comment when the sound of a vehicle approaching snagged his attention. Tierney swiveled and frowned. It was clear she recognized the tall blond-haired man, smiling and handsome, who stepped out of the black Mercedes.

The man's gaze swept over Tierney before fixing on Josh's face. His smile transformed into a sneer. Josh didn't have warm and fuzzy thoughts for this recent arrival. There was something about the guy. He was too slick, or too…something.

"How did you know?" Tierney's voice had an edge to it.

"They called. Cell phones, that wonderful technology you choose to ignore."

"I don't need to be connected to a phone twenty-four hours a day."

"You only need to hide yourself in a room with a computer, and your wonderful creativity will come to life." Again, he favored her with a condescending smirk.

Josh's eyes narrowed. He didn't appreciate this guy's attitude. He took a step forward, but Tierney held up her hand and shot him a warning glare.

She turned back to the newcomer. "Come. Let's go inside." She took him by the elbow and attempted to lead him toward the house, but he shook her off. He turned to Josh, who stood with his hands on his hips.

"Who's this, Tierney? Have you been holding out on me?" The man may have strived for humor, but it didn't come across in his tone. Josh strode toward the intruder just as the other broke away from Tierney. They met on middle ground, hands extended toward each other. The cop spoke first.

"Josh Riddell." He didn't disguise the suspicion and dislike in his voice.

"Monty McGinnis." The man gave Josh a look that radiated superiority.

"Ah, the elusive Monty. We haven't had the pleasure of meeting." Josh didn't hide his sarcasm. The police had tried to track this man since the first murder. The younger Mr. McGinnis seemed to screen his calls.

"He's come to see my parents and catch up on their news," Tierney said.

The directive was clear. She did not want to discuss the murders. This was to be a family reunion. Josh would leave her to deal with her parents and brother. He had to things to do.

"I'm a cop," he stated, sending his own message to the other man. "A homicide detective."

The reaction Josh received was not what he expected, simply because it was nonexistent. Monty McGinnis didn't blink or flinch. He didn't appear shocked or appalled. His breath didn't catch, his eyes didn't widen, and sweat didn't break out on his forehead. He remained in control, and the non-reaction bothered Josh. From a brother, he would have predicted a certain level of concern for a sister.

Tierney, however, looked as if she wanted to chop Josh into tiny pieces and feed him to the birds. She grabbed her sibling by the arm and steered him toward the house.

"Yes, well, that's neither here nor there. Goodbye, Mr. Riddell."

CHAPTER 46

He saw the grin on the old man's face from the end of the driveway. As Josh approached the house, his friend straightened his short, stocky frame and held himself erect. The two men exchanged greetings as Josh settled into a well-worn rattan chair on the sunny porch.

Matt Greyson had been a cop when Josh was in primary school. He was still a cop when Josh joined the force. They had taken to each other from the start. Matt often told the younger cop he reminded him of himself when he was his age, and Matt was everything Josh aspired to be as a police officer and a human being.

Despite the difference in ages, they had forged a bond, one that neither the passage of time nor Matt's retirement had diminished.

The ex-cop still lived in the old house in which he had lived with his wife, in the quiet suburb of Cumberland. Eliza had passed away twelve years ago, and Matt didn't have any pets and few friends, but it didn't bother him. The older man claimed he enjoyed living alone, doing what he wanted to do when he wanted to do it, and the occasional visits he had from Josh were enough to assuage his loneliness.

"What is it? Do you think the old man can't see something's on your mind? I may be retired, but I've still got something in here." He tapped the side of his almost bald, liver-spotted head, wisps of gray hair wafting in the breeze.

"What? Oh no, it's nothing." Josh hung his head sheepishly. "Well, actually, there is something."

"All right, get to it." Matt crossed his arms over his barrel chest.

The question Josh wanted to ask Matt clung to his tongue as if it was afraid to leave the safety of his mouth. He eased into it gracefully.

"I'm working on a case. It's a serial killer. You may have heard of the people who've being killed a few weeks apart, all of them strangled."

Matt's jaw tightened, and he nodded. The news media had discussed the basics of the murders, with no confirmation of a connection between the four killings, or the involvement of a serial killer. But, despite the silence of the police department on the matter, speculation ran rampant.

"There's a woman involved. She's an author of murder mysteries, and it seems as if this guy used one of her books as a road map. The killer is matching the victims to characters in her novel, or at least he's trying to as much as possible." Josh paused for a moment. "There's a problem though."

Matt's eyebrows spiked. "I'd say the fact that a guy's running around killing people because he liked what he read in a book is already a big enough problem."

"You're right, but there's another complication. I'm convinced this woman's life is in danger. I think this guy knows her, and he'll come after her. Someone left a note on her door last night referring to the chapter in her book where an author is killed."

"Could it have been a practical joke?"

"Perhaps, but it's too much of a coincidence. And it'd be a sick joke."

"Seems to me you need to discuss this with Lowe and make arrangements for her."

"That's what I did. But she didn't listen. Actually, she listened, but she claimed her hands are tied by budget constraints, and she'd never be able to justify protecting Tierney."

"I see," Matt replied.

Josh knew his friend saw very well where he was going, and the old man hunted for a way to say no.

"I won't leave her on her own. I just can't. And I can't be with her twenty-four hours a day either. I have a case to solve, and the sooner the better." Josh took a deep breath. "I need to ask for a favor."

"Doesn't she have any family?" The former cop had a note of desperation in his voice.

"Tierney has parents, but they're away on a trip. She has a brother, but he's not around much, and they don't seem to get along. For my peace of mind, I want her to be where I won't worry about her, and this is the one place I can think of where she'll be safe. It'd only be while I'm on duty. At night, she'll stay with me. That wouldn't be so terrible, would it?"

Josh's last words came out in a rush, wanting to spit it out before his friend interrupted him. The old man gazed at the sky and shook his head. Josh understood how much Matt valued his privacy, and he realized what a sacrifice he asked him to make.

Josh also knew Tierney would not only be safe here, but she would be content too. The house was isolated and had a vast property bordering the Ottawa River. There was room for Tierney and Cooper to make themselves at home, and she would get the peace she needed to continue her writing.

"What am I going to do with a woman around here? You know what they're like. They're always sticking their noses into things that are none of their business. And I'll need to be careful of my manners. I'll have to sit at the kitchen table to eat my meals instead of in front of the TV. I won't be able to walk around in my underwear. Christ, my life will be a living hell."

Josh smiled and admitted to himself his friend might have a point, but a bit of feminine influence in his life wouldn't hurt Matt. And it would benefit Tierney to be under Matt's experienced protection. The man may be retired and may have slowed down in the past few years, but his mind was sharp, and his senses were even sharper. Josh changed tactics.

"I guess you're right. I don't think I would've been able to convince her to come here, anyway."

"What? Why not?" Matt straightened his shoulders.

"Tierney doesn't want to go anywhere. She wants to stay by herself in her home. And I'd have a hell of a time convincing her to stay with an old retired cop."

"Why? She has something against cops?" he said, his tone sharp.

"I don't think so, although she hasn't come right out and told me, but it'd be more giving up her privacy and her own way of life to accommodate a crotchety old man."

"First, I'm not crotchety. And, second, I'm no hardship to live with. My wife didn't have any problems, did she?"

Josh had not spoke a word of a lie to the man, but it was all in the delivery. Now was the best time to remain silent and let his friend stew for a while. It didn't take long, but Josh was unprepared for the question that came out of Matt's mouth.

"Are you sweet on her, Josh?"

"What? Sweet? That expression went out long ago. What kind of question is that, anyway? She's involved in a murder case I'm working. That's it. I am not 'sweet' on her." Josh shifted in his chair under Matt's hard stare.

"It's not a good idea to get involved with an interested party in a murder investigation, or any investigation, for that matter." Matt's brows arched. "It's not considered professional."

"We're not involved. I'm concerned. Cop or not, I'm allowed to worry about the safety of another human being." Josh's jaw was tight. Matt had come close to striking a nerve.

The older man grumbled, and Josh leaned closer. "What did you say?"

"I said all right. She can come here, but if she gives me any trouble, I'll let her know, and then I'll let you know, and you'll have to get her out of here."

Josh grinned. "It's a deal, Matt. Thanks."

CHAPTER 47

Clint scowled at the computer screen. The forensic report seemed to annoy him more than it warranted. Josh realized something else bothered his partner. His own recent conversation with Matt led him to wonder if a woman had provoked Clint's foul humor.

"So, how's it going with Lydia?" Josh asked, trying to maintain a casual tone.

"Don't ask." Clint's scowl deepened.

"I guess that means it's not going well."

"I said don't ask."

"I didn't ask. I stated a fact."

"Don't state facts. Especially facts you know nothing about."

Josh's brows headed upward. He had never seen his friend like this. Whatever was eating him had to be serious. "How about you talk to me about it, and then I'll know something about them?"

Clint stared at him for several moments, until his shoulders slumped, and he lowered his gaze. "All right. It's simple. I confronted her. She got mad and left, and I haven't heard from her since. She doesn't return my calls, my e-mails, or respond to her doorbell. That's it. Those are the facts."

"I see." Josh's tone was even. "Now, when you confronted her, what did you say?"

"I tried to be delicate and subtle, but I didn't get very far before she became defensive and hurt."

"You didn't mention the fact you thought she was getting it on with another guy, did you?"

Clint glared at him in exasperation. "No. Not at all. Even I'm not that stupid, Josh."

"Okay. Just making sure." Josh watched his friend sift through papers, without seeing them, or even looking for any information in particular. "So, what now?"

"Nothing. Nothing now. I told you. She won't talk to me. She doesn't want to have anything to do with me. I should have just left it alone."

"Come on, you couldn't do that. Who the hell do you think you're kidding? You can't make me believe you'd want to have a relationship with a woman who spends time sneaking around strange neighborhoods and not do something about it."

"No. You're right. I couldn't. So that's it. It's over. It's old news." Clint leaned back in his chair; his hands splayed to each side.

"Right. Wise decision, my friend. She wasn't worth it."

Josh tossed out his last remark and sauntered away, leaving Clint to glare daggers into his back.

• • •

He had tried everything to get through to her, but she didn't answer his calls. Clint decided the one way to get a reaction would be to make her angry again. And he knew how to do it.

"Lydia, it's Clint. I'm not going to phone you anymore, but I have to get something off my chest before I call it quits. I investigated you and checked out your background to see if you had any previous arrests. I also followed you and saw the place you visited on a regular basis. I just wanted to say I'm sorry for that. Bye."

He'd done it, he thought, after he had left the message and disconnected the call. He had either shot himself in the foot, or he had set a trap she wouldn't be able to keep herself from falling into. Or maybe he had done both. Time would tell.

As fate had it, it didn't take time long to get off its rear-end. Within a half hour Clint's phone rang, and a very irate Lydia screamed almost unintelligibly on the other end of the line.

The epitome of patience, Clint told her to call back when she was calm and hung up on her. Thirty minutes later, Lydia pounded on the door of his apartment. A smiling Clint opened the door only to have the smile he had practiced with such diligence get slapped off his face.

"How could you?"

"How could I what?" He held his hand to his offended cheek.

"Oh, don't be stupid, you big oaf. You spied on me. You followed me. You're disgusting!" She marched past him into the apartment.

"I may be a lot of things, but disgusting is not one of them. Underhanded, perhaps. Disgusting, no."

Lydia swiveled to face him, her fists clenched at her sides. "Underhanded is too mild a word for what you've done. You've invaded my privacy. Poked your nose into my personal life where it doesn't belong."

"I disagree. I think it does belong there."

"You have no right!"

"I have every right." Clint fought to keep his tone low-key and soothing.

"No, you don't. You're so arrogant. You think just because you're a cop, you can follow people around and snoop in their personal business."

"That's not true. It's the first time I've done this outside of work."

She snorted her disbelief.

"It's true, Lydia. I've never cared for someone as much as I do you, so I've never been driven to do this."

"You did it because you care for me?" Her eyes were wide. "Are you crazy? Is that your way of showing affection?"

"It has nothing to do with showing affection and everything to do with worrying about someone to the point of distraction. Do you have any idea how much it bothered me to see you going into that place? I wanted to run in there and drag you out, kicking and screaming if I had to. I was sure I'd be called to a scene and come face to face with your body. How do you think that made me feel?"

For a few moments, Lydia didn't speak. Without a doubt, she digested what he had said. Then the wind seemed to drop out of her sails, and she slumped on the couch. "I wish you had never followed me. My personal business is my own. You don't belong there."

"I want to belong there. It's possible you don't want me there, but I want to be an important part of your personal life. Actually, I'd be thrilled to be the pivot of your personal life, but I'm sure, at this point, that won't happen. Nevertheless, I'm concerned for you. I want to help you if I can. I love you."

Lydia covered her face with her hands. "You can't. Can't you see that? I should never have gotten involved with you. It was a mistake from the start. I kept telling myself I shouldn't, but, somehow, I couldn't stop. When I found out what you did, I realized I should have listened to the voice in my head right from the beginning."

"Why? What's going on? What's so terrible?" Clint settled on the edge of the couch beside her. He wanted to gather her in his arms but wasn't sure if such an overture would be welcome.

"You're a cop."

"I was a cop when we first met. That never changed."

"That's why I should have stayed away from you. Right from the beginning. I can't be involved with a cop."

"What have you done? It must be something illegal. That's what this is about, isn't it? You're involved in something illegal, and you feel you can't talk to me about it."

"I've done nothing against the law. Well, not directly anyway. At least I don't think so."

"Lydia, tell me. I won't let this go. I'll follow you every day if I need to, but I'll sort this out if it kills me."

"I know." She lifted her head and stared at him with a desolate look.

CHAPTER 48

The next morning Josh arrived on Tierney's doorstep just in time to witness the repacking of the car and the extravagant goodbyes. Mrs. McGinnis seemed to have put aside thoughts of Josh's profession and once again looked at him as a prospective mate for her offspring.

"Now, I want you to take excellent care of my daughter while we're gone, if you understand what I mean," Irene said with a smile and a wink. The older woman, once again, trapped his arm against her low-cut neckline, and Josh was worried if he tried to extricate it, something might pop out. "Tierney may seem a little quiet, but I'm sure she's got my genes. You should take advantage of that."

When she went to pass on a few words of wisdom to her mortified daughter, Mr. McGinnis cornered the cop. It concerned Josh the man might question him regarding his intentions toward Tierney, but it turned out he also wanted to make sure his daughter would be well taken care of, yet not with the same undertones his wife had implied.

"Remember now, contact us." Winston pressed a piece of paper into Josh's hand. "That's our information. Anything at all, you call."

"I will. You don't have to worry."

Josh tried to step back while the family members dished out hugs and kisses, hoping to remain inconspicuous, but Irene McGinnis would not let it be. She enveloped him in a cushiony hug, almost choked him with her perfume, and graced him with a firm squeeze on his rear-end. She climbed into the passenger seat of the Toyota Camry, waving as if she was being driven away in a horse-drawn carriage before her admiring fans. Josh couldn't wipe the grin off his face until he turned to find Tierney glaring at him with her hands planted on her hips.

"What are you doing here?" she said. "I didn't expect you back here this morning...unless..."

She faltered, and horror dawned on her face.

"No, there wasn't a murder. I'm here because we agreed you wouldn't stay alone any longer."

"Even during the daytime? That's not what I understood." Tierney's eyes were wide with surprise.

"Not at any time. It isn't safe."

Tierney squared her shoulders and faced the detective full-on. "There's got to be another way. I need to work. I need quiet."

"I have the perfect solution. I found someone who doesn't want you just as much as you don't want him."

"Have you lost your mind?" Tierney's expression was incredulous.

"Not yet, but I'm sure you'll help me with that."

"It won't work. I can't spend my time making small talk with a stranger."

"You don't want me to call your parents, do you?" Josh realized he sounded like a school principal issuing warnings to an errant schoolgirl.

"Don't threaten me." An angry red tint crept up her neck and into her face.

"If it's the only thing that'll work, I'll do it. Come on, I don't have all day. Let's get you packed."

Tierney braced herself in front of him. "I'll make you a deal. I'll leave here and go stay with a friend."

Josh crossed his arms over his chest. "Who?"

"Adam. I'll call him and see if I can stay with him. Or he can come here."

"No."

"Why not?"

"Have you forgotten what happened last time? He left you alone, and the killer got close enough to leave you a note." He was still angry that she had left Faye's without telling him. And to invite Adam to stay with her had only made it worse.

"It won't happen again. He felt terrible about that. Besides, I'll arrange for backup with Faye."

"No." Josh hoped his tone made it clear he was serious.

"This is ridiculous. You want me to leave. I tell you I will, and I'll go live with a friend, just like you wanted me to, and you say no. What is wrong with you?"

"I've already made plans. You'll be out of danger."

"I'll be perfectly safe with Adam too. Besides, I know him, and I'd be much more comfortable with him than with a total stranger. He'll let me work in peace."

"No, and that's that. I'll leave you with someone I trust."

"I trust Adam. We'll be at his place, and no one will even know I'm there. I'll leave Cooper with Faye and Jim."

"You're coming with me. I won't leave you with him."

He wasn't going to add that the thought of Tierney holed up with her ex-boyfriend bothered him more than he liked to admit.

CHAPTER 49

Tierney was too displeased with Josh to ask him questions during the drive. She knew he could carry through on the threat to call her parents, and she had no wish to have them rushing back to protect her from evil.

She decided the best thing was to go along with his idea. If this person did not want to have her stay with him, the two of them would work out an arrangement once Josh was out of sight.

Despite her decision, when they arrived at their destination in Cumberland, Tierney silently and grudgingly acknowledged it impressed her. It was a lovely old farmhouse, not unlike her own home, surrounded by a charming mixture of evergreens interspersed with mountain ash, elm, and maple.

The view included an expanse of open fields behind the house, and in the distance, the river meandered by. Placed on the riverbank to offer the best panorama was a gazebo painted in white with green trim. It wasn't new but was maintained with as much care as the dwelling that dominated the farm.

The house drew her attention, along with a man who sat in a well-worn chair on the wraparound porch. He didn't move while Tierney and Josh remained in the car for those few minutes. She wondered if he hoped she would shake her head in refusal, forcing Josh to turn the vehicle around and leave. The look on the man's face gave her that impression.

Josh shut off the engine and turned to face Tierney. "Since you're so curious, Matt is a retired cop and a good friend of mine. He's dependable and sharp. His house is also isolated. No one will know you're here." He hesitated. "You may find him a little short-tempered at times. Don't worry about it."

They both shifted their gazes toward the man on the porch.

He had lowered his bushy gray eyebrows until they almost hid his eyes, and his mouth was clamped into a deep frown. He had crossed his arms over his chest as if he could single-handedly ward off unwelcome intruders. Tierney glanced at Josh, hoping he had changed his mind regarding leaving her here, but his wide grin surprised her. The cop opened his door and bounded out of the car, shouting a greeting along with a wave of his arm.

"Hey, Matt. Are you glad to see us?"

Tierney shifted her gaze to gauge the man's reaction to Josh's teasing. Matt's posture didn't change, and the frown remained intact, but she thought she discovered a glimmer in the dark shadow of his eyes that may have betrayed a trace of affection for the younger man sauntering toward him. Josh stopped at the porch and leaned forward to place a booted foot on a step and rest an elbow on his knee.

Tierney didn't hear the conversation—one that was one-sided since it seemed Josh did the talking—but the old man clung to his grim demeanor, if only to irritate his young friend. Bracing for a confrontation, while reassuring herself the situation was temporary, she climbed out of the car. The man's gaze moved to her as Josh straightened and turned.

"I'd like you to meet Matt Greyson. Matt, this is Tierney McGinnis."

"That's a strange name," the old man snorted.

Tierney blinked in surprise at the blatant rudeness. But she had grown up in an eccentric household with challenging personalities. She pinned her reluctant host with a hard stare.

Josh intervened with a laugh.

"All right, Matt. You've proven to Tierney you can be a cranky old man, and I'm sure she's shaking in her boots right now. But you agreed to let her stay here, and that's just what she'll do, so you can knock it off."

Matt opened his mouth to retort, but a loud bark from the direction of the car interrupted whatever he had to say.

Cooper's patience had run out. He wanted to investigate this unknown place, and they had kept him waiting more than long enough. Tierney, dismayed she had forgotten her pet, hurried over to open the door. In his excitement, Cooper overlooked the fact he was supposed to be an old dog as he scurried around, sniffing with curiosity at bushes and posts and shrubs until he found one to his liking. He lifted a leg and left his mark while Matt grumbled about having a damn animal pissing on the plants.

"Come on, Matt, you love dogs, and Cooper's just like you. You'll have someone to moan and groan and complain with. It'll be great." A trace of a laugh shaded his voice.

"Yeah, I'll be sitting here comparing recipes for pork chops and watching Martha Stewart on TV while you're having fun looking for a guy who gets his kicks out of murdering people."

Tierney felt as if he had slapped her. She didn't see Josh or Matt with their stricken expressions. Instead, in her mind's eye, Art Landon lay on a gurney in the morgue. A vision of Jennifer Danvers followed it; young, beautiful, and full of hope. She pictured Jeff Lakefield, dead, on his lawn.

"Go ahead," Matt continued. "When you get back, she'll have taught me how to crochet or make those crazy plant hanger things."

Tierney shook herself out of her daze in time for Matt's words to sink in. God, he was difficult, she thought. How his wife had tolerated him, she would never understand. She straightened her shoulders and placed her fists on her hips.

"I don't do crafts. I hate pork chops and Martha Stewart has way too much time on her hands," Tierney said. "You won't need to worry about me. I don't plan on being here long, and while I'm here, I'll be staying well out of your way."

"Good. Let's lay out the rules," Matt said. "I eat what I want, when I want, and where I want. If I have to belch, I'll belch. And if I have to pass gas, I'll do that too. I'm old, you know, and if I try to hold in stuff like that it might kill me. You got that straight?"

"I won't get close enough to you to notice what's going in or coming out. I need peace and quiet. I'll get my own food and do my own cooking."

"Fine," Matt growled.

"Fine."

"Well, since you two are on such friendly terms, I'll be on my way." Josh turned to Tierney. "I'll be back later on to get you."

CHAPTER 50

Matt stared at the hound who inspected him. Josh was right when he stated the ex-cop liked dogs, and he held a special fondness for golden retrievers. Matt and his wife, Linda, had a pet similar to this one for fifteen years. A member of the family, Jasper watched the kids grow up and move out. It was a sorrowful day when the old dog died.

Despite his resolve to be difficult, Matt couldn't resist the big brown eyes and the chin resting on his knee. The old man's hand reached out of its own volition and scratched the dog behind his ears. The pooch rewarded him with a wide doggy-type smile.

"Cooper. What kind of name is that to give a dog? He should have a proper name, like Duke or Rocky." Matt would pet the animal, but he was determined not to be overly nice.

"Gary," was the noncommittal reply.

Tierney sat in the chair next to him, avoiding his eyes, staring toward the river. Matt decided she was an attractive woman, with a fresh-faced, innocent appearance and down-to-earth style. Since she was a crime writer, he had expected someone rougher around the edges.

He also concluded that, despite his friend's denials, Josh was sweet on her. If nothing else, Matt owed her one for that. The young detective had gone through a rough patch, and it was time Josh found happiness.

"What? Gary? What's that supposed to mean?"

"He's named after Gary Cooper."

"Why the hell would anyone name a dog after him? He doesn't even resemble Gary Cooper." Matt was happy Josh had a new love interest, but he still had to keep his reputation as a cranky old man. He caught Tierney's eye-roll.

"I should hope not. My parents love silver screen movies and they named him Gary Cooper. They didn't consider physical appearances."

Matt threw a sideways glance at the young woman. She clenched her jaw shut, and he was certain she bit her tongue, trying to hold back a scathing remark. Tierney had gumption. That counted for something. She would need it if she hooked up with a cop.

Matt regretted his earlier blunder with his comment concerning the killer. The blood had drained from Tierney's face, and he cursed himself for his stupidity and lack of forethought. He'd done his best to distract her, and it looked as if he may have succeeded.

"Gene," he said.

"What?"

"Gene Tierney. That's where they got the name, isn't it?"

"Yeah." Tierney had a wary expression, and he wondered if she expected derision. Matt let his eyes glaze over with pleasant memories.

"Oh yeah, she was quite a woman. A genuine beauty. With a real woman's body. Not like the half-starved things you see on TV nowadays." He turned an appraising eye on Tierney. "You look nothing like her."

"I guess when I was born, my parents couldn't predict how I'd turn out. They could only wait and hope."

"Be happy they weren't into sci-fi," Matt said, his tone dry.

Tierney didn't hold back her brief burst of laughter. "Oh God, I might have been Princess Leia."

"Or Xena."

Tierney chuckled again, but the amusement didn't reach her eyes. "It might have been worth it if they had named my brother Darth or Yoda."

That was a topic for another time, Matt thought.

Her face serious again, his house guest lifted her bags from their position on the porch and headed toward the door.

"I'll put these inside, if you don't mind," Tierney said.

"What is that? You sleeping here?" Matt hadn't noticed her bags earlier, and he experienced a surge of alarm. *Had Josh tricked him?*

"I don't plan to, but Josh suggested I bring a change of clothes at least, just in case. Besides, I needed to have my computer with me." She lifted the smaller bag.

"All right." Matt rose from the chair and stretched. "I'll show you around at the same time."

It didn't take long. Matthew wasn't into giving lengthy descriptions. He stood in one spot, pointed at each doorway, and explained where it led. "It's not very big."

"That's fine," she said. "I don't need much. If the weather's nice, I'll work outside, and if it isn't, all I require is a quiet room."

"Every room is quiet. There's not much going on here."

Tierney asked permission to put a few grocery items in the fridge and cupboards and received a nod from Matt. For the moment, they were on peaceful terms.

• •

Tierney returned from the bedroom where she had set her overnight bag on the small, neatly made bed and noticed Matthew sat in the living area and watched a news show. She retrieved her computer case, slipped out to the porch, and made herself comfortable.

She was soon ready to work on her novel. It wasn't easy. Her gaze strayed to the view of the gazebo and the river. Either there or at the magnificent trees surrounding the house.

Tierney was no stranger to beautiful settings; her own home rivaled the place in which she sat. But she never took that beauty for granted, appreciating every breath of fresh air and every rustle of leaves. The bonus in Cumberland was the sound of the river flowing over the rocks. It was both calming and comforting, and she thought it must be wonderful to sleep so close to that melody with the windows open on a summer night.

Several times she roused herself from her daydreaming and concentrated on the computer, just to drift off again. Sometimes her thoughts strayed in the less desirable direction of the murders. Her stomach clenched, and an ache developed in her chest.

As she blinked away tears, the screen door squeaked to her left, and she realized she was no longer alone. She didn't glance toward Matt, hoping he would return to the house once he saw her, but he settled in the chair next to her.

"I suppose that's how everybody writes books nowadays."

Tierney glanced over to catch him staring at her laptop.

"It's how I do it. I guess you think it's the lazy way to work, don't you?" She expected a lecture on 'the good old days'.

"Not at all," Matt said, surprising Tierney. "I was a cop for a long time, and I experienced a bunch of changes in technology. It made our jobs a lot easier. We didn't have to wait for days to match fingerprints or blood types. And let me tell you, when the whole DNA business came along, it changed the face of solving crimes forever. No, it's not lazy. I think it's smart, and we should never turn our backs on new technology. Now, on the other side of the coin, the bad guys also have their hands on pretty fancy stuff. That's hard to be up against. We have to be faster and smarter than them."

"You enjoyed being a cop, didn't you?" Tierney pictured him as a young cop, full of enthusiasm and grit.

"Yeah." He nodded. "I miss it. I envy Josh when I see him working a case, something that's a real challenge. It's difficult, but it's never dull either. Not when you're in homicide."

"Did you work with Josh for a long time?" Matt had piqued her curiosity.

"Not long enough. My retirement date came along too fast. He's a good cop with a fine intuition. Anybody with any brains should listen to him when he tells them to do something."

Tierney looked sideways at the older man. There was a message for her in that last line, and she wondered if the entire purpose of this talk had been to deliver that missive.

"Were you always in homicide?" She wanted to steer the conversation from Josh and his wonderful intuition.

"No, I had to do my time moving through the ranks, but I guess luck and good timing were on my side, because that's where I ended up and worked there for almost twenty-five years."

His voice rang with pride. "Impressive. You have a lot of experience."

Tierney had kicked into writer mode and realized she sat beside a wealth of knowledge. She didn't know him well enough to be certain he wanted to part with the information, but she wouldn't let that stop her from trying.

For the next two hours, he rewarded her efforts in spades. Matt prattled on about his more illustrious cases and didn't object when Tierney asked if she could take notes. Her fingers flew across the keys as he recounted stories from his term in the homicide division. She didn't interrupt him, deciding that once she went over her observations, she could approach him for further details if needed.

Mid-afternoon, Matt announced sheepishly it was time for his nap, although he used the term 'rest'. Tierney set aside the computer and took Cooper for a walk, at last having the chance to get a closer look at the gazebo.

Once inside, the sound of the river and the view of the countryside entranced her. As much as she loved her home and the peace and tranquility she found there, she admitted these surroundings were idyllic. Too picturesque; Tierney wasn't sure if she could concentrate on writing with such distracting scenery.

The structure was open-air and furnished with durable, weathered, wicker furniture, placed to offer the best view of the river and the rolling hills. Tierney didn't notice the time go by, but Cooper prodded her to explore the growth of shrubs by the water. She urged the dog back toward the house, thinking the end of the day had crept up on her too quickly. She arrived at the farmhouse and spotted Josh's car in the driveway, his long frame folded into a chair beside the older man.

"You don't look any worse for wear, and Matt seems to have survived today without too many battle scars." Josh spoke to Tierney with a wry smile on his face as she and the dog climbed the steps of the porch to join them.

"There's just one way to get along with women, and that's agreeing with everything they want. I've told you that before." Matthew wore an irascible expression upon his face.

Tierney frowned at the old man and shook her head in disbelief. He wouldn't admit they had had a pleasant afternoon. In that case, she was no more eager to let Josh think his idea had been a success, and she followed Matthew's lead.

"The best way to get along with a man is not to ask for help, because you'll only be disappointed." Tierney gave her strongest delivery of a grumpy tone.

"Well, that's good. As long as you know how to handle each other, that's all that counts." Josh stood, grabbed Tierney's bags from where he had placed them on the porch, and headed for the car. "We'll see you tomorrow."

Tierney raised a hand to wave at Matt and felt a rush of pleasure when she received a quick wink in reply.

CHAPTER 51

Josh's apartment was large enough for a bachelor but cramped for two people.

He had been relieved to find both Tierney and Matt unscathed after their first day together. From what he could see, they had gone about their business with a minimum of interaction. It gave Josh hope that the arrangement might be a success.

Now, returning home with Tierney, he saw his apartment through her eyes and worried it was lacking. But, if she was disappointed, she gave no sign.

"Um, I only have one bedroom," he said. "I'll sleep on the couch."

"Perfect. Thanks."

Tierney carried her bags down the hall to his room, and Josh wondered why he experienced a niggle of disappointment. He hadn't expected an invitation to share the bed with her. That would be un-Tierney-like.

Too tired to cook and not having had time to stock the refrigerator, Josh bought takeout fried chicken on the way home. It may not have been classy, but it was filling, and his guest didn't complain.

Tierney didn't talk much at all. Once she made the usual enquiries about the investigation and received the customary response that there was nothing new to share, she became silent and introspective.

"Everything okay?" Josh said.

Tierney looked at him as if he had grown horns. She smiled faintly. "You mean, apart from the fact a homicidal maniac who's using my book to murder innocent people has driven me from my home?"

"Yeah, that's what I mean. It looks as if things went okay today with Matt. I realize he gets crotchety at times, but his heart's in the right place. And, you've got to admit, he's got a nice place."

"You're right, on all counts. Matt's crotchety, has a good heart and a beautiful home. I'm not ungrateful for everything you and Matt are doing, it's just I'm a prisoner of my routine. I like to be among my own things. If I was sure this would be for a day or two, it wouldn't be a problem, but I don't know that. And neither do you."

"We have to make the best of a terrible situation," Josh said with a shrug.

"You're right, and I have. Matt's been telling me about his cases. It's been giving me ideas for my writing." Her smile took on a stronger glow.

"That's great news, for both of you." Josh was happy to see something positive come out of the situation. "I'm always available if you have questions, and Clint has a way of spinning a good tale."

"You and Clint are close, aren't you?"

"Yeah, we made a good team from the start, and we ended up becoming friends."

"Does he have a significant other?" Tierney wanted to move the conversation away from the subject of murder.

The question led to a discussion of Clint's turbulent love life. Tierney had always noticed a sharp contrast between the two detectives, and the more she learned the more it fascinated her to find two opposite personalities as such close friends.

"Do you want to catch a ball game with me?" Josh needed to unwind after his day, and a couple of hours spent in front of a game would do him good, he thought.

Tierney offered him a slight smile.

"No, thanks. I'm not much of a 'ball game' person. I'll go to the bedroom and work on my manuscript."

Josh settled into an armchair and grabbed the remote control for the TV. He admitted he was relieved by Tierney's absence. The atmosphere between them was tense, although their dinner conversation had ultimately veered into a safe territory. He attributed the tension to the fact they both lived through a lot of stress because of the murders. It was a legitimate excuse.

But, if he was honest with himself, he admitted having an attractive woman in his apartment and keeping her at arm's length was a novel experience for him. It created its own kind of tension. Josh hoped Tierney was feeling as uncomfortable, for the same reason, by his presence.

Josh was so invested in the baseball game he had wiped from his mind the fact he had a guest ensconced in the apartment. The sound of footsteps padding down the hallway shook him from his absorption. He turned to see Tierney coming toward him, and his breath caught at the sight of her in an oversized t-shirt that fell almost to her knees. The shirt was far from revealing, but his imagination flew into overdrive. Tierney smiled at him with apology.

"Sorry. I wanted a glass of water."

Josh grunted and waved his hands in the general direction of the kitchen, letting her know she should help herself. His breath left him in a whoosh as she walked out of his line of vision. He used the few minutes to compose himself before her return trip. Tierney issued another good night on her next passing, and his gaze followed her progress down the hallway. Josh tried to decide which view was more appealing, coming or going.

The rest of the evening went downhill from there. The couch seemed to develop lumps that hadn't been there before. It was shorter than Josh remembered, and every time he closed his eyes, he pictured Tierney stretched out in his comfortable queen-size bed. Josh had a sleepless night.

The next morning, he banged around the kitchen, tired and irritated. Josh knew he should prepare a decent breakfast like any host worth his salt, but he was so cranky the most he managed was toast and coffee.

Tierney didn't seem to mind or care. She looked rested after a good night's sleep and a bracing shower. The writer had pulled on a pair of long, baggy shorts and a well-worn t-shirt for the day and appeared more like her usual self.

But Josh now had a different image of what she kept concealed under her loose-fitting clothing, and it only made him more irritable. He looked forward to leaving his guest at Matt's place and joining Clint at police headquarters.

Matt sat in his customary position on the porch when they pulled into the driveway. It was how he began every day. His friend enjoyed nothing more than taking his coffee outside on a fresh summer morning.

Today, the older man had the bonus of Cooper for company, since they had left him on the farm rather than drag him back to the small apartment each night. The dog made an effort to trot over to greet them before following them to the house. Josh dropped Tierney's bags on top of the steps, and after a scant few words of greeting in Matt's direction, turned to go to his car.

"Hey, what's the matter with you?" Matt shouted after him.

"Nothing. I have work to do, that's all."

"You seem grouchy."

"I have to work, and Clint's waiting for me. I've got to go. See ya."

Matt and Tierney watched from the porch as Josh settled into his car and left them.

•   •   •

Clint gave Josh a cursory glance as he passed his desk. "You look grouchy today."

"Why is everyone telling me that?"

"Someone else complained?"

"Never mind. You're looking unusually cheery. What's up?" Josh threw his briefcase onto his desk.

"Nothing." Clint wasn't able to conceal a smug smile.

"Cut the crap. What's going on? Wait. I got it. You and Lydia. You're back on again."

"Yep." A grin lit his face.

"So, what was going on?" Josh dragged over a chair and sat next to Clint, his attention focused on his partner.

"Nothing."

"Nothing? You expect me to believe that? I know something was going on, so what was it?"

"I can't talk about it, and I won't," Clint said. "So, just let it go. Forget it."

"How can I forget it?"

"Just forget it. Don't think about it, don't talk about it. Just forget it ever happened. Lydia and I have patched things up, and it's all that matters."

"What about the mysterious phone calls, the subterfuge?" Josh's voice dripped disbelief.

"It was nothing."

"Nothing. Is that your new favorite word?"

"Yep. Now, shouldn't we talk about the case we're working on?"

CHAPTER 52

"I wonder what's eating him,"

"He doesn't seem to be much of a morning person," Tierney said with a shrug.

"That's funny. I've never known Josh to be anything other than good-tempered early in the day. In fact, he was always the guy at the station everyone growled at because he was too damned cheerful first thing in the morning."

"He slept on the couch. Maybe he didn't sleep well."

Something bothered Matt's friend, and it puzzled him. "How did you sleep?"

"Like a baby. I guess I was more tired than I realized."

"What did you and Josh do last night?"

"Not much. After dinner, I worked for a while in my room, and I went to bed. Josh watched TV. Why?"

"Just curious, that's all."

The day passed as the previous one had, each of them on their own in the morning with Matt taking in his regular TV shows, and Tierney putting a few paragraphs to paper.

After lunch, the writer coaxed more stories from Matt, forming a picture of his previous career as a homicide detective. Again, she took copious notes and marveled at the amount of information he had to share. When he retired inside for an afternoon nap, Tierney and Cooper walked to the river.

Returning to the house, Josh's car wasn't in the driveway, but Matt sat outside in his favorite chair, looking displeased.

"What's the matter?" she said. Her heart was in her throat, expecting the worst.

"Josh called. He'll have to work late tonight, and you'll need to sleep here."

Tierney breathed easier but understood the reason for his frown. Matt had accepted her presence during the day, but he had hoped to have his evenings and nights to himself.

"I could stay at a hotel. Or, I can go back home and get a friend to stay with me."

"No, you're not leaving. Josh would have my hide if he found out you didn't sleep here tonight," Matt said. "It doesn't matter. I can put up with you for one night."

My goodness, so much for giving in graciously, Tierney thought. Although Matt seemed to have warmed to her, he was an old curmudgeon when he wanted to be. She shrugged her shoulders in resignation and went into the house.

Tierney rifled through the groceries she had brought with her to see what she could make for supper, but there wasn't much that appealed to her. She had picked up plenty of things suitable for a light lunch, but not for a main meal.

In the course of her hunt, she found chicken breasts in Matt's freezer and decided to appeal to the man's stomach to bring him around. She combined food from his reserve with hers and threw together a quick but appetizing chicken and vegetable stir-fry with a salad on the side.

Tierney set the table for two before changing her mind. She noticed Matt preferred to eat his lunch meal while he watched the news on the television, and she didn't want to disrupt his routine if he did the same at dinnertime. Instead, she prepared a plate and set it on the corner of the table.

"Matt, would you like to have dinner with me? I borrowed your chicken and made enough for two." Tierney poked her head out the door.

The old man rose from his chair and stretched languidly.

"I might as well. I'm so hungry I could eat the rear-end out of a dead skunk," Matt said as he walked by her. Tierney shot him a bewildered look, unsure if she had been insulted.

"Tell me more about your brother." Matt had eaten his meal with gusto and sat back, replete, his hands rubbing his stomach.

Tierney shrugged. "There's not much to tell. He's a financial advisor. Works for a big firm in Ottawa, loves all the wheeling and dealing, rakes in lots of money."

"Boy, you two must have a lot to talk about when you get together."

"You can bet on it," she said with a short laugh. "We're as different as dogs and ducks."

"I take it you don't get along."

"We do. For a few minutes, until he tells me how my writing is stupid because it doesn't pay enough. And how our parents should sell the place to a developer so they can build condos and make tons of money."

Matt shook his head. "Some people don't realize there are more important things than money. At least you've got a head on your shoulders."

Tierney smiled. Coming from Matt, that was an enormous compliment. It lifted her spirits when they desperately needed a boost.

After the meal was cleaned up, Tierney, feeling inspired, grabbed her computer and retired to the spare bedroom for the evening. She carried out much the same routine as she had the previous night at Josh's apartment. Her goal was to write a few thousand words. When she gave up, she returned to the kitchen to get a glass of water before going to sleep.

Tierney discovered Matt spent his evening like Josh, watching TV, and when she came out of the bedroom, he also looked at her in surprise, as if he had forgotten she was in the house. The difference between the two men was Matt wasn't so surprised he was incapable of speech.

"Do you always sleep like that?" he said.

"I find it more comfortable to lie down first." Tierney tried to make sense of his words.

Matt laughed so hard the tears rolled down his wrinkled cheeks.

"What's so amusing?" Tierney sensed she had missed something obvious.

"Nothing." Matt wiped the dampness from his face.

"Do you always laugh at nothing?"

"I remembered something funny that was on TV. Sorry about that."

Tierney saw him struggle to control himself and didn't believe his story for a minute but let it go. She shrugged and walked back to the bedroom. As the door closed behind her, the old man's laughter reached her once again, and she swore she heard him say 'Poor bugger'.

CHAPTER 53

The routine remained unchanged for a few more days as Matt and Tierney became more comfortable in each other's presence. They took their meals together, their food supplies now intermingled. Tierney joined Matt at noon to eat lunch while watching the news, and they had the evening meal at the kitchen table. Sometimes Josh was there to dine with them. At other times, he was delayed working on the case. Tierney never went back to his apartment.

By unspoken agreement, Josh skimmed over the subject of the murders in their conversations. He relayed the basics to Tierney and Matt, but refused to dwell on the topic, both for his sake and Tierney's. Progress was slow and being reminded of that fact daily was discouraging at best.

Their routine was shaken on the fifth day of Tierney's occupancy at Matt's house. The ringing of the phone interrupted the afternoon session of storytelling and note-taking. Matt reached for the portable device that always sat beside him and answered gruffly, not happy to have his reminiscing disturbed.

Tierney allowed her attention to shift to the view of the rustling trees and the tranquil flow of the river in the background, but she turned to stare at him when she detected a change in his tone.

Matt spoke like a man who didn't want to reveal too much information to the person next to him. His manner was too casual, and his smile forced. Tierney's heart pounded in her chest, and she clenched her fingers on the arms of the chair to keep them from grabbing the phone out of the older man's hands.

When he hung up, it was several moments before he looked in her direction. Instead, he spent the time placing the handset back on the table, adjusting the position of his coffee mug, wiping a nonexistent dirt spot from pants.

"Matt." Tierney's voice was stiff with restrained tension. Her friend took a deep, fortifying breath, and she knew with certainty the words that would come out of his mouth.

"There's been another murder."

Tierney didn't flinch. She scarcely breathed, holding herself rigid, forcing herself to make it through the next few minutes with a semblance of control. "Which one?"

Matt understood what she meant. He hadn't read her book, but he had heard enough about it to interpret the cryptic message Josh had transmitted to him. "The fifth. A man this time."

"He was strangled, same as the others," she filled in for him, her tone flat.

"Yes."

"What was his name?"

"Ted Hill."

"Ted." Her voice hovered just above a whisper. Tierney rubbed her forehead and thought for a moment. Coming up blank, she grabbed the notebook from beside her, and flipped pages until she stopped at a list of names. "It must be Edward."

Tierney's eyes closed, and her head fell into her hands, her control lost. "Oh God, no. What am I going to do? How can I get it to stop?" she said, tears in her voice.

A large warm hand settled on her back, and Matt's voice was beside her ear.

"There's nothing you can do. Be patient and let the guys do their job."

"But how many more will die, Matt? There must be something that can be done."

"There are lots of ways, and they're using all of them, believe me. They'll get him. The killer always makes a mistake."

"I hope it's soon. I truly do."

"We all do."

• • •

Tierney had to be alone. She walked to the riverbank, but instead of sitting in the gazebo, she lay on the grass by the waterfront and stared at a beautiful sky scattered with the whitest of clouds. She couldn't believe such perfection existed when elsewhere there was only evil and horror.

Tierney had learned from Matt that, although the killer had found a victim with the right name, he didn't fall into the same profession. Instead of being a carpenter as written in the novel, the deceased was a mechanic.

It was clear the suspect had trouble finding people to fit her descriptions, and he wasn't able to follow the chronology of the events in the book. Tierney wondered if that was an advantage or a disadvantage for them. It made it more difficult for the police to pinpoint who the next victim could be, but the frustration it may cause the killer might lead him to make an error, one that might benefit them.

As Tierney lay in her tranquil surroundings, an anger built inside her. The first acts of murder had sent a shock wave through her system, followed by a deep sadness and regret, but now she was furious. They had to stop him. There had to be a way to put an end to it.

The next time she saw Josh, she wouldn't let him avoid the discussion. Tierney would insist on being included in the investigation. She wouldn't stay hidden away when there was something more constructive to do instead.

• • •

Josh pulled his car into the driveway to encounter a deserted veranda. He didn't take that as an encouraging sign.

The detective found Matt sitting alone in front of the TV. Josh lowered himself onto the couch opposite him and stared at the ashen face of his friend.

"How is she?" he said.

"Upset. She's by the river. Is there anything, Josh? Any evidence?"

"We discovered a hair this time. It'll help if we find the guy and have to place him at the scene. It isn't much, but at least it shows he's become clumsier. Perhaps he's breaking apart. We can always hope."

"Yeah." Matt's voice didn't convey much optimism. "You don't look good. Is there something you're not telling me?"

Josh looked at his friend, certain the despair was clear in his eyes. "Things have taken an interesting twist."

Matt leaned forward. "How?"

"He wrote on the pages this time."

"What did he write?" The older man's voice was almost a whisper.

"Andrea." Josh forced the word past his lips. "He wrote her name across one page."

"Jesus," Matt breathed. "He knows you."

"Yeah. So, now, it raises another question. Is it me he's targeting or Tierney?"

"Or both of you?"

Josh nodded, his eyes reflecting his weariness.

"Tell me something. Is there a cop that gets murdered in Tierney's novel?" Matt asked.

"There is." Josh lowered his gaze as his shoulders hunched.

The old man sat back in his chair, his breath leaving him in a rush. "The guy's taunting you. He wants to throw you off your game."

"Apparently so. And, the worst of it is, I should have seen it coming. I read the book, Matt. I knew there was a cop in there. I should have seen the signs, but I was so blinded by the need to protect everyone else, especially Tierney, that I didn't see what was going on in front of my face."

"Don't beat yourself up over it."

"Easy for you to say." Josh ran his hands through his hair and leaned back in the chair. "I've screwed up again."

"Don't say that. You haven't screwed anything up." Anger creased Matt's face. "You're too much of a perfectionist. If everything doesn't go exactly your way, you blame yourself. Damn it, what have we been telling that girl?" He pointed toward the gazebo, far in the distance. "This isn't her fault. That's what we've been saying. And it's not yours either. You're a good cop, and you're doing your best."

Josh hung his head. Matt's words, no matter how gruff, had been offered as encouragement, but Josh had a hard time feeling anything other than remorse and responsibility.

Neither of them spoke for several moments. Matt stared toward the river.

"She's been gone a while," the older man said. "You should go check on her."

"I will." Josh pushed himself to his feet. Part of him looked forward to seeing her, and part of him wanted to delay the inevitable. He didn't want to witness the now-familiar expressions of despair and guilt on her face.

Josh found her lying in the grass on the riverbank, her eyes closed, with Cooper by her side. He tried to be quiet, but the instant he lowered himself beside her, her eyes flew open and targeted on his face.

"Oh, Josh." She sat and moved without hesitation into his arms. Tierney grasped him around the waist and rested her cheek against his chest, her head nestled under his chin. They didn't speak. He held her, offering whatever comfort he could give, and taking a portion in return. They remained like that for several minutes until Tierney lifted her head to look at him, and he saw the tears in her eyes. Josh lowered his lips to hers, and a moment later, lay beside her on the lush, green grass.

The emotions that had built inside of him let go, and he didn't rein them in. Tierney reciprocated, and their mouths were hungry while their hands roamed each other's bodies.

Josh sensed a wet coldness against the heated skin of his cheek, and he paused in confusion, until the slathering of a large, unwelcome tongue followed the touch. He lifted his head in surprise to see Tierney was being given the same treatment, but her expression was less surprised and more panic-stricken. Josh interpreted her thoughts. He shoved Cooper out of the way and tried to salvage the situation.

"Tierney..." He attempted to hold on to her as she struggled to sit.

"No, Josh, this isn't right. Let me go, please."

"What do you mean? Of course, it's right. We've moved in this direction from the beginning. I'm convinced we have."

Tierney had become as slippery as an eel in his arms, and Cooper wasn't helping matters, considering it a wrestling match they had invited him to join.

"Go away, Cooper!" Josh lost patience with the animal.

"No, I'm the one that's going away. It isn't right," she repeated. "I'm not in the proper frame of mind."

"Please, let's talk about this. I don't want you to run off."

"I'm not running. I'm walking. I'm walking away from the possibility of complicating my life any further."

She did just that, striding back to the house and out of Josh's reach. The retriever remained behind, looking at Josh as he wagged his tail and hoped for more fun and games.

"Just wait, Cooper. Someday I'll fix you up with a cute little poodle, and when things get interesting, I'll stick *my* nose in there. Not literally, but I'll break it up, and then maybe we'll be even."

The dog, sensing his friend's displeasure, laid his head on Josh's knee and looked at him with a sorrowful expression.

CHAPTER 54

Matt worried about Tierney. She was quiet, even for her.

Incoherent mumblings were all she gave him when she came back from the river, and she retreated into the house looking more distressed than Matt had expected.

Josh arrived a few minutes later with Cooper at his side. Matt questioned him, but the older man had no more luck getting information out of Josh than he had with Tierney. Whatever had happened between the two younger people was something neither of them wished to discuss.

"Tierney will spend another night here, Matt. I'm sorry, but I've got to go back to the station."

"That's all right. I understand."

• • •

As the evening progressed, the silence grew heavier. Matt tried to carry on a distracting conversation, but he stretched his imagination to the limits, and every attempt was unsuccessful. The ex-cop may have experience in a homicide department, but tiptoeing around the female psyche was beyond his capabilities.

Matt met the enemy head-on. "Tierney, stop this business of torturing yourself."

"I'm not."

"Yes, you are. I can see it on your face, plain as day. You're letting this guy get to you."

Tierney turned to him, the full force of her emotions on display.

"That's because I'm responsible for what he's doing, Matt. I've caused this. Why can't anyone understand that? Because of me, those people are dead. How can you not expect it to get to me? I'd need to be made of stone to let it slide off my back. And I'm not."

"I know that, honey. And I realize you believe it's your fault, but it isn't. This guy is sick. If it wasn't your book, it'd be something else. He wants to kill, and he'll use whatever means possible to do it."

Matt saw his speech didn't change her attitude, but he did not give up on her.

"Let me tell you a story. There was a case, years ago, a terrible case. A young woman moved into an apartment building, one that wasn't too bad by most standards. It had the usual security systems; the buzzers and cameras in the lobby.

"Now, this woman had a baby but no husband, a common enough thing, and she loved that little girl with all her heart. But the woman needed to work, because she was the one paying the bills, what with no man around to help her out. So, every day she took the child to a babysitter, someone she'd known for a long time and that she trusted to take the best possible care of her daughter.

"One day, the babysitter called to say she was sick and couldn't look after the baby that day, so the mother asked the next-door neighbor if she could take care of the little one. She seemed like an agreeable lady, very polite, in her fifties, had three grown kids of her own, and she said she'd be more than happy to babysit the beautiful little girl."

Matt paused for a moment. Tierney lifted her head to stare at him. Once he was sure he had her full attention, he continued.

"Well, the mother came home from work and went to the next-door apartment to pick up her daughter, but the door was locked, and no one answered. She convinced the building manager to open the door, and it was awful. The woman had disappeared, and the poor little baby was dead, murdered by a crazy woman. I'm telling you, the mother never got over it and never will."

"Are you trying to cheer me up, Matt?" Tierney's eyes brimmed with tears.

"What I'm telling you is the woman never stopped blaming herself. It was as if she'd killed her own child. She kept saying if she hadn't moved to that apartment building, it wouldn't have happened. And if she had stayed home from work that day, it wouldn't have happened.

"And, in a way, she's right. But that doesn't mean she's responsible for her baby's death. She'd have given her own life for her child, and she'd have never brought harm to her, but she didn't kill the baby. A madwoman did. Would you blame that woman for her kid's murder? Would you?"

Tierney shook her head.

"So there, if you don't blame her, you can't blame yourself." Matt scrutinized Tierney for a moment. "You just need to remember to keep everything in perspective."

"You sound like my mother."

"Your mother must be a very sensible woman." Matt raised his brows in surprise when Tierney burst into laughter. He didn't understand what he'd said that was so funny, but it was nice to see a smile on her face.

CHAPTER 55

Tierney pitched one way and the other for hours before she drifted off to sleep. A few minutes, or several hours later, she wasn't sure which, she awoke.

She had heard a noise. *Had it been a bark? Or did something fall and break? Had Cooper knocked over a dish? Or, perhaps, it was Matt getting up to go to the washroom.*

Not wanting to intrude, but thinking she should investigate, she pushed back the covers, grabbed her jeans, and tugged them under her baggy t-shirt. Tierney pulled on her slippers and tiptoed to the door of the bedroom. If Matt was on his way to or from the bathroom, she didn't want to startle him.

As she stretched a hand toward the knob, the door burst open. Tierney swallowed a scream and took two steps back when a dark shape loomed in front of her. Her first thought was of Josh, until it registered that the person in the doorway appeared shorter and slighter than Josh.

"What..."

A gloved hand wrapped itself around the back of her neck, and cold metal was pressed against the front. "Don't move and don't make a sound. Not one sound, or I'll kill you right now."

Tierney realized it was a knife, and she had come face-to-face with the killer. She was afraid to breathe, terrified she would tremble, and the blade would slice open her throat.

The murderer stood inches away from her, but she couldn't see his face. Everything was black; the room, him, her thoughts.

Tierney fought to gain control of her fear. It was the only way to survive. She focused on his voice, trying to place it, but it meant nothing to her.

Tierney knew this person was deranged, a maniac who had killed several times and had no qualms about taking her life. The only leverage she possessed was her knowledge of the novel and the killings so far.

"Who are you?" Tierney's voice held more bravado than she felt.

"Never mind that. I have to get you out of here."

"What do you want with me? Where are you taking me?"

"Come on, Tierney. You wrote the book. You should realize what's going on," he said with a chuckle.

Tierney had to keep him talking, to delay when he would take her from the house. She needed time to make a plan.

She wanted to get him away from Matt. Her mind searched for a way out without bringing harm to the ex-cop. "Just because I wrote the book doesn't mean I understand you. I want to make sense of it. Explain it to me."

The man laughed. "You think I'm stupid enough to fall for that? I won't blurt out my plans for the old man to hear. I want them to figure it out," he said. "I want the cops to work for this. They haven't been very good at it so far. But maybe they'll get lucky this time."

Tierney caught the laughter in his voice.

"You won't get away with it. They'll find you," she said.

"I doubt it, but if it makes you feel better to think it, go ahead. I won't stop you."

Holding on to Tierney and pressing the knife to her throat, he moved until they emerged into the hallway. She kept her gaze on his face, waiting for the moment the sliver of light from the bathroom revealed his identity.

Instead of a revelation, she saw a smirk and evil eyes peering out from behind a black mask. Dark clothing encased his body. There was nothing to identify him, apart from his height, build, and eye color.

"What do you want with me?" She forced the words from between clenched teeth.

"Don't be stupid. It's your turn. Didn't you figure out your time would come? You wrote the book, T.L.," he said again. "And, I rewrote it to take care of unfinished business." An eerie chuckle escaped from behind the mask.

Tierney sensed a movement in the passageway and was careful to keep her gaze fixed on his face. Matt stood behind him, and she prayed he handled the situation without getting hurt. There was still a sharp knife held to her throat. She was no help.

She flinched when a deep voice boomed from behind the killer. "Drop the weapon and turn around with your arms in the air."

Tierney realized by the look in the man's eyes that it wouldn't work. Within seconds, he spun her around and pressed her back to his chest. He again placed the knife against her neck.

"No, *you* should drop the gun and put *your* hands up."

Matt's gaze met Tierney's. She read the desperation in it. She nodded, absolving him of any responsibility, and tried to send him the message to cooperate. The last thing she wanted was to have something happen to this man who had become her friend.

There were several tense moments as no one moved until Matt tossed the gun onto the floor in the hallway and lifted both arms in the air.

Tierney cried out when the man raised his arm to deliver a blow to Matt's head, sending him crashing down the stairs. She struggled and tried to pull his knife arm away from her, but he twisted her arm behind her back, making her yelp in pain.

Tears of frustration and fear rolled down her face. He hauled her to the stairs, as she stumbled and fought to keep herself upright and safe from the threatening edge of the dagger. Tierney whimpered as he dragged her past Matt and Cooper, both of them lying inert on the floor at the foot of the stairs.

The man didn't come to a stop until they were outside, standing behind a black SUV. Her assailant released her arm but kept the blade pressed against her throat.

"Don't move a muscle. This knife is sharp, and we wouldn't want to slit you open by accident, would we? That's not the way it's supposed to play out. It was you who decided to strangle your victims. I'm just following your lead." She detected a trace of humor in his voice.

Tierney tried not to budge, but it was difficult to prevent the tremors of fear that threatened to shake her body. She breathed in rapid gulps of air, not giving into the impulse to sob. The man rummaged in his pockets for something, and he made a slight cry of triumph when he found it.

He grasped her left arm and twisted it behind her again. At the same instant, he removed the knife from her neck and shoved her against the vehicle with his body. The man pulled her other arm behind her and she heard the rasp of tape being removed from a roll. With her arms taped behind her, he opened the door of the rear hatch and tossed her inside, grabbing her ankles and securing them in the same way.

"I won't bother gagging you. I don't care if you scream, and I'd enjoy a chance for us to chat on the way." The door banged shut.

* * *

Josh felt guilty for his behavior of the previous day. He hadn't been fair to Tierney, unable to stay on an even keel after seeing Andrea's name scrawled on the paperback page. Memories of the other woman's death assailed him. His sense of guilt in relation to Andrea's death was never far from his mind.

Tierney had been right to put a stop to everything. She was vulnerable, and though Josh had not set out to take advantage of that vulnerability, he should have held himself back.

It wasn't very generous of him to leave under those circumstances without talking to Tierney and trying to work out their differences. Josh would make a point of doing so today. He also owed Matt an apology for his less than gentlemanly behavior.

For the second time in two days, the detective pulled up to the house and found the porch chairs empty. It was early, just past dawn, and even Matt wasn't always outside at that hour.

As Josh climbed the steps, he saw the inside door stood ajar, and he had a terrible sense of foreboding. Something was wrong. The sound of a weak whimper from the other side of the door made his heart rate spike. He bolted into the room to find Cooper perched on the floor, licking Matt's unconscious face at the bottom of the stairs.

CHAPTER 56

The confusion in Clint's voice was noticeable. Josh realized he had woken his partner from a sound sleep. His own tone resonated with distress.

"Tierney's been taken. Matt's unconscious. I've called it in."

A few minutes after the ambulance arrived, Clint pulled in and parked behind three police vehicles.

"What happened?" Clint joined Josh in the living room of Matt's house. His hair pointed in every direction and his t-shirt was on inside out, his face creased with concern.

"I found Matt on the floor, unconscious. It looks as if he may have fallen or been pushed down the stairs. Tierney's gone." His last words came out like a choke.

Josh felt his partner's hand on his shoulder, giving it a reassuring squeeze, but there was nothing anyone could say or do to comfort him.

The crime scene investigators would analyze every corner of the house for a trace of the person who had taken Tierney.

After calling 9-1-1, Josh had taken the stairs two at a time to check out the spare room at the top. Tierney's belongings were there, most notably her laptop computer. She hadn't left the house of her own free will. There was no doubt in Josh's mind someone had abducted her. Matt had tried to protect Tierney but had been struck down, Josh was sure of it.

"There doesn't seem to be any blood that doesn't belong to Matt. Nothing in the bedroom. It has to be a good sign." Josh brought Clint up to date.

They both turned when a groan came from Matt's direction. One of the two paramedics bent over him, leaning next to his ear. "Mr. Greyson, can you hear me?"

"Goddammit, why are you yelling in my face like that? Ow! What are you doing to me? What the hell happened?"

"Lie still, Mr. Greyson. You're injured."

"Matt." Josh kneeled beside his fallen friend and placed his hand on his shoulder.

The old man looked at him, and Josh saw from his expression that his memory of recent events had returned. "Tierney. Oh my God, Josh." His voice broke; his eyes filled with anguish. "Is she...God, please don't tell me she's dead."

"She's not dead, but she's gone."

"He took her?"

Josh nodded, fighting to keep his face expressionless. "You've got to tell us everything you can."

"We need to get Mr. Greyson to the hospital," one of the paramedics said. "His arm is broken, and he'll need x-rays."

"Get the hell away from me." The ex-cop winced in pain as he tried to shove the man aside. "A woman's been abducted by a known killer. We don't have time for your foolishness."

"Give us a few minutes, would you?" Clint appealed to the medical personnel. "Time is important."

The two men nodded and retreated but kept a close eye on their patient.

"What happened, Matt?" Josh said.

"Dammit, I can't tell you an awful lot. I woke around three in the morning. There was a noise. I stepped into the hall, saw Tierney's door was open, and heard a man's voice. I went back in my room and got my gun. I'd been keeping it under the pillow since she came here. I thought maybe it was you, Josh, but I didn't want to take any chances."

Matt drew a shaky breath, his face lined with pain.

"I didn't recognize the voice. I came up behind him, but he was fast. He had a knife, and he used her as a shield. I had no choice. I dropped the gun. He backhanded me down the stairs. I don't remember anything after that."

"Can you describe him?"

"Six feet, slender build, dressed completely in black. He wore a ski mask. All I saw was his mouth and black eyes."

Josh's shoulders slumped.

"I screwed up. I'm sorry." Matt's voice had weakened.

"You did your best." Josh meant it, certain Matt would never have stepped aside and allowed harm to come to Tierney. He was a victim and lucky to be alive. Josh realized nothing he said would wipe away the sense of responsibility that plagued the older man.

"Anything else you can tell us, Matt?" Clint asked.

"He laughed. There was a part I couldn't make out. Then he said it was her turn, and she should have known because she wrote the book. He said something about rewriting it to take care of unfinished business."

Josh swore under his breath. "I should have seen it coming."

"We were doing our best to get him," Clint said. "No one is responsible here. The important thing is to use what we have to catch him."

"It's time to move him out of here, guys," a paramedic said. They had waited long enough to get the patient to the hospital. The two detectives stood to the side as the medics laid their friend on the stretcher and prepared him for transport.

Clint squeezed the older man's shoulder. "Don't worry, Matt. We'll find her."

After the group left the house, Josh turned to Clint, no longer needing to hide his desperation for Matt's sake. "Damn it, we might be too late, and I have no idea how to find her."

"There's a good chance we're not too late." Clint's tone was even. "Tierney's a smart girl, and she's tougher than she looks. We can't give up hope."

Josh drove his hands through his hair, wishing Clint's words reassured him, but his mind lunged for the worst-case scenario.

Clint's words pulled him back. "Josh, we need to be practical about this. Let's put our personal feelings aside and do what we can to find Tierney. You read the book. Where was the victim, the author, attacked?"

Josh swallowed and forced the words around the constriction in his throat. "In a public library."

"A library?"

Josh saw the disbelief on Clint's face and imagined the thoughts running through his head. There were a lot of libraries, both public and private, in the Ottawa area. *How would they be able to search every one and get there in time to prevent Tierney's murder?*

"Is there anything else you can remember that might narrow it down?" Clint said.

"I need to get the book and we'll check. It's in the car."

"Okay, never mind that for now. First, we'll talk to the CSI team to see what they've found."

Clint had taken over, and Josh was grateful. Images of Tierney lying dead, strangled like the others, terrified him.

There wasn't more to learn from the professionals who combed the house and its surrounding area. They still dusted for fingerprints and scoured for trace fiber, but it would be hours before they eliminated the legitimate hairs and prints from what they found. Only then would they discover if there were any that belonged to the killer.

The intruder had broken a pane of glass on the back door to reach in and unlock it. They weren't sure how he kept Cooper from alerting someone to his presence, but Josh saw the dog wasn't himself. He had trouble staying steady on his feet, which led the cop to suspect the killer had drugged or immobilized him somehow.

Josh returned from the car after fishing in the glove compartment for the book that had become a constant companion. While he thumbed through it, looking for the correct chapter, Clint peered over his shoulder. Josh skimmed the details, trying to find something that would give them a hint of where the killer and Tierney were headed.

"All right. Here it is. A library; a public library. There's nothing more than that."

"We'll send out teams." Clint said.

"There must be something more specific." Josh flipped through pages, wanting something to pop out at him.

"Come on, we'll study it on the way to the station. We've got to regroup."

At headquarters, Lieutenant Lowe met them, her expression concerned. "We'll do everything to find her." She directed her words to Josh. "How badly was Matt hurt?"

Josh realized Lowe had worked with his friend for many years, and her interest was genuine. "Matt should be okay. He has a broken arm, possibly a concussion, but he's tough."

"We need to concentrate on finding Tierney." She looked Josh in the eye, letting him understand he had her support.

Clint filled in the assembled team on the likelihood Tierney had been taken to a library, perhaps a public one. The group brainstormed probable sites. Clint set up teams and disbursed them to each location.

Josh didn't object to Clint taking the wheel. His head spun, and he needed to concentrate.

Something bothered him. The search left Josh with a strange taste, but he didn't know if it was because they had too many places to investigate, or if they were off track. Something niggled in his brain, and he couldn't figure out what it was.

Clint turned the car into the parking lot of the largest public library in the area. The plan was that each team would do a preliminary check of their assigned sites, and if they noticed any suspicious activity, they'd call for backup.

"No." Josh stared through the windshield at the building. People circulated, parents with children, older people on their own, couples.

"I agree. It's dangerous with this crowd," Clint said.

"I mean, no, this isn't right. We're not supposed to be looking at libraries."

"You're the one that said it'd happen at a library."

"Turn around. Head east, out of the city. I'll call Lowe and get the teams moving."

CHAPTER 57

Tierney couldn't concentrate on what was happening to her. She wanted to keep track of how long they drove and over what kind of terrain, but her thoughts were scattered. She pictured Matt on the floor and Cooper lying by the kitchen door.

Tierney trembled with terror, imagining at least one or perhaps both of them were dead, and it broke her heart. The tears wouldn't stop. She worried for her friends, both human and canine, and she feared for herself. *Would she escape the killer? Why should she be different from the people who had suffered by his hand?*

Despite the man's remark about wanting to chat with her, her abductor was quiet on the way to their destination. He muttered to himself, but he never spoke to her.

Tierney realized where the killer intended to take her. It would be a library, although she didn't know which one. This gave her an advantage over the other victims, being aware of what to expect. *But would it help her? Would she be able to use the knowledge to her benefit?*

After half an hour, they drove over rough terrain, possibly a gravel road, before coming to a full stop. This puzzled Tierney. She hadn't expected crushed rock. Was it a patch of road work?

The door opened, and Tierney gained her first view of their location. It appeared to be a large sand pit or quarry. *What was he doing?* Again, he veered from the novel.

Yet, it gave her hope. There should be workers; someone would see them. *But why would he bring her somewhere where they could be seen? Was it abandoned?* Possibilities tore through Tierney's mind. She knew she needed to pay attention and discover a way to escape.

Her captor came into view, the ski mask still hiding his face. Again, it gave Tierney a spark of hope. If the killer didn't want to show himself, he might intend to let her live.

The man yanked the tape from her ankles. He tugged her from the SUV and stood her upright, her hands still taped behind her back. Tierney almost lost her balance. The one thing that prevented her from falling on her face was a sturdy grip on her arm.

"Come on," he said. "We have quite a walk ahead of us, and I don't want to carry you, so stay on your feet."

Tierney did not understand where he intended to take her, but she had no intention of going with him. From what she could tell, the man was unarmed, unless he had a weapon concealed on his body. If he did, she hoped it wasn't easily accessible. She figured this was her one chance, no matter how slim.

The man stood behind her, so she swung around on one foot and kicked at his left knee with her full strength. He grunted and fell to his side. Tierney didn't hesitate. She turned and ran in the direction from which they had arrived. Logic told her the exit was that way.

As luck would have it, Tierney had miscalculated two things: how much slower you run with your hands tied behind your back and how soon a maniac recovers from a kick to the knee. Within moments, he tackled her from the rear, and a moment after that, everything went black.

CHAPTER 58

Tierney opened her eyes. It took several seconds to orient herself and remember what had happened. *Where is this cold, damp place?* It was dark. Not pitch black, but gloomy enough that her vision needed a few minutes to adjust before she made out her surroundings. She didn't move, afraid of alerting the killer to the fact she had regained consciousness.

Tierney appeared to be in a small cave. The floor was hard; the walls made of densely packed earth. A few feet away lay a ragged-looking duffle bag. A half-eaten package of potato chips peeked out, along with other indistinguishable objects hiding underneath. She assumed the entranceway was nearby. A glimmer of light peeked around the corner. There was no sound, no wind, no movement.

Tierney presumed the killer wasn't in the cavern. It was deathly quiet. She took a chance and tested her limbs to determine if she had any injuries of which she was unaware. Everything seemed to work, apart from the fact her arms and ankles were tied. Escape was doubtful at this point, but she hoped to wiggle her way toward the mouth of the cave to find a sign of her aggressor.

Tierney spent several long minutes crawling around the corner and closer to the entrance. On the way, she looked in the duffle bag, awkwardly using her taped hands to forage for something to use as a weapon. The sunshine streamed in like a lifeline and sweat dripped down Tierney's back as she struggled to reach it.

She peeked her head out through the opening, glimpsed the vast expanse of the quarry, and let out a short, high-pitched shriek. A few inches from Tierney's face was that of the monster who had abducted her and murdered several people. His rancid breath hit her when he laughed.

It took a moment to grasp that the man no longer wore a ski mask. Tierney noticed his smug expression as he waited for her to remember him. It started with a trace of recognition. Tierney dug through her memory for a context that fit until it struck her. Her mouth fell open, and she gasped.

"Took you a while, didn't it?" Nick said, laughter and pride in his voice. "Who would have imagined it? I'm the invisible man."

Tierney admitted to herself he had always been almost imperceptible to her. She would never have guessed the unassuming coroner's assistant was the evil behind the murders. Nick was what her mother might describe as a nice young man. Inconspicuous, bland, with an unobtrusive personality. She didn't remember ever hearing his voice. He had stood beside Chris Abbott, carrying out his duties in a mechanical, deferential manner.

Tierney now faced a different person, one who appeared to become more dangerous as time passed. The eyes she had seen through the ski mask at Matt's house had looked normal compared to the crazed expression in them now. The killer's hair was untidy, his clothes dirty and torn in places.

Tierney realized this was the real Nick, and the one who worked with Chris had been the imposter. This man had murdered innocent people while remaining unremarkable, able to function unnoticed in the actual world. *Why hadn't she put him on the list of suspects?* The assistant had never entered her mind.

His lips curled into a sneer. "Thought you'd get away, did you? I knew you'd come around soon and want to meet me. How do you feel?"

Tierney refused to answer, glaring at him, hoping the look of fury on her face masked the terror humming through her body. She knew she was in the presence of a killer, and her life meant little or nothing to him, just like the lives he had already taken.

"Don't want to talk? That's all right." His voice rang with a cheerful tone. "Despite what you say, T.L., I know you very well. I've been watching you for months, following you for weeks. You're surprised, aren't you? You never noticed me." He giggled, a ghoulish sound. "No one does. But I saw everywhere you went. It was too easy."

Tierney's mind raced, imagining this monster spying on her and following her every move. Her stomach roiled.

"As you've no doubt figured out, I'll kill you here." Nick looked at her with an expectant expression and continued when she didn't answer. "I can read your mind. I'm supposed to follow your intentions, not alter them."

Tierney couldn't keep quiet any longer. "It's a novel, a work of fiction, not an instruction manual. Don't you understand that?"

"Of course I do, T.L.. I'm not stupid. And neither are you, by the way. Your killings were brilliant, although the police arrested the killer in the end. That's not the way it'll happen this time. But I guess you had no choice. You have to create a happy ending. I get it. It's what readers want. But I'll help you get it right."

Tierney had known he was crazy, but now she saw the true extent of his insanity. Nick lived in a fantasy world, imagining he was immersed in a novel. Her thoughts tumbled over each other, hunting for a way to use that fact to her benefit.

"You had a little trouble, didn't you, Nick? You couldn't follow the book the way I wrote it." She spoke in what she hoped was a conversational tone. Annoyance streaked across his features.

A red hue crept up the man's neck and into his face. "It's difficult to match the names with the professions and the looks and to tie it in with the proper location. It takes a hell of a lot of planning and research. I had no choice but to deviate. Besides, I took what you wrote, and I made it better. You should appreciate what I've done to improve your work."

Nick leaned forward until his face was inches from hers. His eyes were glassy with madness. "And I have a double purpose, killing two birds with one stone. So, when things didn't work out perfectly, I made sure to kill the other bird." His cackle sent a shiver along her spine.

Tierney wanted to gag, but realized she had to keep up the act. She would die if she didn't. "But what of this?" She scanned the quarry. "This is more than a minor aberration. I killed the author in a library, not in a place like this. And what about Jeff? He didn't even fit into a chapter."

"Ah, yes. I'll start with the question concerning your charming neighbor." He changed position, settled his back against a rock, and stretched his legs out in front of him, feet crossed at the ankles. As he got comfortable, Tierney's joints screamed in pain.

"Jeff's death was his own fault, but it served an important purpose. I don't know if you caught onto it, but Jeff was infatuated with you. He loved the fact you're a crime writer, and you're pretty, and all that other stuff." Nick waved his hands in a dismissive gesture.

"He wanted to prove himself to you. Lakefield came to the lab one day, thinking he might do research for you, wanting to impress you with his knowledge. I don't understand how he slipped by Gentle Ben, the formidable security guard, but Dr. Abbott wasn't there. Just little old me, Mr. Invisible. Unfortunately, Jeff was a quiet bastard. He snuck up on me while I inspected Marsden, enjoying my artwork, and I guess I was muttering to myself. I have a tendency to do that when I'm alone." Nick's thin lips twisted into a wry grimace.

Tierney's heart sank into her stomach. She saw where this was going.

"I did a marvelous job of covering up, but I was concerned about Jeff knowing too much. I realized the fact he was your next-door neighbor gave me the opportunity to add spice to the investigation. It got boring; didn't you find? I even resorted to having a little chat with a journalist to add some excitement to the mix."

Nick looked at her, as if expecting a response, but Tierney didn't react. The horror of what he said numbed her.

"Anyway, I tried to match dear Jeff to a chapter, but he didn't fit. Besides, everything is working out exactly as I wanted." An eerie smirk made her shiver. "Now, what was the other question? Oh yes. Why are you here instead of the library? Can't you guess?"

Nick stared at her until Tierney shook her head. She needed him to continue, despite dreading the explanation.

"We're both aware your friend Josh expected you to be on my list. And you always were. But the library? You should have written something more original?" His face twisted in disgust. "I had to improve on it, T.L.. And, once again, killing you here serves a double purpose."

Nick leaned forward onto his knees and stretched his long neck toward Tierney, eyes gleaming with anticipation. "Did you hear Josh's story?"

Tierney frowned. *What was he talking about?*

"He didn't mention Andrea to you?" he said. "Oh, this will be fun." Nick rubbed his hands together and grinned. "Our mutual friend Josh has a past."

He paused, as if wanting to ensure he had her attention. "Before he worked in homicide, they assigned him a case that involved a young woman by the name of Andrea. She was a pretty little thing." An expression of fond remembrance spread across Nick's face.

"Poor girl was being stalked. A nasty man followed her, left her notes, and made a pest of himself. Andrea went to the police, and Josh got the case. Unfortunately for both of them, the stalker was smart, and they couldn't catch him. In the meantime, Josh fell in love with her." Nick's smile was horrid.

Tierney's breathing spiked. She had a terrible premonition of where this story was headed. She wanted to stop him, even as she needed him to continue.

"The police took the case away from our friend Josh. They gave it to homicide. Why? Because Andrea was murdered. Right here in this pit." A grin split his face.

Tierney's heart tripped. "Did you...were you...the one who killed her?" She flinched when his laugh echoed off the rocky walls of the quarry.

"Let's just say I was very involved in that case." The smirk disappeared, and he returned to his position, lounging against the rock. "I decided killing you here will add a pleasant touch. It'll bring back memories for Josh, don't you think?"

Tierney shuddered. "Why Josh? Why are you doing this to him?"

"I enjoy putting him in his place. Riddell's supposed to be such a hot-shot. Dr. Abbott is always talking about him as if he's a special friend. But I'm the one who's special. I learned everything from Dr. Abbott. I'm the one he should praise, not a stupid cop."

Nick got to his feet and paced across the compact space in front of Tierney, his hands flapping by his sides. "When Andrea died, everyone felt sorry for him and made a fuss." He sneered. "He's not such a big guy, is he? Riddell didn't save Andrea. He hasn't solved these murders, nor has he found me, and he never will. I've thrown off the wonderful detective, despite all the clues I left for him. Who's the hot-shot now?"

He took a few deep breaths and wiped a sheen of dampness from his forehead.

"I'm changing the initial plot, but next time, it'll go as planned. I can promise you that." A thin finger pointed her way.

"Next time?" A trickle of sweat ran down her back. "There'll be more?"

"Of course. I don't leave a job half finished. Ask Dr. Abbott." His grin displayed straight, white teeth. "Oh, I forgot. You won't be seeing the good doctor again."

Tierney dreaded probing this depraved mind, but she needed to engage him somehow. "Have you chosen the rest?"

"Yes, I have." His smile melted away, and a storm gathered in his eyes. Tierney's body tensed, readying for an assault. "You were supposed to be last. You and Riddell. But he screwed up my plans."

Nick took up his pacing again. "He told Dr. Abbott he was reopening Andrea's case. He wanted to check for a connection. I had to change my strategy." He stopped in front of her, his chest heaving. "It doesn't matter. It's better this way. They'll never figure it out. I was more careful this time."

Tierney suspected his last words were meant to convince himself, not her.

Nick's eyes brightened with excitement. "I'd like to start over, but I'd match them perfectly, and I'd follow the instructions to a T."

Tierney didn't bother to remind him again that the book didn't involve instructions. She worked furiously on a blossoming idea and hoped to succeed. "I could help you, Nick."

The killer's gaze swung to her. "Don't try to convince me to let you live. It won't work. You're the one who made an author die. You realized it would be you. You planned this."

"I didn't plan this. You remember, don't you? The writer in the novel was an older woman with gray hair. Her name was Theresa, not Tierney. And she wrote romances, not mysteries. She's not like me."

"I don't care." His eyes flashed with fury again. "We both know you referred to yourself. Besides, I don't know any other writers."

"But I do," Tierney said. "I know all the people in the book."

"You do?" Nick's eyes narrowed. "But I heard you. You said Art wasn't the right person. You said I wasn't inside your head. But I am."

"You are," Tierney lied. "Something about Art didn't fit. In my mind, he looked different. I have to say, I think you made the better choice. And,"

Tierney said, leaning closer as if to convey a special secret. "You got the first one exactly right."

Nick's eyes glowed. "I did? Are you saying Jennifer was the one? The actual person in your book?"

"The same. That's why it amazed me. I didn't understand how anyone else knew of her. How did you find out?"

"I guess I just had a hunch it was her," Nick stammered.

"Unbelievable." Tierney's eyes widened; her voice filled with awe.

"So, you're saying every character in the novel exists?"

"Yep."

Nick turned to stare across the pit, and Tierney imagined the thoughts churning through his head. She had planted the seed.

"Let me help, Nick," she said.

"Why?" he asked, his gaze pivoting back to her.

"Because you'd be making the book real for me. I created the dream, but I'm not strong or brave enough to turn it into reality. You could do it for me. You have a dream too. I could help you experience it." Tierney's smile cemented their conspiracy. "We'd make an impressive team, don't you agree?"

Nick nodded his head, his brow furrowed. "You may be right. It might work. We have a lot of planning. I want to do it perfectly." He jumped to his feet. "Come on, let's go. We can't waste time, and it'll take us a while to get out of here. I carried you down, but I won't carry you back."

CHAPTER 59

A phone call to Lieutenant Lowe redistributed the teams according to Josh's instructions. The dogs were on their way.

When Josh and Clint arrived and encountered an empty SUV, it confirmed Josh's worst fears. Inside the vehicle, the police found rope, tape, and a bottle of something that may have been an anesthetic liquid. By the time the other cops got there, Clint had mapped out grids and assigned the teams to each one.

In the meantime, Josh paced, his mind racing over all the events of the last several weeks. His stomach churned, and every muscle in his body was tight. He couldn't believe this was happening. Again. He wouldn't survive it twice; he felt it deep in his soul.

The cop checked his watch for what seemed to be the thousandth time and resisted the urge to scream at the others to get their shit together. The only thing that stopped him was the certainty Clint was moving mountains to organize the search.

Getting a hand signal from Clint, he hurried to join the group.

"Okay, we're ready to go. Josh, you and Pete will take this section on the north side." Clint pointed to an area on the large makeshift drawing of the pit. They hadn't had time to get the actual layout. "Everybody stick together. Move as fast as you can but be quiet and careful. The man's armed, and he's got a hostage."

Josh's skin chilled with those words.

"If you see anything, radio it in, and other teams will join you," Clint said. "Don't take any unnecessary risks. Once you've completed your allotted section, return here. Any questions?"

There were nods all around, and the officers split into teams of two. Josh left with Pete, and they made their way northward, scouring the terrain for signs of recent footsteps or a struggle. The two men inspected the walls of the pit for hiding places.

As they climbed over rocks and slid down embankments, Josh listened for an alert telling him another team had found Tierney. A rumble and a muffled shriek broke his concentration. He swung around to find Pete lying on the ground amid a pile of rubble that had loosened and landed on top of him.

Josh rushed back and kneeled beside his fellow police officer. "You hurt?"

"My leg." Pete's face twisted in pain.

Josh brushed away gravel to reveal a bloodied leg bent at an unnatural angle. Pete wouldn't go any further. He grabbed the radio from his belt as he scanned the area around them and called for help.

With the news they were sending a stretcher, Pete met Josh's gaze and spoke through clenched teeth. "You go ahead."

"I'll stay here."

"Don't be crazy. Find her. You can't waste your time here with me."

Josh wavered, torn between loyalty to another cop and the need to find Tierney.

"Listen to me," Pete said. "I have a gun. If something happens, you'll hear me. Go."

Josh stood, hands on hips, and looked at the vast space before them, filled with hollows and piles of sand and stones that presented endless possibilities for hiding places. As each minute ticked past, Josh became more frightened for Tierney's life.

He shifted his gaze to the officer on the ground beside him. A large rock hid Pete, and he should be safe. Josh made his decision. "I'll leave you the radio. You'll need it to guide the guys to you."

He nodded at the injured cop and set off in the direction he had chosen. The pit was immense, and they had their work cut out for them if they wanted to find Tierney. Josh scrambled over piles of sand, his boots filling with it.

The bulletproof vest was hot and uncomfortable, and he would have preferred to remove it, but he assumed the killer was armed. Josh wouldn't be any good to Tierney if her abductor shot him dead and left him in the bottom of the chasm.

Pebbles rolling down an embankment sounded to his left. Josh took a step backward until he hid his body from the sight of anyone approaching from that direction. It might be an animal or another police officer who had wandered out of his territory, but Josh wouldn't take any chances. His gun was secure in his right hand, and he focused his attention on the oncoming footsteps.

"Watch your step. I wouldn't want you to get hurt, T.L." The voice spoke with a hint of a chuckle that belied his last words.

Josh's heart leaped with relief when he realized Tierney was just a few feet away, and she was alive. He needed to choose his moment with care, uncertain what he might face when he stepped from the shelter of the rock. He assumed the man was armed, but he didn't know with what.

Josh leaned to the side and discovered Tierney unbound and following a few feet behind a tall, slender man who carried a duffle bag. Josh lifted his gun and pointed it at the man's back.

"Drop the bag and put your hands in the air where I can see them," Josh shouted.

Tierney gasped and spun to face him, her expression a mixture of relief and fear. Josh had expected the relief, but not the fear. Her ordeal would soon be over.

He was wrong. The stranger, with surprising speed and strength, yanked Tierney toward him. Josh hadn't noticed the cord tied around her waist. He caught the wince of pain that crossed her features as the rope tightened against her bare skin. The killer dragged her back, tugging her body in front of his before Josh recovered from his surprise.

Tierney was once again a shield for a dangerous killer and at his mercy. Josh had a gun aimed at the man's head, even as he acknowledged he couldn't take the risk of using it. The man reached inside his jacket pocket and withdrew a pistol that he pointed at Josh.

"I suggest you drop the gun. Someone might get hurt." The killer chuckled at his own lame joke.

Josh had no choice. He lowered his weapon and threw it to the ground.

He figured he had two hopes. One was that the man would turn and leave with Tierney without taking the time to kill him, or one of the other cops prowling the pit would rescue him.

The latter was a dim possibility, and the former was so improbable there was no point considering it. He could fire a warning shot to alert the other searchers, but he wouldn't live long enough to enjoy it, and he might endanger Tierney further.

Before he came up with another alternative, the sound of Tierney's voice interrupted his thoughts. "Don't hurt him, Nick." Her tone was firm and in control, surprising Josh. He expected her to be pleading for their lives, not commanding them.

"Don't tell me you have a soft spot for this cop. I realize you've been hanging out together, but I didn't imagine you'd like him."

"It's not that." Tierney frowned and shook her head. "I thought we had a plan. Killing him will ruin everything. How can we stick to the agenda if you keep straying from it? That's been your problem all along. We had an agreement and I expect you to honor it."

Tierney's voice became angrier and more forceful with each word she spoke, sounding like an exasperated schoolmarm. She twisted to glare at her companion, whose gaze moved from Josh to her, but she was still too close to the killer for Josh to take a chance on retrieving his gun and trying to shoot him. He wouldn't have time to complete the move. Whatever Tierney referred to, it distracted the man, and it was the best Josh could hope for at this point.

"We have a plan, T.L., but this guy's gotten in the way. What are we supposed to do with him? If we let him go, he'll ruin everything, and then no amount of planning will be any good to us."

Tierney paused and seemed to consider the dilemma. Josh didn't say a word. This was her game, and he trusted her to make the right play.

At last, she spoke. "How about this? We'll tie him up and leave him. It might be days before anyone finds him. By then, the coyotes would've made quick work of him, or he'll have starved to death."

"What if he's not alone?"

"We'll hide him to be sure they won't find him."

Josh worried. Tierney sounded convincing; her intentions toward him appeared far from honorable. Cold-blooded treachery seemed to be second nature to her. The detective drilled her with his gaze, hoping to discover a sign she was still on his side, but she wasn't giving him any clues. What he witnessed was an icy determination and an iron will.

"Do you have any more rope?" Tierney enquired of her apparent partner in crime.

"No, I don't," Nick said, glancing at his bag with a frown.

"Do you mind if we use this one?" Tierney gestured toward the rope tied around her waist, the other end still in Nick's hand. He shrugged. "I guess so," he replied.

Nick moved to stand beside her, keeping the gun trained on Josh, while Tierney struggled to untie the knot that secured the rope around her body.

The killer instructed her to tie Josh's wrists and ankles and attach him to a tree that grew alone in an isolated area on the side of the pit. Tierney did as she was told, fastening the ropes as tightly as possible. Josh didn't make eye contact with her. He needed to trust her.

The killer scrutinized her workmanship and seemed pleased with the results. Tierney knotted a bandana around Josh's face, gagging him and preventing him from calling out for help. Finished with her handiwork, she stood and stepped back with a look of smug satisfaction.

"Take away his phone," Nick ordered. "We can't leave him with that."

"He won't be able to talk on a cell phone with his hands tied and his mouth covered," Tierney said.

"I don't care. I'm not taking any chances. Give it to me."

The man bounced from one foot to the other, vibrating with nervous energy. There was something familiar about him, but Josh couldn't place him. *Where had he seen this guy?*

Tierney leaned across Josh and pulled the device from the holder on his right hip. She handed the phone to her accomplice, who turned it off and stuffed it into his jacket pocket.

"Okay, that's enough. Let's get going. You walk ahead of me," the killer said to Tierney.

They took several steps before Tierney came to a standstill and turned to face the man.

"Wait, I have to check something," she said. Without waiting for a response, she jogged toward Josh, refusing to look him in the eye. She kneeled beside him and sifted through the dirt at his back until she seemed content with the results of her examination. Nick came up behind her.

"What are you doing?" His voice was tense and suspicious.

"I forgot to check for rocks or sharp objects he may get his hands on, but everything's okay."

The killer bent and inspected Josh's tied hands and appeared satisfied nothing was out of the ordinary. Without warning, he swung his arm back and the butt end of his gun connected with the side of the cop's head. White dots danced in front of Josh's eyes, and he worried he would pass out. He struggled to hold on to consciousness, knowing if he didn't, he might never wake.

"That should help," mumbled the man. He seemed pleased with the blood dripping down Josh's face. He glanced at Tierney, who had a complacent look on her face, and gestured for her to precede him once again.

Tierney did as she was told.

CHAPTER 60

Josh waited until they moved out of sight before he removed the knife Tierney had slipped into the waistband of his pants and covered with his shirt. He was thankful the weapon was sheathed in a leather holder or he would have lost part of his left buttock.

Josh hadn't flinched as he endured her movements behind him. Instead, he kept his eyes trained on the man with the gun who approached them. If Josh had seen any sign of suspicion on his face, he was prepared to throw himself in front of Tierney to protect her. Hopefully, someone nearby would hear the shot and rescue her.

Tierney's ruse worked, and Josh awkwardly used the knife to saw at the rope. It took several minutes too long, but eventually he was unrestrained and making his way in the same direction Tierney and the killer had taken. He was still dizzy from the blow to his head and wasn't happy about the fact the man had taken his gun.

Josh reached a point where he could no longer track them. The terrain had changed from sand to gravel. He struggled to keep out of sight as much as possible while keeping an eye out for the two fugitives or another cop who would help him.

"Dammit," he said in frustration when he slipped and twisted his ankle.

Josh needed to get to them before they reached a car and make good their escape. A rumble of movement came from above him and, looking upward, relief flooded his body as his partner made his way down an embankment.

"Are you okay?" Clint glanced from the dried blood on Josh's forehead to the ankle he favored.

"Did you see them?" Josh ignored Clint's concern.

"Who?"

"Tierney and the killer."

"You found them?" Clint's hand went to his holstered gun as his gaze swiveled around the immediate area.

"They got away. He's armed with at least two guns now and possibly another weapon."

"Who is it? Did you recognize him?"

"No, but there's something about him...wait a minute...his name's Nick."

"Chris Abbott's Nick?"

"Dammit. That's who it is. I knew I'd seen him somewhere."

Clint returned to the subject at hand. "Are you sure they came this way?"

"No. We'll have to radio the others and have them block the exits from the pit."

Within seconds, they updated everyone and barricaded the exit routes. Clint led Josh to the road that took them to where the teams had been told to gather. Only a few officers had made it back, but they observed others moving like ants through the pit, heading to the meeting place.

Josh worried the killer would see the same movement, and it would ignite a spark of violence. A sense of helplessness swamped him. *How could he help Tierney when he had no idea where to find her, and the area to cover was so vast?* She had been so close to him he could have touched her, yet she had slipped through his fingers, and her life was no more guaranteed now than it had been.

The police officers talked among themselves, regrouping, when a scream echoed through the pit, bouncing off the walls of sand and rock and making it impossible to figure out the origin. A second shriek followed it.

Everyone spread out, splitting into groups and taking different routes, not knowing what they might find. Josh's heart beat triple time. He ran a quarter mile east with two other men before his radio squawked, telling him all units were to head to the west entrance. The group changed course and moved in the opposite direction.

Josh prayed they found Tierney unhurt, but his hopes crashed when he saw a group of officers standing at the edge of a cliff, looking down. Josh came to a standstill and fought to push air through his lungs. His body wanted to cave in upon itself.

He had narrowly survived the last time, and now he had to relive it again. Josh doubled over, his hands on his knees, his shoulders sagging.

"It's okay. I'm here. Come with me." Clint's voice seemed to emanate from inside a tin can. Josh's vision blurred, and his stomach churned. His partner tugged on his elbow. "C'mon. Let's get you to the car."

Josh's mind zeroed in on the sympathy in Clint's tone and figured the worst had happened. Tierney was dead, lying at the foot of the cliff. It was a repeat of Andrea's death.

Josh pushed through the group and dropped to all fours on the ground. His throat tightened at the display before him.

Lying at the bottom, sprawled like a tiny tin soldier, was Nick, without a doubt, dead. It was inconceivable to fall such a distance and survive. A more horrific sight for Josh was Tierney, draped in a precarious position on a ledge twenty feet below the top. She lay motionless, and from this far, Josh couldn't see if she breathed or not. Her right arm was extended and bent at an unnatural angle, and her legs were twisted awkwardly. Her injuries were impossible to assess at this range.

A wave of dizziness passed through Josh as he saw the size of the tiny ledge. By a miracle, Tierney had landed there and hadn't yet plunged to certain death. One slight move and she would plummet downward to join the killer below. He needed to get to her. He had to find out if she was alive. If she was, he had to bring her to safety as fast as possible.

Another surge of light-headedness assailed him. Josh realized he needed to overcome his fear of heights, push it aside long enough to bring Tierney back, dead or alive. He closed his eyes and whispered a silent prayer to give him the strength to do what was required of him. His eyes flew open as a hand landed on his shoulder, and Clint's voice sounded in his ear. "I'll get her."

"No, I'll do it." Josh tried to make his statement sound stronger than he felt.

"You won't help her if you pass out on the way down. I'll go."

Josh closed his eyes and nodded his head. For all his good intentions, deep down, he understood his friend was right. He had made too many mistakes today, struggling to be a hero.

Someone brought a rope to Clint and secured it around his waist. A team of policemen lowered him down the wall of the cliff while Josh waited at the top, his heart in his throat. When Clint drew level with the woman, he placed two fingers on the side of her neck. Josh released his breath in a whoosh when his partner looked at him with a grin.

"She's alive!"

The men cheered, all except Josh, who was too relieved to make a sound. If they got her to the top unharmed, he would shout with joy.

CHAPTER 61

Tierney moaned. A sharp stab of pain made her open her eyes to find Clint's concerned gaze staring back at her. *What was he doing here? Why was there something strange about him?*

"Clint?"

"Hey, sweetheart. How are you doing?"

Clint's question made her analyze her condition. When she attempted to move her extremities, agony coursed through her body, starting with her right arm. The uncomfortable impression that her bones had been jostled and left to lie on a hard surface followed it, along with the sensation not all her limbs touched solid ground.

"Don't move. Stay still."

Tierney ignored Clint and twisted her head to take in her surroundings. Open sky filled her vision, except for one wall of rock along her left side.

Then she remembered.

Nick had led her out of the pit, climbing the rough gravel road, uneven and full of potholes caused by heavy equipment and many years of neglect while the quarry remained abandoned. Tierney didn't understand what his plan was for her. It was possible he would strangle her, despite her efforts to convince him she wanted to be his partner. *Would she escape?*

Every once in a while, Nick stopped and pulled her against the wall of the quarry, his gun pressed to her side. It compounded Tierney's suspicions that he didn't trust her. When he seemed satisfied the coast was clear, they moved on to whatever destination he had in mind.

When they reached the summit, she looked for a car, hoping they would leave, but what she saw was a vast surface of sand and rock. Tierney tried to find an exit, something that might lead her to civilization, but Nick tugged her arm, pulling her along, distracting her from her purpose. At last seeing where he headed, she dug in her heels, but the killer was too strong for her, and he dragged her behind him.

"Come on, I don't want to carry you."

"Nick, what are you doing? We have to get out of here. The place could be crawling with police!"

"That's why I don't have a lot of time."

"What are you talking about? We had a deal. An arrangement, remember? I'll help you."

Nick stopped and turned to face her, a knowing smirk on his face. "Did you imagine I'd fall for that? Do you think I'm an idiot? If it hadn't been so pitiful, I would have laughed."

"I'm serious. I want to do this. Why don't you believe me?"

Nick was angry, his voice a low growl. "Because I understand you, that's why. You said I'm not in your head, but you're wrong. I am. And I realize how upset you are for the people who died. I always knew you would be. That was part of the fun. Don't you get it? I wanted to turn it against you. And I did. I succeeded."

His rant stunned Tierney into asking, "But why? Why me? Why my book?"

"Jesus, T.L.! I saw you with Dr. Abbott. The skilled doctor and the wonderful author, working together to create a piece of fictitious drivel to entertain the masses. It's fake. It's all fake! I wanted to show you reality is better, so much more entertaining. And it has been.

"People have followed the story in the news with bated breath, talking about it at work and in restaurants. The city dedicated an entire police force to the investigation. They've hired experts to work on it. You've never commanded such attention, and you never will, not anymore. You'll have your fifteen minutes of fame on the evening news as the latest victim, and that'll be it."

Tierney swallowed. "You never believed me? What about Josh? Why did you let him live?"

Nick laughed. "Just for fun. As you said, it wasn't in the book. But I don't plan to let him survive. I'll go back and finish him off, slowly and painfully. Did you forget one victim is a cop? Josh was always the one. It was part of my plan. I've been teasing him, but I'll strangle him like the others. It'll be fitting for him to die here with you, where Andrea died."

"No, please. Let us go. Please…"

Nick gave her a vicious tug, and Tierney found herself in his arms, her back against his chest, and the cavernous view of the pit ahead of her. The force of a large hand around her throat extinguished her scream.

Tierney didn't want to die. She thought of Josh and hoped her plan would work. Things could go wrong. The blow to his head could have knocked him unconscious. What if he had fumbled with the knife and lost it somehow? She couldn't be sure.

Tierney decided not to give in. Any attempt to struggle might send her over the cliff to the jagged rocks on the bottom. But the alternative was to die by strangulation and let her killer go free to murder others, including Josh.

With a burst of strength, her elbow lunged into the solar plexus of her assailant. In response, his body bent forward, curving over hers. She lost her stability. Tierney twisted her body to the side, trying to dump the heavy load pressed on her back.

She succeeded. Nick's scream echoed in her ears, and she witnessed his body tumbling through the air, bouncing off the rocks and outcroppings on its way to the bottom. Unfortunately, her own nose-dive hampered the view of his descent as she lost her battle with balance and somersaulted down the gravelly side of the pit.

• • •

Tierney realized where she was perched, and her breath caught. No wonder Clint appeared so peculiar. He floated in the air, hanging by a rope, and she lay half on and half off a tiny ledge that didn't look strong enough to hold her weight.

"Clint?" She swallowed convulsively.

"It's all right, honey. Look at your fan club standing on top. We'll get you up there, okay?"

Tierney shifted her gaze upward and focused on Josh's face among the many above her. The fact he was safe and healthy bolstered her spirit, and she would do whatever possible to join him on solid ground. Clint's voice drew her attention back to him.

"Listen, I have to move your arm. I'll bend it and place it on your stomach. I won't kid you. It'll hurt like hell. You following me?"

Tierney appreciated his honesty, but she did not look forward to the pain. Her limb was broken, bent in such a grotesque position moving it wouldn't be a picnic. She clenched her teeth and nodded.

Nothing prepared her for the blinding agony, and despite her determination, she screamed. Thankfully, she blacked out.

•   •   •

The look Clint sent to Josh held an apology. It pained him almost as much as Tierney to have to do it, but there was no way for him to lift her from the ledge and carry her without securing her arm. Josh nodded, his expression grim. They both understood it was better the woman was unconscious, and they should hurry before she came to or she'd only suffer more pain.

Clint slid his arms underneath her shoulders and knees and pulled her against his chest. When he was sure he had a firm hold on her, he signaled to Josh, who instructed the team of men to pull them upward.

Clint braced his feet against the side of the cliff to avoid banging against it as they lifted him upward. When he reached the top, he relinquished his precious burden to his partner.

•   •   •

It took several minutes for Tierney to regain consciousness. Her first sight was of Josh as he gazed down at her. He forced a comforting expression onto his face, but he didn't fool her. Tierney was sure she was not a pretty vision, and it would take a while before her body healed from the battering it had taken. She recalled the sequence of events and had a question for Josh. *Was it possible she wasn't the only one to survive the fall?*

"Nick?"

"He's at the bottom. They've gone to get him, but I'm sure he didn't make it."

Tierney nodded and closed her eyes against the anguish, both physical and emotional. In the distance, a siren screamed, and she understood it was for her. She focused on the fact they would take care of her, and she would soon put the entire ordeal into the past. It was small comfort while she lay on the hard ground, her body wracked with pain, and the image of Nick in her mind.

CHAPTER 62

Tierney stared at the ceiling for at least half an hour. She realized she was in the hospital and they had performed surgery to set her arm. The doctor had informed her she was a very fortunate woman, having survived the fall with only one broken appendage, cracked ribs, and an unspecified number of cuts and bruises to her credit.

Thankfully, her legs were unbroken. The arm break was nasty, she was told, but it would heal, and she would regain full use of the limb with physiotherapy. Yes, she was lucky. Tierney would overcome the physical injuries. It was the damage to her mental health that would require more time, she thought.

The door squeaked and roused her from her musings. From the corner of her eye she spotted a tall, colorful figure approach and turned her head to get a better view. A wide grin lit Josh's face as he strode toward her carrying an enormous bouquet.

"Hey, you're awake. Finally. I waited here forever and decided the room needed a little redecorating. How do you like them?"

"They're beautiful," Tierney whispered.

Josh crossed the space to grab a vase. As he moved into the washroom to fill it with water, he spoke over his shoulder.

"How do you feel? Has the anesthetic worn off?"

"I'm good... as long as I don't move, that is."

Tierney waited for him to return to her side, and, as he took her hand and smiled at her, her expression grew serious.

"Josh, I dread asking you this, because I'm terrified of the answer, but is Matthew..."

"Matt's fine. It'd take more than a blow to the head to get rid of the old codger. You can sign each other's casts." He nodded toward her broken arm.

Tierney exhaled a huge breath of relief.

"Oh, thank God. I was so worried. I remember him lying at the bottom of the stairs, and he looked as if he was dead. I'm so glad he's all right."

"Don't worry. He's already at home grumbling and complaining about one thing or another. He misses you, that's all."

Her smile was weak. She still felt terrible for causing Matt's pain.

"How did you find me?" she said. "How did you know to go to the quarry?"

"Matt told me Nick said something about unfinished business. Everything fell into place, all the little things that had bothered me. He realized the first location we'd scour would be the library. But he'd been taunting me. I didn't tell you, but he wrote a name on the page found at Ted Hill's murder scene."

"Was the name Andrea?" she said.

"He told you?"

Tierney raked Josh's face for pain, regret, lost love. "Yes, he told me about her being stalked and her death in that pit."

"There had been something about this case that rang an odd chord for me. It started with Penny. She worked in the same boutique as Andrea had. I chalked it up to coincidence. Then there was Arthur at the theater. I had been there a couple of times with Andrea. She loved going to the theater. He killed Bill Marsden in a blue Honda Civic, the same color and model of car she drove. All these things drove me crazy, reminding me of her at every turn. But there was a reason. He had set it up that way."

"So that's what he meant." Tierney felt a rush of awareness. "He talked about clues he left behind, but I didn't understand. There had been no clues, as far as I knew. He also said that if he couldn't get the murder to match the book, he would kill another bird with the same stone."

Josh's eyes darkened with grief. "Yes, that's what he was doing. He was taunting both of us. You with your book, and me with Andrea."

Tierney moved her good arm to take Josh's hand in hers. "I'm sorry you had to go through that."

"It was a tough time in my life. I won't deny it, but his hints finally sunk in and led me to finding you, and I'm grateful for that." He smiled at her. "Now, I have a question. Where did the knife come from?"

"I saw it in the duffle bag when I was in the cave. Nick taped my hands behind my back, so it wasn't easy, but I got it out and slide it into my jeans. I waited for the perfect opportunity. It never presented itself for me, but I was certain you'd make good use of the knife."

"Brilliant."

His smile beamed with pride, but Tierney needed to get the rest out of the way.

"Josh, he knew everything about Andrea, and jealousy of you consumed him," Tierney said. "I asked him if he killed her."

Josh frowned. "What did he say?"

"His answer was cryptic. He neither admitted nor denied it outright. But he said the reason he had to kill us both, earlier than planned, was because you were reopening Andrea's case."

Josh gazed out the window, his face engulfed in sorrow. "It's over, Tierney. I'm almost certain he killed her, but we may never prove it. He may simply have wanted to wave her death in front of my face to torment me. I'm reopening the case to see if I can find a connection, but, as far as it concerns you or me, Andrea's story is in the past. She's dead. Nick is dead. We have to put it behind us."

Tierney closed her eyes, a wave of fatigue washing over her. She was confident they would find the connection; Nick had convinced her of that, but she didn't want to think about the killer's conquests at the moment.

"Thank God you were there to help me. I wouldn't have survived on my own." Her eyes flew open. "Poor Clint. He carried me. Is he okay?"

"He's fine." A look of embarrassment crossed his face. "I wanted to do it, but..."

"I know." Tierney laid her hand on his and smiled, remembering the incident in the garage.

"You can thank Clint some other time." Josh tightened his fingers around hers. "Right now, he's with his lady love."

"They're back together?" Tierney's eyes widened.

"It turns out it was a false alarm. Lydia's brother had spent time in jail as a juvenile for drug possession. He had been offered leniency by a cop in return for turning in his dealer. Unfortunately, the cop didn't keep his end of the deal and the kid did time. He doesn't trust cops anymore, rightfully so, and Lydia dealt with some of that mistrust too."

"So, it was her brother she visited on Debra Avenue?" Tierney asked. It seemed she and Lydia had troublesome brothers in common.

Josh nodded. "He's still got a lot of problems. He's an addict and unemployed. Lydia supports him as much as she can. Her biggest fear was he'd find out she's dating a cop. He'd never forgive her. She also worried about him being arrested again."

"Clint wouldn't betray her. She had to understand that." Tierney was affronted on Clint's behalf.

"On one level she did, but she had listened to so many stories from her brother of how the cops had screwed him over, she didn't know which way to turn," Josh said. He gave a quick laugh. "Clint's so relieved Lydia isn't involved in a hideous crime, he's ready to jump through hoops to help her brother."

Tierney smiled. "It'll work out for them. I'm glad." Her smile disappeared, replaced by a worried frown. "What about Cooper?"

"Cooper's great. We found a stun gun in the SUV. We assume it's what Nick used to immobilize Coop. But he's another tough old bugger. No wonder he and Matt get along so well." Josh wiggled his eyebrows and leered. "I fixed him up with a cute little poodle. You should see them. It was love at first sight."

Tierney laughed, wincing when she felt a stab of pain in her arm. "He's too old for that."

"What? You're never too old. I'll be chasing you around the kitchen table when I'm eighty."

A smile lit Tierney's face. "You promise?"

"Count on it. I'll even let you chase me once in a while."

Josh lowered his head toward hers, but before his lips made contact, a loud guffaw of laughter echoed from somewhere down the hallway. Tierney stared at Josh, a question in her eyes.

"It's your mother. She's entertaining the troops."

Tierney rolled her eyes. "I can just imagine."

"Half the men on this floor are in love with her, and the other half are trying to avoid her."

"And I suppose Dad is standing by, smiling indulgently."

"You got it."

"Welcome to my childhood."

"You didn't turn out that bad."

Tierney gave a quick laugh. "You should see me when I do my Bette Davis imitation."

Josh's expression softened, and he bent his head toward her again, only to have the instigator interrupt them once more.

"Oh, she's awake! My little angel!"

Despite the velocity of her entrance, the hug Tierney received was surprisingly gentle, her mother taking into account her battered bones.

"Hello, Mom."

"Sweetheart, promise your father and me you will do nothing like this again."

"It wasn't my choice. I'd never have set it up on purpose."

"Oh, we realize that. But you have to be careful of the people you become involved with. Surely you can just stay at home and write books without having to do outside research. I mean, what in heaven's name is the Internet for? That's much safer, isn't it?"

"You're right. It is. Besides, I don't have the stomach for writing crime novels anymore. Not after having a genuine life experience."

Tierney's father frowned. "What are you going to do? Go back to teaching?"

"No, I'll still write, but I may switch to romance instead of crime."

Josh and Tierney watched with amusement when a look of crafty understanding swept over Irene's features. The older woman sauntered over to Josh with a sway of her hips. Tierney inwardly cringed, not sure how her mother would assault the cop.

Josh, however, smiled bravely and, with noticeable relief, accepted Irene's arm around his shoulders.

"Now, that sounds like an excellent idea. And if you need help with researching the steamy, trashy parts, I can give you a few tips."

"Duly noted, Mrs. McGinnis, but Tierney and I can handle most of the research on our own."

NOTE FROM THE AUTHOR

Word-of-mouth is crucial for any author to succeed. If you enjoyed *By the Book*, please leave a review online—anywhere you are able. Even if it's just a sentence or two. It would make all the difference and would be very much appreciated.

Thanks!
A.J.

ABOUT THE AUTHOR

A.J. McCarthy grew up with books by Agatha Christie, Sidney Sheldon, and many other masters of mystery and suspense. She's an award-winning author with four published suspense mysteries to her credit and plans to have many more to come. She's a member of *International Thriller Writers, Sisters in Crime*, and *Crime Writers of Canada*. For more information about A.J. and her work, please go to www.ajackmccarthy.com.

Facebook – https://www.facebook.com/ajackmccarthy/

Twitter – https://twitter.com/ajackmccarthy

Instagram – https://www.instagram.com/a.j._mccarthy/

Website/Blog – www.ajackmccarthy.com

LinkedIn – https://www.linkedin.com/in/a-j-mccarthy-208a20164/

Pinterest – https://www.pinterest.ca/ajmccarthy0125/

BookBub – https://www.bookbub.com/search/authors?search=a.j.%20mccarthy

Thank you so much for reading one of A.J. McCarthy's novels.
If you enjoyed the experience, please check out our recommended
title for your next great read!

Legacy of Fear by A.J. McCarthy

"A must-read for anyone who wants to be thrilled!"
-J.L. Canfield, award-winning author of *What Hides Beneath*

View other Black Rose Writing titles at
www.blackrosewriting.com/books and use promo code
PRINT to receive a **20% discount** when purchasing.